NOTHING LAST

No secret can sta

Vish Dhamija was born and raised in Ajmer, Rajasthan, but his nomadic inclinations have made him encamp in Jaipur, New Delhi, Chennai, Jamnagar, Mumbai, Dubai, Tel-Aviv, Manchester and London, where he currently lives with his wife, Nidhi. He is an alumnus of St. Anselm's Ajmer and Manchester Business School, UK and holds dual citizenship - British and Overseas Indian.

For more info visit: www.vishdhamiji.com

NOTHING LASTS FOREVER

No secret can stay buried...

Vish Dhamija

Srishti
PUBLISHERS & DISTRIBUTORS

SRISHTI PUBLISHERS & DISTRIBUTORS
N-16, C. R. Park
New Delhi 110 019
editorial@srishtipublishers.com

First published by
Srishti Publishers & Distributors in 2010
Fifth impression 2015

All characters in this book are fictitious, and any resemblance to real persons, living or dead, is coincidental.

Printed and bound in India

"I dedicate this book to my wife Nidhi for, so patiently, being a guinea pig for the plot and endless sub-plots in the story."

— Vish Dhamija

"All men dream, but not equally. Those who dream by night in the dusty recesses of their minds, wake in the day to find that it was vanity: but the dreamers of the day are dangerous men, for they may act on their dreams with open eyes, to make them possible."

— Thomas Edward Lawrence

Acknowledgements

Nothing Lasts Forever would have never seen daylight if it hadn't been for the numerous kind souls who helped me to write it and put it into the shape it is in today, so I express my deepest gratitude to Victoria, Trudy, Sudesh, Rana, Charlotte and Akansha.

My sincere thanks to Lisa Simmonds, for the cover design.

I am indebted to my mum and dad who taught me to read and, more importantly, to write.

I thank my literary agent, Ritika Bajaj, and Srishti Publishers: their belief in the novel has enabled it to be published.

Last, but not the least, I thank all of the readers who have picked up a copy of *Nothing Lasts Forever*. I hope you will enjoy reading it as much as I enjoyed writing it. I have taken some liberties in using the names of certain institutions, public figures, cities and brands to provide authenticity to the backdrop. All characters, however, are my own creation and any resemblance to anyone living or dead is unintentional.

—Vish Dhamija

PART ONE

Reality is merely an illusion, albeit a very persistent one.'

— Albert Einstein

1

The Hilton, Orchard Road
Singapore, August 19, 1996
03:57 hours

The phone rang for some time before it woke Serena. Even a casual glance at the bedside clock couldn't miss that it was an unearthly four in the morning. She had arrived in Singapore on a short business trip the night before and partied with her colleagues in the Kaspia bar in the hotel lobby. Having long held that the Kaspia had one of the largest collections of vodkas in the world, she never missed an opportunity to entertain people there when in Singapore. The bar stocked a diverse assortment; its opulence was in fact too much to take in in a single night and even if one tried, one ended up indulging oneself wantonly.

That night, by the time Serena had ultimately lost her duel with a bottle of Chopin and returned to her room, it was midnight.

Who could be ringing at this hour?

She yawned, struggling to switch on the side lamp to locate the receiver. The ringing stopped the moment she turned on the light.

'Goddamn it.'

It rang again.

'Mrs Kumar?' a male voice on the other end enquired.

'Yes.'

'Mrs Kumar, I am Michael D'Cunha - Senior Inspector of Mumbai Police...'

'Police?' Serena gasped. 'What is it about?'

'Mrs Kumar, I have some bad news for you… there was an accident at your flat in India and your husband Raaj…'

'What? What happened to Raaj?' She could sense the hesitation in the police officer's voice.

'Mrs Kumar, I guess there's no easy way to say this. Your husband has passed away.'

There was a knot in her stomach. The tears struggled to flow but an inexplicable numbness overtook her.

'Mrs Kumar? Are you there?'

'Good morning madam, how may I help you?' The receptionist sounded cheerful even at this hour.

'I need a ticket for the next flight to Mumbai please.' Serena was sobbing.

'Is everything alright madam?'

'Please get me the first flight back to Mumbai.'

'What class madam?'

'Does not matter,' she said, in a clipped tone. Class was the last thing on her mind and for a moment the mention of it made her feel even more helpless.

'The Singapore Airlines flight for Mumbai is at seven-thirty in the morning,' the receptionist browsed through the list, 'and they only have availability in Business and First class, but you will have to leave now if you want to be on this one madam. Alternatively…'

She cut him off. 'Book me on this one and confirm it. Could you call a cab and get my bill ready please? I'll be down in fifteen minutes.'

'Okay madam.'

Changi Airport
Singapore
06:00 hours

Changi Airport always smelt the same. The clinical precision of the décor, the pervading aroma of perfume and the bustle belied the hour. It was lively even at six in the morning. With flights to over a hundred destinations it was hardly surprising that every legitimate flying hour of the day was equally busy, especially if one added shoppers that stayed just a little bit longer before checking in or out.

After going through Immigration, Serena picked up a cappuccino from a café, and, with no inclination to shop, went straight to the lounge at the boarding gate and sat down. As she looked at her watch, she was reminded of how Raaj had bought her the Omega on their recent trip to Switzerland, earlier in the year. It had a black dial with real diamonds around its platinum square case. She had insisted until the last minute that they save some money, but Raaj, as always, was extravagant. He never stopped himself when it came to what Serena wanted. She stared into the dial and the memory of the scene came back to her.

'It's too expensive.'

'But you like it,' Raaj explained.

'We don't have to buy everything I like.'

'You only live once, sweetheart.' He finished the argument, by which time he had concluded the deal and promptly placed the watch in Serena's hand.

With her eyes brimming with tears, the only thing Serena did not see in the watch was the time. One memory led to another, until shortly after seven, her thoughts were abruptly interrupted by the boarding announcement.

Everyone was on board the flight by the time the airhostesses closed the doors at twenty past seven. Fortunately, the flight was on time. Serena was totally spent with the alcohol she had consumed the previous night, the lack of sleep, and then the news. It would be well past noon in Mumbai before she got anywhere near home. She felt her body flag to a very obvious slumber even as the aircraft taxied the runway. Her fatigue prompted her to close her eyes but the thoughts of Raaj kept her disoriented.

Sahar International Airport
Mumbai
10:20 hours
The flight descended on the dot but had to hover over the airport for

an extra ten minutes to get a landing slot. Once it was cleared, the captain started his landing spiel: 'Ladies and gentlemen, we have reached the Sahar International Airport at Mumbai. The temperature outside... time is... past ten. Please remain ... halt and the seat belt signs are switched off. If you... to contact our ground staff at the help desk... wish you a very pleasant stay in India... Singapore Airlines... hope to see you on board again soon.'

The long announcement hardly registered with Serena. Bits and pieces of the voice faded away and she could sense herself becoming irritable with each passing moment. She got up as soon as the aircraft stopped rather than waiting for the seat belt sign to go off. Despite often showing her liking for Changi, she had at all times insisted that comparing Mumbai's Sahar International airport to Changi was not fair. Mumbai was never designed to be a traffic hub and that was evident in all aspects – the infrastructure, the staff, the services and the facilities.

'You just flew out last night,' the duty officer at the passport control remarked, looking at her landing card.

Serena nodded.

'Was it a business trip?' he asked.

'There's been an accident at home.' Serena was almost in tears, cutting the officer short.

'I'm sorry to hear that. Hope all goes well.' He stamped the passport quickly and gestured to her to move on.

Serena was out of the airport by half past eleven and hailed the first cab she saw.

'Worli, please.'

'Yes madam.'

At any other time, Serena would have booked a better car through her office, but this time it was different, completely unplanned. She knew from experience that coming out of the airport was a nightmare. The narrow road had a unique blend of bullock carts and luxury cars that slowed the pace; add to that a million bicycles, pedestrians and trademark auto-rickshaws and you had a situation in which even the most adventurous foreigner would hardly dare to be at the wheel. Moreover, every possible space on the roadside was covered by hawkers who sold everything from cigarettes to bangles, and those who by stopping to buy and browse, took up whatever small and valuable driving space was left. This ancient cab, based on the same design as the Fiat 1100 of the sixties, was not even air-conditioned. The windows were open, and the noise, traffic fumes and smell of open drains made the journey anything but peaceful. On any other occasion, Serena would have complained throughout the journey, but she was overwhelmed with thoughts about the accident back home and nothing else bothered her.

12:10 hours
'Two hundred rupees madam,' the cabbie mentioned, taking out her small trolley from the boot.

Serena took the money out of her purse and handing it over to the guy then rushed to the lift. As she came out of it onto the fourth floor, she saw a crowd in front of her cordoned-off apartment, which had been completely wrecked by fire. The white exterior wall was shades of grey and black; the door had been broken open and the little wooden nameplate was lying in a corner like a piece of half-burnt charcoal. There was a complete hush the moment that they all saw her. Kim, a long time friend of Raaj and Serena, moved forward and hugged her before they both broke down. A police officer stepped forward and took off his cap. 'Hello Mrs Kumar, I am Michael D'Cunha. We spoke last night.'

Serena looked up with tears in her eyes and nodded in acknowledgment. D'Cunha did not match the caricature of any Indian police officer she had seen in newspapers or magazines. Wearing the classic khaki uniform with polished tan shoes, he was neither bald nor had a potbelly; nor was he chewing tobacco. Given his lean frame, one could guess that he took regular exercises at the police academy fairly seriously. With a full mane of salt and pepper hair, he appeared to be in his forties. Although his exact age was hard to make out, the manner in which he conducted himself revealed a mellowness that comes with years.

'I can understand you're upset at your loss, Mrs Kumar, but as part of the formalities, I need you to visit the morgue in Lilavati Hospital to identify Mr Kumar's body,' D'Cunha continued.

'Identify?' Serena almost screamed, wiping away her tears.

'It's a legal formality, madam. In the case of any unnatural death, we have to complete the investigation.'

'Yes,' Kim joined the conversation. 'Though the partially charred body and face are recognisable, the police want you - as the wife and only family - to identify the body as his, before they take it for postmortem investigation.'

'Confirm what? When can I see Raaj?' Serena asked, trying to move towards the police-sealed apartment.

'Mrs Kumar, I am sorry but you cannot enter your apartment until the investigation is complete. For your information, there is nothing much left in the apartment anyway after the fire. In fact, it must have been burning for quite some time before the neighbours raised the alarm – considering the damage it did. The structural engineer has been in to confirm that it did not damage the mortar in the walls or we would have had to evacuate the whole building for safety reasons.' D'Cunha paused for a breath. 'The fire has stripped most of the walls in the master bedroom and in what looks like an office or a study, so we have sent for a forensic archaeologist from Delhi to visit the apartment to take DNA samples. In this situation, do you have any relatives or friends you can go and see to wash-up and then visit the morgue? I need you to come to the mortuary today so that we can complete the formalities quickly and send the body for postmortem. I can understand the state of shock that you might be in; you might want to rest…'

'No. I want to see Raaj, now,' Serena pleaded.

'Calm down honey,' Kim started, 'you are not seeing Raaj. It's an awfully burnt body... it will only make you…'

'I want to see my Raaj please.' Serena was getting hysterical.

'Okay Miss Kim, could you ask your driver to take you both to Lilavati Hospital in Bandra West please?' D'Cunha suggested.

Serena sobbed throughout the journey to the hospital, intermittently muttering 'Raaj'. No amount of consoling from Kim helped.

D'Cunha, travelling in his patrol vehicle, met them at the hospital reception. Compared to the government hospitals in India, Lilavati looked like a clean hotel, although Serena and Kim could detect the distinctive stench of formalin from the portico itself. The receptionist, taking down their details, directed them to the mortuary, which had another little nondescript reception area. The three of them signed a register and donned appropriate clothing – dreary white robes - before entering the room. The mortuary was not dissimilar to those that Serena had seen in movies – air-conditioned to an almost freezing degree with large, white, cold steel drawers in which the bodies, apparently, lay.

D'Cunha, a few steps ahead, checked the number on his key, unlocked one of the drawers and pulled it out.

'Mrs Kumar…' he said, glancing into the drawer first to confirm if it was the right one.

Serena ran to him and peeked into the drawer, followed by Kim. The scream filled the room before Serena fell down.

Kim glanced in the drawer, closed her eyes in revulsion and slammed it shut instantly. There was a melancholic silence – the kind death always brings. 'Are you okay?' Kim knelt down beside Serena to comfort her, while D'Cunha stood there looking at the two women.

'Is it...?' He started.

'It is my Raaj.' Serena confirmed tearfully.

'This is one of the few things on him that survived.' After a few moments, when Serena got up and looked, to some extent, calm and collected, D'Cunha handed over the wedding ring found on Kumar's body.

'Yes. This is our wedding band. I have the other one... we exchanged these on our wedding day, three years ago.' Serena offered her finger for D'Cunha to see.

'Could I take it from you for a couple of days please, Mrs Kumar?'

'You can take it forever now.' Tears streamed down her face as she closed her eyes and took off her band of memories.

'Thanks for your help in the identification of the body, Mrs Kumar. I will now send it to a pathologist for postmortem examination to verify the clinical identity and cause of death. The only picture of Mr Raaj Kumar we could find in the house is on his half-burnt passport. Would you have any more pictures of Mr Kumar on you?' D'Cunha pulled out Kumar's passport from his pocket and showed it to Serena.

It was certainly damaged. Although some portions of the passport had yellowed and blackened, Kumar's picture was definitely recognisable: Serena needed only a momentary look to nod and say, 'yes.' She opened her bag, pulled out a picture of Kumar and herself from the wallet, and handed it over to D'Cunha.

'I have some in my house, if you want?' Kim chipped in.

'It will be great if you could bring them along the next time we meet.' He looked around to ensure he had not left anything unattended. 'You can leave whenever you want,' he finally offered.

'Why God... why?' Serena kept sobbing, as they left in Kim's car.

'I know. We always discussed that you were an ideal couple. You guys had everything going for you.'

'I used to tell him not to drink so much and smoke those bloody cigarettes…' Serena banged her wrist on the car window.

The driver took them to Kim's place in Versova. Kim was an up and coming model and was generally home unless she was on a shoot. Fortunately she had no appointments that day so she could take care of her friend. She had a three-bedroom apartment. Of course she did not require all the space, being single, but the size of the house also mirrored her position in society. An up and coming model living in paying guest accommodation would not reflect the persona she sought to project. Moreover, she needed the space for all the lavish parties she threw. She had bought it only a year ago and had been careful to select one of the best buildings in the locality. She knew she could not afford an apartment in South Mumbai and even if she did manage to scrape up enough cash for it, she would have had to live in a single bedroom or studio apartment in some dilapidated building, probably with a leaking roof. However this apartment, newly built, with Italian marble flooring in all the rooms, was a delight and she had done it up really well.

There were two antiquated carpets in the living room that added immense richness to the whole place. The carpets matched the jacquard silk curtains in red, which whether drawn or open, added the required colour to the whole room. Kim had got an uneven thick glass shelf fitted in the wall, which stacked her candles. A first-time visitor to her house might have mistaken it for an aromatherapist's, given the number of candles it had. She was well versed in lighting the correct ones together to blend the fragrances. She had found a small outlet in Mahim that made lampshades, so she had them make four lampshades in the same material as the curtains, in different sizes. Consequently, the four lamps in her living room, although different in their designs and shapes, looked like a family. She did not mind going out of her way for such effects that echoed her taste in house décor and reflected her flamboyant personality. Some of the furniture in her house was sourced from various places in Mumbai, like the chest of drawers that stacked her CD collection. She had bought it from an antique shop that specialised in old colonial furniture. It came with a certificate of age proving it to be from the Edwardian era. The piece adorned one of the shorter sides of the room, next to her little bar. Her music player sat on it with speakers that extended to all four corners for a perfect acoustic effect.

On one of the walls of the rectangular living room was a piece of original signature art, which she had received as payment for a modelling assignment. She had seen it as she had come out of the studio after a shoot and fallen for it in the first glance. It was an ancient nude by Raja Ravi Varma. Like most of his works in museums all over the country it was hideously expensive, but she readily signed a three-year contract for a client in lieu of money. She had a fascinating story for each one of her special acquisitions. She felt an uncanny empathy for this painting; she always said that it resonated with her life, since she thought that an up and coming model in a city like Mumbai was as vulnerable as the nude in the painting, yet confident of herself despite her nakedness. It was her pride and joy, and if there was one thing she wouldn't part with, it would be this painting; to a certain extent this was because of the financial value, but more importantly because she genuinely believed what she told people about it. Just opposite the painting and of the same size, was something that caught the eyes of every living man, a dazzling photograph of her running on the beach in a black bikini. It was from a lesser-known print advertising campaign she had done a few years back that had been carefully edited to eliminate any association with the local tyre brand trying to copy Pirelli. Kim looked devastatingly beautiful. If one were to analyse them, the pictures belonged to the same genre, though one was a painting and the other a photograph; even though they were over a hundred years apart, they captured in essence the beauty of the female form. Being the connoisseur she was she had spent a small fortune in getting a similar frame that paired with the painting on the other wall, unlike most people who would just mount a photograph of this size. Both the pictures were the focal points of the walls they adorned and it was hard to imagine the starkness that would result were the two pieces not there.

There was a door on the fourth side of the room right before the balcony for access to the other parts of the house. The views from her balcony could only be described as breathtaking. There was nothing between the building and the Arabian Sea. If one looked straight as far as one could see, there was the vast stretch of water. It was a view that only the privileged could afford on a daily basis. She had a sitting hammock in the corner usually occupied by her, to have her morning tea or read a book, or to listen to music when she was alone in the house, which was not often. Life in the fast lane; life as one aspiring to be among the glitterati of Mumbai, takes its toll. Maybe not on Kim's body, but essentially on what she chose to do and what she could finally do. The hammock, more often than not, went unutilised, a mute testimony to much else in Kim's life that had come to be relegated. But Kim didn't seem to mind this. She loved her flat; it was her sanctum sanctorum and doing it up was a ritual for her, regardless of how much time she spent in it.

2

It must have been nine in the morning when the phone started ringing. A cup of tea was all that Serena and Kim had shared before retiring to their individual rooms the previous night. Serena still felt bludgeoned after the previous day's trauma and any kind of interaction with anything or anyone that reminded her of Raaj was unwelcome.

'Good morning Inspector… yes, she's awake. Oh yes, let me call her… Serena – it's Inspector Michael for you.' Kim was at Serena's door with the phone.

D'Cunha informed Serena that the postmortem report would be released by noon and it would be ideal if she could be at the hospital by then. He reminded her that depending on the report, she might be required to answer a few questions, but everything need not necessarily happen the same day. Considering her state of mind, he could accommodate any delays.

To Serena's surprise, Kim had carried a few pictures of Raaj and handed them over to D'Cunha as they arrived at the Lilavati hospital. D'Cunha looked at them carefully for a minute before placing them in the file he was carrying. 'The partial face and body recognition by the neighbours and Miss Kim plus your identification confirm that the body belonged to Mr Raaj Kumar. We have sent samples for DNA testing to our joint laboratory with the Metropolitan Police in London, as we do not have the facility here. The cause of death is given as asphyxia. The body got burnt after the death, which is only logical.' D'Cunha continued. 'The report also confirms that the dead person had a blood-alcohol content of 0.38 percent, which is enough for most people to lose consciousness. The cause of the fire is not known, but as Mr Kumar was a heavy smoker, it is presumed that either he was smoking when he fell unconscious or accidentally threw a lit cigarette in the house that led to the accident.' He handed over a copy to Serena.

Serena quickly read the report again, as her eyes were suffused with tears.

'Mrs Kumar, as I mentioned earlier, the DNA reports will take up to three weeks, therefore the case is not yet closed till they give us conclusive evidence. We also need some time to investigate and ensure that the death was caused by an accidental fire…' D'Cunha started again.

'What do you mean?' Kim asked.

'Let me explain. Mr Kumar was a successful man. He was a flourishing finance and stock broker with good cash reserves in the bank and investments, an apartment facing the sea at Worli, two luxury cars, a happy marriage and a wife that works for a foreign bank in a senior position. One would be counted among the demented, were he to miss the motive to end his life,' he said, as straight-faced as possible.

'Are you saying, this could be a…?' It was Serena this time who spoke.

'Who knows, Mrs Kumar? We, in the police force, are paid to doubt everything… everyone's guilty, unless found innocent,' D'Cunha misquoted eloquently, and with aplomb, and carried on. 'Though, whoever set fire to the apartment, accidentally or otherwise, had no intention of taking anything valuable. I cannot determine if this is an arson investigation or a murder inquiry or both.' He paused for a moment to look at Serena and Kim carefully before continuing. 'I need to ask you some questions when you are ready.'

'Would tomorrow be okay?' Serena appealed. She was positively not in the state to answer any questions after reading the postmortem report.

'Okay by me. I shall see you at the Worli police station at eleven, tomorrow morning. Have a good day.' D'Cunha started walking away.

Serena still appeared shocked as she sat in the car. 'Does he really suspect that someone might have killed my Raaj...?' Serena said.

'I am sure he's trying to check everything; as he said, he's paid to doubt everything,' Kim tried to calm Serena.

Next day

The Worli police station was no better, or worse, than Serena or Kim had expected. Like all other government buildings and offices across the country, the plain and uneven white walls carried pictures of the Mahatma and Nehru. Some of the national offices had started displaying a photograph of Mrs Gandhi from the late eighties, but surprisingly it was missing in this one. The station was sparsely furnished with outdated wooden furniture to accommodate the few people that visited the place and both women knew that the Indian police weren't exactly known for their hospitality. When they walked in, a little before eleven am, the inspector was there in his room. He sat at the other end of a large office table that had precisely two chairs for visitors on the other side and a sofa behind them.

'Good morning, ladies.' He forced a smile.

'Good morning.'

'Tea or coffee?' he asked.

'Tea, please. Thanks,' Kim said.

He looked at Serena for a corresponding answer. She nodded.

'Three teas, please. Quick,' he ordered a constable, who walked out of the room with a familiar, but inexplicable, saunter to send someone to the nearest roadside vendor to get the tea.

It was eleven now.

'Miss Kim, ideally this should be a private session between Mrs Kumar and myself, but I can see that you are very close to her and I can allow you to sit through this on one condition that you will not speak or answer anything on Mrs Kumar's behalf, no matter how compelled to do so you may feel. Is that okay with you?' D'Cunha asked looking at her for confirmation.

'Okay.'

'Are you okay with Miss Kim being around, Mrs Kumar?' D'Cunha turned to Serena.

'Yes,' Serena nodded to confirm.

'Okay. Miss Kim, could you sit on the sofa there please?' He said pointing behind Serena towards the cheap blue faded vinyl sofa, kept with its back against the wall with a table of sorts in front to lend a semblance of comfort.

Kim got up, kissed Serena on the cheek and walked towards the back of the room.

'Mrs Kumar, tell me, how long had you known Mr Raaj Kumar?' asked D'Cunha.

'Eleven years. We met in 1985.'

'I would like some details please, Mrs Kumar.' D'Cunha made it clear that he wasn't looking for monosyllabic responses.

'We had met in college when we had got admission in the Faculty of Management Studies, the highly ranked FMS, Delhi in 1985. As we came to Delhi from different places, we got introduced as classmates. I remember seeing Raaj for the first time; he had a verve in him that radiated life, fun and energy to everyone around. He was extremely good looking, ambitious and enchanted most who met him with his conversational skills. In the course of the next three months, we fell in love. It was the love story of the batch. Raaj was a numerical genius and his passion for numbers led him to finance, which he topped in business school, and got him a job in investment banking at Barclays in London...'

'He didn't join that?' D'Cunha sounded surprised.

'No. He was very attached to his mother and was not willing to leave her alone in India. The UK authorities declined to issue a visa for his mother as she wasn't dependant on him, so he took up a job in Mumbai instead. His mother was the only living blood relative he had that he remembered. He was broken hearted when she passed away in 1990.

'For the six years that he was in Mumbai, he worked for a bank and then an investment company. I initially got a job in Delhi and we met every couple of months. I was there till 1991 and then got transferred to Mumbai. We decided to get married in 1993 in a civil ceremony in Jaipur, attended by my parents and a few mutual friends.

'Raaj quit his job before the wedding and once we were back from our honeymoon he set up his own investment consultancy. He had been dealing with a lot of high net-worth clients, who were willing to offer their wealth management to him as an independent consultant because of his personal involvement, rather than go for bigger names with a limited service. As you know, the business flourished, and we bought the apartment in Worli.' Serena was in tears again as she spoke about Raaj.

D'Cunha waited for her to compose herself before he posed the next question. 'When did you last see Mr Raaj Kumar?'

'He had driven me to the airport for my flight to Singapore on the morning of the 18th, a Sunday. He dropped me at the airport at around ten; my flight was to take off at noon.'

'Did he drink on Saturday night?' D'Cunha quizzed.

'He had a few beers at a party. Kim was there too.' Serena turned to look behind at Kim.

Kim nodded in agreement as D'Cunha shot a glance.

'Was he planning to party on Sunday after you left?'

'I don't think so. He said he was tired and wanted to sleep.'

'Mrs Kumar, was Mr Raaj seeing someone… some other... woman?' D'Cunha deliberately softened his pitch, as if that would take the aspersion out of the question.

'No. He wasn't. We were very much in love,' Serena insisted, her voice perhaps the strongest and loudest it had been in the last twenty-four hours.

'I wasn't suggesting that Mrs Kumar. Apologies for any confusion here, I am only trying to…' D'Cunha tried explaining.

'It's okay.' Serena had sobered a bit after the shocking question from D'Cunha.

'Was he expecting a visitor on Sunday?' D'Cunha continued probing.

'No.'

'You guys had a loud fight on Saturday night – would you like to tell me about that?' D'Cunha pinched the bridge of his nose.

'It was a normal husband-wife tiff, Inspector. Sometimes we used to bicker and one of the main reasons was Raaj's drinking.'

'So he had had more than a few beers at the party on Saturday night...' D'Cunha made it sound like a question.

'Yes.'

'Your neighbours always regarded you as a loving couple, though they did report occasional fights,' D'Cunha declared. 'Do you know anyone who could gain by harming Mr Raaj Kumar?'

Serena shook her head.

'Were there any problems he was going through?'

'What kind of problems?' Serena asked.

'Like someone blackmailing him. Or, had he lost money in business recently? Something that might make him consider suicide?' D'Cunha was reticent to offer examples, but was doing it just the same. To Serena each submission was more bizarre than the previous one.

'No way, Inspector. Raaj could never commit suicide. He just wasn't the kind. He was so full of life, he would never even think along those lines.' Serena sounded confident.

'I am sure you know that the insurances, both house and personal, could be invalidated if the investigation reveals that it's a suicide,' D'Cunha explained.

Serena nodded stoically to affirm that she understood this.

'So, Mrs Kumar…' D'Cunha sighed, rubbing his right temple with his index finger, 'according to you, there is no reason for suicide, there seems to be no foul play, the victim had no enemies, the victim had a habit of occasional excessive drinking, he was a heavy smoker, who in a drunken state accidentally set fire to the house, thereby killing himself.'

Serena listened to him as she wiped her tears with a tissue.

'Thank you, Mrs Kumar. I think that should suffice for the time being. I shall be in touch. Are you planning to travel in the next few weeks?' asked D'Cunha.

'I am certainly not in a state to go to work, so I won't travel.'

Kim realised she could join the conversation now and got up to sit next to Serena. 'Are there any restrictions on her travel?' she asked.

'Yes. I would advise you not to leave the country without informing us till the investigation is complete. We might need to speak to you again,' said D'Cunha.

There was silence in the room, which indicated that there were no more questions.

'Can we go now?' Kim looked at D'Cunha, then at Serena.

'Of course,' D'Cunha said abruptly and then, as if to recover his composure, he offered, 'would you care for another tea or coffee?'

'No, thanks.' Serena declined politely.

'Serena, I have been trying to say this to you, though I know I don't need to, it's just that… look, I know what you are going through and I don't want you to be alone, so please stay with me for some time. As all your belongings and clothes were in the burned–out apartment, I don't know how long you can survive living off the luggage you brought back from Singapore. You can always take my clothes till we are in a state to go out to buy some for you…' Kim broke the silence on the way back from the police station.

'Thanks Kim. Thanks for being such a good friend. I appreciate the support. Raaj has… had been a part of my life for so long now that I cannot even imagine living without him around. I almost grew up with him… how could this happen? How could this happen to us?' Serena's voice was breaking.

'I didn't even get a chance to say good-bye.'

'He was so young still.'

'We had all our lives ahead of us, he was only thirty three.'

'How will I live without him?'

'I hope this is a nightmare that is going to end soon.'

'Why?' Serena kept talking to herself about the good times gone by, about Raaj and college days, about their marriage and honeymoon and vacations and travels…

It was almost five by the time the women got to Kim's place.

'Take a quick shower and have a drink. It will calm your nerves,' Kim suggested as they sat in the living room with their cups of tea.

'You're right.' Serena got up. 'Do you have some comfortable pyjamas or shorts? I am tired of wearing these jeans.'

'Of course.'

The women entered different rooms. Kim locked the room from the inside and broke down. She had put up a strong appearance for her friend all through the day, but she was equally shocked and disturbed. Seeing the usually cheerful Serena in a state of mourning grieved Kim. It was a relief to let go of herself in the privacy of her room. Crying suddenly seemed to assume a meaning in her otherwise happy life, with which the normally welcome sound of the wind chime on her balcony, jarred.

3

Serena, at almost thirty, was beautiful. She had aged quite graciously. She looked no less than a model and frequently received compliments on her figure and complexion. Her slender frame, mesmerising almost-black eyes, and straight, espresso-coloured shoulder length hair, lent her a quaint charm. Although her job did not allow her as much time as she would ideally have liked to spend in a gym, she ate cautiously to maintain her weight. The overall impression was that of a distractingly attractive woman.

Kim was almost as good-looking as Serena, only taller, darker and younger. She was regular at her workouts and had an hourglass figure. She had a nice defined jawline with a flattering smile and brown shoulder length hair. Startling to look at and exceptionally well groomed, her countless attributes were augmented by the fact she knew her charm worked on almost every man. She had a way about her that was nothing short of alluring. With a body and legs like hers, she had no inhibitions about flashing some extra skin every so often. At any party, she was always the best-dressed woman, whether in a long black backless dress or a really short one, and being single, she had no dearth of admirers. Every living man tried stealing an opportunity to get close to her.

Raaj was an exception. He danced with her occasionally, but there was a difference in the way he held her. Kim always told Serena that Raaj was not like other men. He could make women like her feel comfortable even when he was close. There was something in his hold that never felt lecherous, even when he was drunk. One of the reasons for this was probably Raaj's rock solid marriage with Serena. Obviously, the couple had their share of misunderstandings and nitpickings. That was normal. They were socially very visible in the Mumbai corporate and advertising circles and there was always something about them that set them apart.

Kim, being part of the entertainment crowd, frequently invited the couple to her parties, each one of which was a sensation; a delectable blend of the best food, the best wine and the best music. The coterie mostly comprised of bankers, a few investors, some advertising and media professionals, Sonny, a chef from the Sheraton, and a bevy of aspiring models and television stars.

Kim often teased Serena, saying that she would only get married if they could find another Raaj Kumar. No other man would ever be able to give her that feeling of reassurance or love that Raaj was capable of. She knew that their doting relationship was mutual, but she absolutely believed she could play the wife's part with finesse if she found the right guy. She had had a few relationships in the past but none of them lasted long. One guy was jealous of her career; another could not bear the thought of her stripping for a soap advert; a third could not put up with the luscious jeering during one of her locally arranged ramp walks and got into blows with other men. Kim wasn't willing to give up her career for anyone. She recognised the fact that being a single model gave unnecessary signals of being available to chauvinist males, especially first-generation, middle-aged, pot-bellied, balding industrialists whose products she promoted. There was this one particular guy running a third grade detergent cake factory, who had succeeded in making his product into a strong local brand and in the process acquiring substantially good reasons for his social mannerisms. The fellow's new-found success made him predictably arrogant and of course, swollen-headed. He tried his best to get into bed with Kim, offering any amount of money. When that failed, he made the ludicrous offer of giving up his twenty-five year old marriage and two teenage daughters to start again with Kim.

Kim was very comfortable with herself irrespective of whatever outlandish outfit she wore at parties or at ramp shows. She knew how to ward off unnecessary attention. She had met Serena through Ogilvy when the latter had handled the marketing communications for her bank in January 1994. They had clicked immediately.

'Oh God, you're gorgeous. Wish I were a man,' Serena had quipped.

'Thanks. You're no less yourself – actually I thought you were a model too.'

'I am Serena Kumar – I work for the client.'

'The bank?'

'Yes.'

'I am…'

'I know – you are the famous model Kim. Who doesn't know you?'

'You embarrass me darling, I am far from famous,' Kim had said.

Later that evening, as they lay in bed, Serena had told Raaj about meeting Kim.

'That sexy model…' Raaj could not control his reaction.

'Yes. And she looks even more gorgeous in person.'

'When can I meet her?'

'Someone's got an itch?' She had teased.

'Darling, it will take more than a dozen Kims to take me away from you. You know that, don't you?'

'Yes sweetheart.' And she had melted in his arms.

Serena's second meeting with Kim was also in the agency where they had both been invited for the storyboard. Serena was there as a client and Kim decided to come along, as she was sceptical about playing a young mother for this campaign. Her career till now had consisted of assignments with local brands portraying a carefree girl. Transforming her profile for this project could jeopardise her career. Her objective was to establish herself as a glamorous fashion model. Modelling for a bank as a young mother was not on her agenda and did not appear to be the right thing to her. She was seriously considering dropping the offer when Serena stepped in. Serena was aware that the banking industry's stodgy image was deflating Kim's motivation. Their bank was purposely trying to morph its image from stodgy to sexy by investing in upgrading the dull branches into upmarket ones, like retail stores. The challenge of communicating the changes in the bank's service strategy and repositioning it as a bank to identify oneself with, rather than a commodity service provider like all other banks, was a task given to Serena, who was convinced that Kim could make all the difference. They needed an attractive face – a face and personality like Kim's to carry it off.

'I can understand your concerns about modelling for a bank as a mother…'

'I am not sure if I am the right choice. I don't want your campaign to fail because the consumers might not accept me in this role,' Kim had explained.

'I am confident they will welcome the idea of a financially savvy yummy-mummy. The world is changing and so are perceptions. People no longer expect women models and film stars to be single all their lives, which explains why so many married women are coming back into modelling and movies after marriage and kids. But you have to be convinced. I can guarantee that we will make sure that you look very attractive. And don't forget, it is a multinational bank with a big budget, so you would be more visible in the media than ever before.' Serena passed on the media budget sheet for Kim to see.

The penny dropped as soon as Kim saw the media budget.

'You are a great saleswoman, Serena. Let's do it.' Kim had signed up.

Back at home, Serena had boasted to Raaj about signing up Kim as the new face of the bank.

'Guess what? Kim has signed up for the campaign.'

'I am surprised she's taken up that role.'

'I convinced her.'

'Someone's ego is a bit charged up tonight,' Raaj had mumbled, taking her into his arms.

4

Both the women showered and came out of their rooms in about an hour. Serena was in a white V-neck ribbed sleeveless T-shirt and knee length khaki shorts. Kim's pyjamas were too long for her to manage. Kim was wearing a natural-coloured linen casual dress with a long slit on the right side. She was sans any make-up for once.

'What can I serve you, my darling?' Kim asked Serena as she walked towards her well stocked bar.

'Vodka, please.'

'With?'

'Could I have one straight on ice, please?' Serena asked.

'It's only six; if you have vodka on ice, you will be drunk in no time.'

'Do you still imagine I want to be in my senses?' Serena asked. 'Let me have one straight. I promise I will have the following ones with cola.'

'Okay. I'll have the same.'

Kim went into the kitchen to get some ice from the refrigerator. A minute later, both the women were sitting comfortably on the sofa with their vodkas, and in another five, the first round of drinks was already over.

Kim once again disappeared into the kitchen, this time for cola, and made up new drinks in tall crystal tumblers.

'Thank you Kim… very beautiful glasses,' Serena acknowledged as she took the drink and had her first ample sip.

'I bought them on my last trip to Bangkok. In fact, I was modelling for them, they plan to launch in India by the end of the year. They have a large range, like all other crystal manufacturers, but some of them are really exquisite designs that would stand out even in an overcrowded market like ours.' Kim was happy that Serena had started a conversation about something other than Raaj for the first time in so many hours.

'Bangkok… uh… I have such fun filled memories of the place. Raaj and I went there for our vacation in '93. I still remember the Menam Riverside Hotel we stayed in, it was gorgeous, right on the river. It is still so fresh in my mind, like it was yesterday. I can still hear the ripples break the silence. Raaj took me around to the infamous Patpong district for an authentic flavour of the place.' Serena was on the verge of breaking down but she calmed herself with a long sip of her drink. The iced concoction went down easily and soothed her. She felt better after two more generous sips.

'Oh honey,' Kim comforted and moved on quickly, 'I am surprised Raaj took you there, most men would not take their wives, its a kind of… red-light… area, isn't it?'

'It is. But you knew Raaj – he was comfortable with everything. In fact, after reaching there I figured out that I wasn't the only wife there. There were lots of men with their partners – Patpong has become a tourist spot for all the wrong reasons now. It's more than just a pick-up joint. Actually, Raaj and I went into a strip joint for a show too, where girls perform all sorts of tricks…'

'Is it safe?'

'Of course. The country survives on adult entertainment and that is the backbone of its tourism. I am sure there are some horrifying places too in that area but Raaj decided to go to the ones titled Kings. His explanation was that in a monarchy, no one would use the word 'King' blasphemously. They even accepted American Express…'

'Did the naked Thai girls not offend you, as a woman?' Kim got up to refill their glasses for their third drinks.

'Not at all… if Moulin Rouge doesn't bother people this shouldn't either, although this does not have the same grandeur and sets; it's a strip joint with pesky girls bouncing their perky tits. The only difference is that if you buy drinks for these girls they come and sit in your lap and some men can be disgusting even in public, but that's life. I admit some of the tricks were repulsive…'

'Like?' Kim wanted to know the details of the explicit tricks, obviously, deriving a vicarious pleasure from Serena's narrative.

'Well, there was one act, for example, where a girl blows out candles on a cake using her...' Serena said, pointing between her legs.

'How do they do that?'

'Don't know. I never tried it,' Serena retorted, with a faint smile; the first time since she had done so since she had known about Raaj's accident.

'Gross.'

'I know. Let's talk about something else.'

'Okay honey.'

'Another drink?' Serena asked.

'You're going way too fast girl… and making me catch up with you. We will both get drunk soon.' Kim got up to fix yet another drink. 'What will you have for dinner? I can order some Chinese or a pizza.'

'Pizza will be fine, Kim. Thanks.'

'Let me call up for cola and cigarettes,' Kim said and dialled out.

Mumbai's home delivery service can be compared to the best room-service available in hotels; one can order, virtually, anything and the local corner shop would send it promptly and without any delivery charges. The colas and cigarettes arrived in no time. Kim lit up almost immediately as she paid the guy off at the door. 'I've been dying to have one for hours now,' she said.

'Could I have one please?' Serena asked.

'Of course honey.'

Both the women sank into their seats once again.

'Did you hear from Raaj after the Saturday night party?' Serena suddenly asked as she took a sip.

'No. I had gone for a shoot at the Taj on Sunday, that's why I left early on Saturday night – remember? It was supposedly a three-hour assignment but the creative director revised his story and my costume. You know how it is in this profession; it was for a new range of depilatory cream and the initial shot was of me using it on my leg but the client thought it would be better if I were shown using it on my bikini line to demonstrate it can be used on sensitive areas of the body. I don't think he was totally wrong, though you cannot rule out his secondary motive of getting to see a female in a scanty string bikini… I had to call my agent to amend the contract and terms; they've now agreed to shoot it tomorrow afternoon.'

'You love that, don't you?' Serena said, in a matter of fact tone.

'What?' Kim queried.

'The attention.'

'Who doesn't like a little admiration?' Kim responded with a glint in her eyes as she lit up another cigarette. It was almost seven now. 'Let me know what time you would like to have dinner? It takes at least an hour to deliver,' Kim mumbled through the lit cigarette in her mouth.

Serena bent forward to pick up the packet of Bensons to light one herself. 'How drunk could Raaj be that he managed an accident like this?' she started again.

'Oh honey.' Kim got up and sat next to Serena with an arm round her to give her friend much needed support.

'What was the need to drink so much in my absence? I wish I had been around that day to save my Raaj…'

'I know Serena. But you will have to be strong.'

By the time the pizzas arrived, it was past nine and the two women had almost finished the bottle of vodka. Kim poured the last drink from the bottle for both of them before they sat down for dinner. With their stomachs full of the liquid, they barely had more than a few slices and then stumbled into their rooms.

The telephone ring, once again, shattered the morning calm in the oasis. It wasn't as early as the hangover made it feel. It was nearly eight.

It was Inspector D'Cunha again. 'Good morning Miss Kim. Could I speak to Mrs Kumar please?'

'Good morning Inspector. She's in the washroom - do you want to hold on or should I ask her to call you back? Kim asked.

'I'll hold.' D'Cunha was firm.

Kim knocked on the door and handed the cordless telephone to Serena.

'Hello Inspector.'

'Good morning Mrs Kumar. What time could you come over to the Worli police station today?'

'Again?' Serena asked.

'Yes, morning would be good for me, as I have to attend a meeting on security arrangements in South Mumbai later in the day,' D'Cunha carried on without answering Serena's question.

'We will be there by eleven…'

'Not *we* Mrs Kumar, just you... please come alone. I'll see you at the Worli police station at eleven.' D'Cunha made it adequately clear that he wanted to see Serena without Kim.

'What did he want now?' Kim asked as Serena came out of her room to the dining table as Kim had already made tea.

'He wants to see me again.'

'What for?'

'Don't know… he said if I could make it by eleven, it would be good.' Serena took a sip of the hot tea, holding the cup between her hands.

'Okay. The driver said he would be here by nine and we can leave right away if we get ready. Let me call up and cancel my shoot for today.' Kim picked up the phone that Serena had just kept on the dining table.

'You don't have to come along. I should be fine,' Serena suggested, recalling Michael's instructions.

'You sure?' asked Kim.

'Yes.'

'Don't bother about my schedule, it's easily changeable.' Kim insisted that she came along.

'It's okay Kim, I'll manage. Why don't you drop me at Worli police station and carry on? I will meet Inspector D'Cunha and catch up with you at the Taj after your shoot.'

'Good idea.'

5

Serena wore a borrowed blue and white floral full-sleeved top that had slightly flared cuffs with a round neck and big buttons fastening it in the front. It went well with her tight blue jeans. Kim dropped her at the police station and asked again if she should come along but Serena convinced her to carry on with the shoot.

'Hello Mrs Kumar.' D'Cunha politely got up to welcome Serena.

'Hello.'

'I needed to see you alone.' D'Cunha looked into Serena's eyes and said with a straight face.

A man arrived with a kettle of tea at D'Cunha's desk, poured it into cups and left.

'Mrs Kumar – I am sure I have asked this before and I trust you to have told me what you believe, but was Mr Raaj Kumar seeing someone else... any other woman?' D'Cunha apologised for repeating the question, albeit a bit differently.

'I don't think so. I am worried about why you are asking me the same question again?'

'Let me rephrase the question for you, Mrs Kumar. Was Mr Raaj Kumar seeing Kim?'

'What? That's even crazier. Kim is a mutual friend, the reason we've been friends with Kim for so long is that we trust each other. Kim has been a true and reliable friend for years now.' Serena sounded disgusted.

'Relax Mrs Kumar. I told you, I have to make sure of everything.'

'What made you even think on those lines?'

'Do you know that Mr Kumar was insured for four crore rupees, which is approximately one million US dollars?' D'Cunha continued.

Serena nodded.

'Do you know who the sole beneficiary of his insurance policy is?'

'Me.' Serena broke down.

'Do you know that your Worli residence was insured for over a crore of rupees – another quarter of a million US dollars?

'Yes.'

'Do you now realise why I need to ask you so many questions?'

'Yes Inspector. Are you insinuating, in any way, that *I* am responsible for my husband's death?'

'No Mrs Kumar, I am not. But someone else could be responsible; someone who knew about it and his other assets... someone like Kim who was witness to his will and knew the amounts involved. To get some part of a million dollars, people can sleep around in order to blackmail and when everything else fails, turn to the last resort – murder - to finish any evidence,' D'Cunha clarified.

'I don't think so.' Serena shook her head.

'It's not what you think that matters Mrs Kumar. I've spoken to a few of your mutual friends in the past twenty-four hours and some of them did not deny that Kim and Mr Raaj Kumar could have been romantically involved although, I acknowledge, no one confirmed it either. Some of them strongly believe that Kim had a kind of control on Mr Kumar at parties, especially the ones you did not attend due to your business trips or whatever. They have been seen dancing closely together in your absence; they even arrived and left the parties together… sometimes…' D'Cunha slipped in the '*sometimes*' as an after thought, perhaps, realising that he had gone a little too far in his insinuations.

'I told you she's been an equally good friend to both of us. I could trust Raaj with anyone. He wasn't the sort of guy who sleeps around with other women, Inspector.'

There was a short silence in the room.

'I admire that Mrs Kumar.' D'Cunha started to rummage through a file. He sifted a few papers and pulled out one, looked at Serena and continued. 'After Mr Kumar dropped you at the airport around ten on

August 18th, he made five calls to Kim from his mobile phone between then and eleven. Five calls in one hour.' He highlighted the calls on the paper before passing it on to Serena.

Serena looked at the paper and broke down. This was the last thing she wanted to hear about Raaj. She, sobbingly, told D'Cunha about buying the mobile phone for Raaj earlier in the year on his birthday. Raaj had a fascination for new gadgets, and since the whole technology had only been a year old in Mumbai, he was as excited as a kid with his new toy. She went on to disclose that she had only innocently asked Kim the night before if Raaj had called in her absence, and she had said no.

'He called five times, not once.' D'Cunha's voice was a little more confident now that his line of inquiry seemed to break some of Serena's confidence in Kim.

'Do you have the record of any of the conversations?' asked Serena.

'No.'

'Going back to your conversation with our friends, who actually thought Kim was involved with...?' Serena intentionally avoided Raaj's name in the question.

'I am sorry but I cannot reveal that, Mrs Kumar.'

'So where do we go from here?'

'I need to get permission from the department to keep a watch on your friend Kim for a few days and we will inevitably bring her in for questioning. There is no other option. I recommend that you do not probe her on this topic by asking her why she lied to you regarding the phone calls from Mr Kumar in your absence that Sunday...'

'Why not?' Serena asked before D'Cunha could finish.

'For two reasons, one, it might, or should I say it would, spoil your relations with Kim and second - she might get a clue that she could be under surveillance. So for those reasons I strongly advise you to stay out of this for a few more days till we get some more evidence. I fully understand what you are going through, but your confrontation with her could ruin the investigation,' he explained.

'Okay.' Serena nodded.

'That's all for today. I am afraid I will not be able to close the case, as quickly as I thought, to provide you with all the paperwork to proceed with the insurance; I need to present all documentation before any insurance money is paid out. It's not a case of what you and I believe, it's more how the insurers work – they want a completed investigation before they can proceed,' D'Cunha informed her.

'That's fine, Inspector. I am in no hurry. I loved Raaj and will love him for the rest of my life. His wealth is of little significance to me without him. I would like the culprit, if any, to be brought to book first.' Serena broke down again.

'I am sorry, Mrs Kumar. Could I ask for another tea for you?' D'Cunha tried being as sympathetic as he could possibly be.

'Yes please.'

Serena got up to leave as soon as they finished their second cups of tea.

'Could I drop you somewhere?' asked D'Cunha. 'As I said, I am off to Cuffe Parade for a security briefing now.'

'I am off to the Taj to meet Kim at her shoot.'

'Great. I'll drop you at the Taj,' he offered.

'Don't bother Inspector, I'll take a cab.'

'It's not a bother at all. I am going that way.'

'That is really nice of you.'

Mumbai traffic can become a car park sometimes. They quietly sat in the backseat as the driver changed lanes constantly to negotiate through the cacophonous traffic at a snail's pace.

'She is gorgeous.' D'Cunha pointed at a huge billboard with Kim endorsing some toilet soap.

'She certainly is.'

'It would be difficult to refuse a woman like that, if she insisted on…'

'Sleeping with a man?' Serena solicited.

'Yes.'

'Not my man, Inspector. I don't believe that one bit.'

'I did not say Mr Kumar was sleeping with her. I am only saying that *some* of the evidence is pointing towards such a possibility,' D'Cunha clarified, though he knew well that he didn't need to.

'I hope it is not true.'

'Me too, Mrs Kumar.' D'Cunha put a supportive smile on his face. 'In my entire police career, there has not been a single case that I haven't closed in three months. I am a second-generation cop, Mrs Kumar; I promise I will not let this case break my record.'

'I can only pray...'

'There you are Mrs Kumar – the Taj. Say hello to Kim and remember to keep yourself calm.'

'Thanks Inspector.' Serena got down from the car.

6

Serena walked to the reception desk, as Kim had suggested, and asked if she could attend the shoot happening in the Rajput suite.

'You must be Serena,' the receptionist volunteered, sounding confident, after a brief glance at her register.

'Yes, I am Kim's friend.'

'I know; she left a message to let you in. Could you wait for a few minutes please? I will have to ask someone to take you up there as they normally wouldn't allow anyone on that floor during the shoot.'

'I'll wait there.' Serena pointed at the lobby sofas.

The shoot was over by the time Serena got to the suite. The crew was packing up and the director and the client were chatting with Kim, who looked comfortable in her shoot costume; it was just as pink but even scantier than she had described earlier. Hovering around was, unmistakably, the middle-aged nouveau riche entrepreneur, whom Kim had depicted so graphically that it was no effort for Serena to recognise him. The moment Kim saw Serena she excused herself and started walking towards her with her arms wide open in anticipation of a hug.

Michael was right, as all the others were; Kim looked gorgeous, and even more so without clothes.

'Hi Serena, I'll just change and be with you in five minutes,' Kim announced and said goodbye to everyone before she disappeared into the Ladies.

'Are you a model too?' asked the chirpy client, who was not in a mood to leave yet.

So now you want me to strip into a tiny bikini too. You filthy minded soul, Serena thought.

'No. I am a banker by profession,' she answered firmly; she was in no mood for letting a past-middle-aged lunatic make passes at her.

'Really?' he continued. 'You look stunning… sorry, I forgot to introduce myself. I am Adi.'

'*Mrs* Kumar,' Serena stressed.

'If you wish to pursue a career in modelling, I can offer you some assignments for our other product ranges…'

Kim came in assertively, but sweetly, as soon as she got out of the changing room to save her friend from the discussion that was getting nowhere. 'Thank you very much for the offer. Even I've asked her a few times but she is not interested in modelling at all,' she told Adi.

'How nice to see you again, Kim.' Adi looked at Kim and continued. 'In my opinion you looked better in the costume we provided. Don't you think so Mrs Kumar?'

'Thanks.' Kim smiled. 'Adi, we need to rush for some lunch quickly, as we haven't had anything to eat since morning.'

'Why don't I take you both out for lunch?' He wouldn't give up.

So he wants an orgy now?

'Some other time please. Serena has just had a tragedy in her family and this is not the right occasion for a social event,' Kim tried explaining.

'I am sorry to hear that. Could I help in any way?'

Yes you can Mister. Please leave us alone, Serena wanted to say.

'Thanks for the offer. We'll keep that in mind.' Kim wanted to leave.

'Okay ladies. Have a nice day. Let's have dinner together some evening Kim,' Adi offered and quickly turned to the agency personnel asking loudly, 'When are we meeting for the review of the photographic assets? I would like to see the shoot results along with Kim, please.'

Kim and Serena walked out.

'He's horrible,' Serena said as they sat down for lunch in the restaurant.

'I know, but I guess it is a standard trait in most first generation entrepreneurs, especially those who dropped out of school and started small. They got married to the girl their parents chose for them. And now, when they have all the money at their disposal, they want to have some fun on the side.' Kim almost sounded like she was apologising for Adi.

'But would you?' Serena questioned.

'Would I *what*?' Kim noticeably did not understand Serena's question or what was coming next.

'Would you have fun with someone like him?' Serena was almost probing now.

'You mean Adi? No.' Kim was defensive.

'Or anyone else who showers money or promises you a lucrative modelling contract?' Serena went on.

'It depends on the man, not the money.'

'If Adi was Raaj, would you?' Serena was on a mission now.

Kim was speechless at the direct question. 'Would and wouldn't. I would, since Raaj was so charming. I wouldn't for the reason that he was married to you and we are very close friends,' Kim stated.

'Have you never had fun on the side with someone like this?' Serena stayed focused.

Kim did not say anything for a few minutes, but her smile and expression were enough for Serena, or anyone else, to draw a conclusion.

'I am not sure why you are asking me all these questions, Serena. As a friend, you should not be assessing my morals. I am a single, independent woman and I make my own decisions. Some of which are right and some not, but I guess the answer to your question is *yes*. I have slept with married men,' Kim said, without being embarrassed. She did not want to be a torchbearer or a moral ambassador. In fact, to be fair to her, she had never made any claims to be either. She was attractive, young, single, independent and unabashedly promiscuous.

'I am sorry Kim. I did not want to upset you. I don't know what made me ask you such obnoxious questions after meeting Adi…' Serena apologised, remembering that D'Cunha had requested her not to voice his suspicion. Even subtle unrelated ones like these risked revealing too much to Kim.

'I can understand, my friend. I know you are going through a really rough time. I should have asked you to meet me at the reception, rather than come up and get pulled into conversation with Adi.'

'So, where are you meeting him for dinner?' Serena retuned to Adi's parting conversation.

'In his dreams for sure.' Kim laughed it off.

The lunch was sparse, as expected for the two women, and it finished quickly.

'Coffee?' asked Kim.

'Yes please.'

'Kim, you've been extremely nice to accommodate me in your apartment, but it's time I made my arrangements,' Serena started, as they were sipping their cappuccinos.

'What's the rush, honey?'

'I mean, the longer I live with you the more I will not move on with life. Moreover, you need privacy too.' Serena was fully aware of the imminent situation of Kim being called in for questioning. The relationship might not remain friendly beyond that point and it would be awkward to live with Kim and equally uncomfortable to move out later.

'You mean privacy for Adi to have dinner with me?' Kim smiled. 'I don't have any issues. You are welcome to stay with me as long as it takes; it's only been a few days. And if you move into a hotel or a guesthouse, how would that be any better? I suggest you stay with me till you join work. Meanwhile, the police formalities regarding the accident will also be over and...'

'That might take too long,' Serena filled in.

'Why? Isn't it a clear case of an accident?' Kim was quick.

'I meant, I am neither leaving the country, nor in any haste to collect the insurance, so why wait for police formalities to complete. I need to learn to move on.' She evaded Kim's question with an indirect response. She felt a tear forming and pulled out a tissue to wipe it away.

'Suit yourself. Whatever makes you comfortable - you know I am always there for you.'

'Thanks Kim.'

Kim called out for the bill. 'Let's go home now.'

'Could I have a drink please?' Serena asked even before they entered Kim's apartment.

'Of course you can, but please do not use it as an escape from reality.

That is how addiction starts.'

'Vodka with cola, please.' Serena ignored the unsolicited advice.

'Okay madam.'

Both the women went into their respective rooms to leave their bags and wash up. Kim was already fixing the drinks when Serena came out of the room. She picked up her drink and carried it to the sofa. Kim followed her.

'We still have an apartment at Linking Road in Bandra. It's been closed since the last tenants left in June. I will ask the estate agent to get it cleaned and send me the keys,' Serena mentioned as Kim sat down opposite her.

'You've made up your mind, haven't you? Okay, we'll organise that soon.'

'Thanks for understanding, Kim.'

Both had their first sips and lit up, one after the other.

7

A few days later

Serena moved into her old apartment in Bandra. It was the one she had moved in with Raaj after their marriage in 1993. As business grew and money started coming in, they had bought the larger apartment on Worli Seaface by the end of 1994, and Serena had suggested they sell the Bandra property.

'Why should we sell? We don't need the money now. The investment in property will only grow and who knows when one might need it.' Raaj was decided.

He couldn't have been more right. The prices had only gone north in the last couple of years and the rainy day that the flat might have been required for had arrived. With the Worli apartment completely gutted, the only property they owned was this. Luckily, it had been vacant since the last tenants had left in June. The estate agent had been asked to get it repainted before letting it out. It was a small accommodation with two bedrooms, but it was elegantly furnished, so Serena did not need to buy any household stuff immediately except a few bits and pieces in the kitchen and some clothes and personal belongings. Living alone once again would be painful, she knew, but one had to start. At least she was independent, and more importantly, she did not have to be with Kim if, and when, the enquiry turned ugly.

Fortunately, the estate agent had got it painted in a neutral colour – ivory. He had also seen to it that all the electronics worked. The old apartment brought back a million memories for Serena, like the time they had bought a new television after the wedding, or the new bed they had ordered, and even the first toast Serena burnt in the new toaster. Each memory was freshly redolent and yet increasingly painful with each passing minute. In no time her mind was a collage of blurred images.

Serena called up her office and her manager GK was very supportive of her taking some time off after a loss like this. He offered her his condolences and asked if she required any assistance from him or the office staff. He would be more than happy to help, he assured, but Serena could think of nothing to say but the clichéd thank you.

'I'm fine. I just need some time to get myself together. That's all.'

'That's okay, Serena. But do let me know if you need anything?' he asked.

'It's not important. But if there is any post for me, could you ask our office courier to drop it at my Bandra apartment, please?' She was sobbing as she made the request.

'I'll ask someone to do that immediately, don't worry. Be brave and take care of yourself.'

Sonny the chef, called on Serena the day after she moved in. It was a surprise to see him at the door at seven in the morning, without him announcing his intention to visit.

'Hi Sonny,' she said, almost in tears as she opened the door.

'Hello,' Sonny said taking her in his arms for a consoling hug before breaking down himself. 'I have been feeling terrible since I got the news. I just couldn't get myself to face you, somehow.'

Serena suddenly realised that she wasn't appropriately dressed for Sonny. She had expected the new cleaning woman when the bell rang and had opened the door without bothering to wear anything apart from the T-shirt she had worn to bed. 'Give me a minute Sonny. I'll quickly change and come. Why don't you make yourself comfortable?' She started walking away.

'It's okay. I'll leave in a few minutes.' Sonny tried stopping her.

'I'll only take a minute,' she said, as it was certainly not okay to her since the T-shirt was barely long enough to cover her knickers, even after pulling it down.

Sonny's eyes were fixed on her back till she had disappeared into the bedroom. He had been close to Raaj for many years after meeting him at a party through mutual friends, before Raaj's wedding. They had briefly stayed together in this very apartment before Raaj got married. He was one of the few friends who had attended Raaj and Serena's wedding in Jaipur three years ago. Roughly the same age as Raaj, Sonny was less well maintained in terms of his physical appearance – he was bald and a bit overweight even for his nearly six foot frame. He had been in a few relationships in the past, though no one had actually met any of his girlfriends. Their friends had frequently joked that Sonny was always scared that his girls might fall for Raaj or someone else in the group therefore he never introduced them to others. Serena had tried fixing him and Kim up a few times but they just weren't interested in each other.

Sonny was born in New Delhi with a silver spoon in his mouth. Almost literally. Being the only son of an industrialist father, he had inherited enough money to last generations, but he declined running his father's empire and went into catering. He gradually came up the ranks in the hotel industry and was now a chef overseeing two of the restaurants at the Sheraton.

Serena was out in a few minutes wearing jeans under the T-shirt. He was sitting on the settee in the living room gazing at her blankly with moist eyes.

'I cannot imagine Raaj doing something as careless as that,' he started as soon as Serena sat down. If there was one careless person in their social circle, it was Sonny.

'I know. I still cannot believe the whole thing.' Serena burst out crying, holding her face in her hands.

Sonny got up and put his arm around her. 'Calm down, Serena. One cannot change destiny. I know the biggest loss is yours, but I feel I have lost a brother. Raaj was such a good friend.' Sonny tried comforting. 'You have to be strong.'

Serena just nodded. Words were difficult to come by.

'Do the police suspect anything?' he suddenly asked. 'Do they suspect anyone?'

'It's strange you thought about it. It never occurred to me, though the police are investigating.' Serena looked at him in surprise.

'I'm sure successful people like Raaj always evoke envy and malice in others. Was anything stolen… papers or jewellery?'

'Who knows? There wasn't anything left in the apartment after the fire. The police did not even let me enter. Did Raaj have anything that you are particularly looking for?' Serena asked.

'No. I was only asking… In fact, Raaj dropped all my shares and papers at my place a couple of months ago.'

'Did he return the motorcycle we had borrowed a few days back?' Serena remembered the last bike-ride she had with Raaj only a few days ago.

'Yes but I wasn't around, so he put the keys through my letter box with a thank-you note.' Sonny clarified he hadn't come looking for his papers or vehicle.

Serena broke down again.

'Raaj was much more to me than my financial consultant, Serena,' Sonny continued after a brief pause.

'Yes,' Serena sighed. 'How did you know I had moved in here?'

'I asked Kim. Why are you living on your own? You know you can move in with me for as long as you need.'

'Thanks Sonny, but I want to be on my own for some time. Could I get you some tea?'

'No. I'll leave now; I have to get to work. I thought I'd see you before that. If there's anything I can do, please let me know. I am still your friend.'

'Of course you are, Sonny.'

Sonny got up to leave. He hugged Serena one more time, then quickly turned away with tears in his eyes and walked out of the door. Sonny's departure gave her time to reflect. Long after she closed the door, she couldn't stop herself from contemplating Sonny's insinuations - he had made her think along the same lines as the police inspector, though he had added a dimension of theft into it.

Inspector Michael D'Cunha had been working overtime to gather all he could to justify calling Kim for interrogation. He was honest when he had mentioned to Serena that he had closed all the cases in his career in less than three months. He had uncovered another case like this earlier, one that had seemed like an accident but was actually manslaughter. Moreover, he was due for a promotion and knew that high profile cases like these, where one showed perseverance and tenacity in terms of making discoveries, always helped.

'Miss Kim? I am Inspector D'Cunha. I am afraid you will have to come down to Worli police station to help us with our enquiries,' he stated bluntly.

'But I have other appointments…' Kim started in an attempt to excuse herself.

'Change your plan, Kim. I am not offering you another modelling assignment; I am calling you here for an investigation of a recent case. If you cannot find time, I will have to send constables to bring you here. See you here at two sharp.' D'Cunha noticeably dropped the *Miss* in addressing Kim and assumed an intimidating stance to convey his mood.

'He wants to see me. I am not sure for what, but he was downright rude. All his politeness has suddenly evaporated. Do you know anything about it?' Kim called Serena immediately.

'No. I guess you'll know when you get there.' Serena kept it simple. 'Should I come along?'

'No. He wants to see me alone.'

'Let me know how it goes,' Serena told her.

Kim was at the Worli police station before the appointed hour, but D'Cunha was busy with someone else and called her into his office a few minutes later.

'Nice to see you again Inspector,' Kim lied. There is nothing nice about having to see a police inspector for an enquiry.

D'Cunha was in no mood to exchange pleasantries.

'What is it that you wanted to talk to me about alone regarding the accident?' Kim was nervous, but remained nonchalant.

'Accident, arson, suicide or murder… it's an open case till I investigate and close it. Sit down,' D'Cunha cut her off. 'Let me make this very clear. We have been keeping a watch on you for the last few days and some of the information collected suggests there was more than a friendly relationship between you and Mr Raaj Kumar. That might or might not have anything to do with his sudden death, but we would like to look at this case from all angles… '

'What?' Kim couldn't hide her disbelief.

'Kim, for the purpose of this investigation, may I request you not to hide any facts. As this isn't yet a formal cross-examination, you don't need a lawyer present,' D'Cunha explained.

'Okay.' Kim had already gone weak at the knees.

'Kim, did you have any relations with Mr Raaj Kumar that were beyond ordinary friendship?' D'Cunha started the onslaught.

'No.'

'No?' he asked, sarcastically.

'Serena and Raaj were good friends and that's it, Inspector.'

'Did Mr Raaj Kumar ever make a pass at you?'

'Never before… but on the day Serena left for Singapore…'

'August 18th?' D'Cunha offered.

'Yes. He was a bit different. He called me up from the airport after dropping Serena and made some rude remarks that were totally inconsistent with his behaviour till then,' Kim stated.

'What kind of remarks, Kim?'

'He wanted to get together with me for a good time. He said Serena was away and we should play around a bit, as no one would know.' Kim was almost trembling and fighting back the tears as she spoke.

'Why would he do that? A reasonable man and a dedicated husband until now… suddenly call up for a bit of fun? How long had you known him?'

'Over two years.'

'And he had never acted in this manner before?'

'No.'

'Strange, isn't it? What happened after that?'

'I told him I wouldn't do anything that would hurt Serena, but he kept insisting.'

'Did you give in?'

'No Inspector. I am Serena's friend...'

'So what you are saying is that the only reason that stood between you and Mr Kumar was your friend?'

'It was the main reason.'

'What is the other reason Kim? Have you never slept with a married man?'

'That's got nothing to do with this.'

'Don't tell me what's to do - or not to do - with this case Kim. Have you or have you not?' D'Cunha raised his voice to establish his authority.

'I have.'

'Did Mr Kumar know about it?'

'Yes.'

'Was this the reason he called? He might have thought that if other guys can get into your bed, why not him?'

'Yes. He said that if I refused, he would spill enough beans that would give me a difficult time in our social circle.'

'So what did you do next?'

'I said *no* and slammed the phone down.'

'Did he call again?'

'Yes, a few times.' Kim was quaking in her boots.

'Five times,' D'Cunha stated, passing a packet of tissues towards her. 'The telephone company records show that he called you five times in that hour.'

Kim was shocked that the police knew about the calls and the information D'Cunha had. She herself had not kept a count.

'What happened next, Kim?'

'It was basically the same conversation Inspector. He insisted and I declined and in the last call I told him to go on and tell whoever he wanted, but I would not get into bed with him.'

'But you did?'

'No.'

'I told you not to hide anything Kim. The security guard in your apartment complex met Mr Kumar around eleven in your building and has confirmed that he saw Mr Kumar's car parked for the next two hours before he saw him, Mr Kumar, leave.'

'What?' Kim was exasperated.

'Don't act so innocent Kim. He was with you in your apartment for two hours. I am sure he must have convinced you to...' D'Cunha did not complete the sentence.

'He never came to my apartment, Inspector.'

'Stop lying. We have already established your morals, so there is no reason for you to act virtuous.' D'Cunha raised his voice again.

Kim felt humiliated and stripped of all decency. 'In fact I had an appointment at the Taj at one and I left home at noon.' The stress had clearly pushed her to the brink and her voice trembled.

'Now that is interesting. You guys had fun for an hour. You left at noon and Mr Kumar left an hour later so that no one saw you leaving together.'

'Raaj never came to my apartment that day Inspector. Believe me.'

'Believe you?' D'Cunha's tone was even more cynical than before.

'Yes.' Kim had stopped herself up until now but she eventually broke down.

'You're lucky. If you had been to his apartment, I would have taken you in custody and asked you all these questions in a different manner. We can make even the dead talk Kim. But for now, you will be doing yourself a favour by not hiding anything. Do you understand?' D'Cunha said insensitively.

Kim was so scared that she found it difficult articulating; she sat there speechless for more than a minute.

'Did you tell Mrs Serena Kumar that her husband called after she left for Singapore?' D'Cunha queried.

'No.'

'May I ask why not?'

'What was the point? Raaj passed away and I did not want Serena to have any bitter feelings towards him especially after he was gone – she adored him.'

'Oh, so you wanted to be a perfect friend?'

'I've always been a good friend.'

'Really? Tell me what happened in your apartment that day?'

'Raaj never came to my apartment, Inspector,' Kim insisted.

'I don't believe you, but carry on.'

'I left for my shoot at noon.'

'Did you see him later that day?'

'No.' Kim was firm.

'Okay,' D'Cunha concluded. 'It's your decision. I can assure you that I will definitely get to the bottom of this. You might be needed for further questions, hence you are not allowed to leave the city till the investigation is complete.'

'Can I leave for now?'

'Yes, you can.'

D'Cunha was on a call with his senior almost instantly. 'I have questioned the model, sir. I think she is lying about her relationship with the deceased, for reasons we can understand. I will let the team keep a watch on her for anything suspicious and bring her back in, if required.'

'Okay.'

8

Adi was waiting for Kim to arrive to start looking through the photographs from the shoot last week. 'There you are, gorgeous!' He was up on his feet as soon as she arrived. 'What's the matter with you? You look upset.'

'I am okay.'

'Sure? We can postpone this.' Adi offered.

'Let's see them now.' Kim was adamant.

'Okay.'

Adi could not keep his mouth shut even for a minute, as Kim's photographs were flashed on the big screen in front. He whistled, he groaned, he made comments…

'I wish I could make a wallpaper of these pictures for my office.'

'I wish we could go for a vacation on a beach – just you, me and that bikini.'

'You have an awesome body.'

Three photographs were shortlisted for print and billboards. There wasn't any budget assigned for television commercials, so that was it. It was seven in the evening by the time they finished. 'Have dinner with me tonight,' Adi requested when they waited for the elevator to take them down.

'Okay Adi.' Kim did not want to be alone. It had been a long day for her and she was still disturbed after the police questioning.

'Should we drive to Bandra?' Adi could not believe his luck.

'Yes.'

'Ask your driver to take your car home. I'll have you dropped later.' Adi seemed to enjoy his newfound position of control. He was delighted, as well as surprised, by Kim's unusual complaisance.

'Okay Adi.' Kim succumbed.

As they finished the meal Adi once again asked if there was a problem and if he could help. 'Actually there is…' Kim gave in. 'I am sure you must have read about the recent accident involving Raaj Kumar in the local newspapers. I was very close to him and his wife, Serena. Remember her? You met her the other day at the Taj?'

Adi nodded.

'The police inspector called me in for interrogation. That's why I had to postpone the meeting to the evening. He was rude, bordering on being nasty; he humiliated me by probing me about whether I had something with Raaj on the side…'

'Which police station is handling the case?' Adi demanded.

'Worli.'

'Who's leading the inquiry?'

'Inspector Michael D'Cunha,' Kim mumbled.

'Why don't we go to my company guest house and I can sort that out for you. I need to understand the situation a little better before I start making calls, you see…' Adi clarified.

Kim knew that going to the guest house would mean that Adi would make a few calls and the police would never bother her any more. But Adi wouldn't do her any favours for nothing. As his driver picked them up from the restaurant, Adi placed his hand on Kim's thigh, leaving no ambiguity about what those calls would cost her. Once at the guest house, he asked the caretaker to fix drinks for them and get the bedrooms ready. After the caretaker served drinks and disappeared, Adi opened his briefcase and shocked Kim by taking out the little pink bikini she had worn for the shoot the other day. 'I've been waiting for an occasion to see you in it again. Why don't you go into one of the bedrooms and change? I will be with you in a few minutes.' He pointed towards a room on the right.

'Okay Adi.' Kim got up; she did not require any convincing.

She went into the bedroom and took her clothes off to get into the bikini. She felt sick that Adi had carried the costume, she had worn, in his briefcase. However, fear, one of the most potent causes of desperation, convinced her that it was better for her to spend a night with Adi than to spend one in a police lock-up with cops and inmates. What if D'Cunha got a warrant against her? The police were known to behave like an occupying army and a single woman like her could end up totally defenceless against the whole system. Besides, she had heard of custodial rapes and deaths, and she was quite sure of what she couldn't handle and what she could. Adi, at this stage, seemed easier to handle than the police.

Adi was in her room in ten minutes. He whistled as he saw her trying to reach her back to tie the lace. He came close and held her shamelessly from behind pressing himself against her barely covered bottom with his hands feeling her all over and his lips moving down her neck.

'We can even make the dead talk.' Michael's words echoed in Kim's ears.

'I have pulled the right strings for you, Kim.' He picked her up in his arms. 'Let me pull some here now.' He slowly pulled the pink strings of her bikini as he got into bed with her.

Kim closed her eyes.

'All sorted.' Adi called Kim the next day around lunch. 'You shouldn't get any more calls from that inspector or any police station at all. In case you do, please let me know and I will see to it that I attend the session along with my lawyer. Okay Kim?'

'You're great Adi.'

'You were great in bed last night.'

Kim knew that Indian bureaucracy did not work on facts. It worked on who had better connections and lawyers. Adi, obviously, funded a large number of local politicians for their election campaigns and a few calls got him the guarantee that a small time police inspector would not follow a useless trail and harass a vulnerable single woman.

A month later

'Hello Mrs Kumar,' called D'Cunha.

'Hello Inspector.' Serena recognised the voice.

'Mrs Kumar, I have the DNA report from our UK office. They have confirmed, as we already knew, that the body found in the accident on August 18th belonged to your husband, Mr Raaj Kumar. I am sorry that it took so long for the reports to come back. I also wanted to let you know that all our investigations prove beyond doubt that it was an accident. In fact, the calls to Kim that I mentioned when we last met were a miscommunication. She received no calls from Mr Raaj Kumar on the day; the telephone company's lines were entangled, hence the misunderstanding – they've got a new cellular technology and are still inexperienced at using it. We would have been better off in the days of the simple landlines,' D'Cunha lied convincingly.

'That's ridiculous. It could have led you down a totally unwarranted investigation, spending time and money in vain. Anyway, thanks for clarifying Inspector. I've been unnecessarily suspicious of Kim ever since that day. She's been such a good friend. I can only blame myself for sharing your apprehensions in the first place.' Serena sounded relieved.

'It's okay now. I told you I have a record of closing all cases in less than three months, didn't I?' D'Cunha boasted.

'Yes, of course.'

'I will be sending my report to the authorities before the end of the week. This case is now closed,' he said.

'Thank you.'

After the call to Serena, D'Cunha reflected on the events that had occurred the day after the meeting with Kim at the police station. He had been having breakfast with his wife and kids in their cosy two-bedroom apartment on the fourth floor in the Mumbai suburb of Andheri East. Theirs was a thinly furnished house with inexpensive furniture and drapes. Even some of his junior colleagues lived far more lavishly than he did, but he was different. He was clear that his aim in life was not to accumulate wealth; he had joined the police force to serve honestly. His father had retired as the Additional Commissioner of Police for Mumbai and Michael D'Cunha had ambitions to reach even higher. To him, his father was symbolic of strength of character, having grown through the police ranks, like him, and reached the pinnacle of his career solely on the basis of hard work and commitment. The senior Mr D'Cunha was still revered by some of Michael D'Cunha's superiors, a number of whom had trained under his father. When D'Cunha joined the police force, he was under tremendous pressure to live up to his father's reputation. Much of it was from the expectation of his peers and senior colleagues, but he, predictably, had never let them down. He had built up a reputation of a tough cop, who lived with the clichéd motto of *service before self.* And, he had not done badly. He was still in his forties and, given his track record, he was already earmarked for his next promotion. It was only the red tape taking its time now.

The telephone ring killed the breakfast conversation with his family. D'Cunha looked at the clock, on the wall across the modest wooden dining table laminated with some cheap plastic veneer, and it was fifteen minutes past nine.

'Michael?' It was his immediate supervisor.

'Yes Sir,' D'Cunha said.

'What have you found out about the recent incident of the fire at Raaj Kumar's apartment in Worli?'

'Sir, we are still looking into it. In fact, as I told you yesterday, we questioned this girl Kim and she could be a vital thread in…'

'Forget it,' his supervisor barked, discourteously, cutting him off in the middle of the sentence. 'The girl has nothing to do with this case.'

'But sir… I think we've got a point…' D'Cunha tried explaining.

'No Michael, in my opinion you're missing the point – it was an accident. Raaj Kumar is dead. It does not matter if the girl slept with him or not. In any case, she was nowhere near Worli at the time of the accident. She was on a shoot at the Taj Hotel in south Mumbai and she has more witnesses than you can count. Perfect alibi.'

'I understand that sir, but if we can prove that she could benefit from Raaj's death in any way…' D'Cunha tried convincing his supervisor politely.

'Michael. Kim is an up and coming model who is connected to some really powerful people in this city. I am under excessive pressure to inform you that you will not be doing the department, or yourself, any favours by pursuing that line of inquiry. On the contrary, the girl has access to some of the best lawyers who would, in turn, charge you with defamation and drag you to court. Now, you don't want that, do you? You're due for a promotion. One wrong move on your part can destroy your prospects in this department.' He knew how to make a real impact.

'Okay sir.' D'Cunha was a smart man. He knew he had been pinned.

'I do not want you to contact Kim without my permission. Is that understood?' his superior asked.

'Yes sir.'

'Good day.' The boss slammed the phone down.

Fortunately, it was a Sunday, as D'Cunha l was in no mood to go to the office after that hostile call. Sleep eluded him for a long time as he lay in bed later that night. His mind was battling between the truth and the pressure. He could still go ahead with his investigation with Kim but, the whole bureaucratic machinery would turn into an enormous headwind to provide overwhelming obstacles and he would only exhaust himself struggling against it. Even if he, somehow, managed to continue his search and eventually found nothing at the end of the winding road, he would have to pay a rather heavy price. Maybe Raaj Kumar and Kim had a fling. So what? He wasn't in the moral police force. An extra marital affair was not what he was investigating in this case. Frustrated by powerlessness, he convinced himself he should focus his endeavours towards any suspicious movements around Kumar's apartment in Worli that ill-fated evening.

He wasn't abandoning the case; he was only diverting his efforts to solve it, he persuaded himself.

The inspector had put Serena, too, under observation and had run a comprehensive investigation on her; being the only beneficiary of all the insurances, she could hardly be excluded from suspicion. His team came back with a report that she had either been brooding, sobbing or mourning since the beginning – she hadn't met anyone except Kim and a chef from the Sheraton who was an old mutual friend of she and her husband; the only calls made were to her office, Kim, the estate agent and a few to the local grocers. She had merely gone out shopping once, for some essentials, with Kim. Her passport clearly showed that she had travelled to Singapore on the fateful day and returned after D'Cunha had called her about the accident. She had been married to Raaj for three years. None of the friends questioned suspected her of any extra marital affair. On the contrary, all of them reflected that Serena and Raaj was an ideal couple, barring a few envious people who had earlier given him the otiose tittle-tattle on a plausible romantic liaison between Raaj and Kim. However, when police had probed these imbeciles later, they confessed that they could have been wrong in their assessment.

None of the neighbours interviewed had seen anything suspicious. The security guard of the building in Worli remembered seeing Raaj only once during that day, driving out in the morning, with his wife. He wasn't aware what time Raaj had returned but on one of his rounds of the building after lunch, around two in the afternoon, he had seen both the cars in the basement car park that indicated Raaj was back in the apartment before that time.

One of the viewpoints was to probe into suicide, but no one who knew Raaj accepted the theory, even for a minute. There were no grounds to doubt his mental state after meeting his family physician and there had been no family history of such tendencies. Moreover, his business was flourishing and there hadn't been any losses in the recent past that would make him take a desperate step.

After having exhausted all suspects and all other lines of enquiry, D'Cunha contemplated the possibility of Raaj disappearing from the country after leaving another dead body with no one, including his wife, knowing of it. But, the chances of that were very slim – a lot of people had recognised the face and the DNA report was conclusive enough. There wasn't anyone reported missing the same day, hence producing a dead body in itself was intriguing and impossible. Besides, Raaj's passport was found burnt in the apartment so he could not have left the country. Also, there wasn't a motive; the insurance sums weren't credible if one took into account his promising business and his contented life with his wife and friends.

D'Cunha deliberated for quite some time before convincing himself to close the case and sign the papers.

9

Serena met Kim for coffee. Both of them were casually dressed in jeans, only their tops were different. Kim was wearing a floral fitted shirt that contoured her shape. It was neatly tucked into her jeans. Serena wore a skinny-fit light blue T-shirt.

'How have you been darling?' asked Kim in her usual friendly tone.

'Fine thanks. I've been trying to come to terms with reality. Sorry I haven't called for some time. I wanted to be alone to sort things out.'

'I understand.'

'I will start at the office again from next week. Hopefully, it will get me back into life, as I need to start living again. Why don't you move in with me for a week before I start?' Serena proposed.

'I am game. Let's go buy some office wear for you.'

Kim moved into Serena's apartment the same evening. Both the women went to Shoppers Stop for some quick buying. It was certainly not one of the legendary shopping trips that they had indulged in together in the past – shopping binges, which lasted a full day and ended in a spa or club in the evening where Raaj usually joined them. In fact, Raaj was a happy man since Serena had befriended Kim. He could now escape Serena's infamously long shopping sprees, which he detested like most men.

'You always loved to take me shopping when were dating,' Serena had

pointed out once when her shopping plans had been vetoed vociferously by Raaj.

'Correction, my dear... I loved to hang around with you when we were not married and shopping was good as it lasted longer than a meal or a movie. Now that we live together I think we can do better than going out shopping,' Raaj had explained.

'But, don't you have to buy some shirts?'

'I'll pick some up on my next trip. You know it is a ten-minute job. You girls make a ritual of trying on everything before you buy. For us, a collar size is enough to buy a shirt.' He had walked away into the study.

The mood was very different today. They had a set purpose to pick up some office clothes for Serena, as she had nothing left after the fire in the house. If she was to begin work from next week, she needed respectable clothes. She had been living out of her suitcase and some borrowed clothes from Kim for a month now. There was no way she could have managed it any longer. It was extremely nice of Kim to have agreed to come shopping with her, or else she would have had to do it on her own.

'Black suits you,' Kim commented as soon as Serena had picked up a skirt suit.

'Thanks.' She walked towards the changing room with a few hangers.

A few shirts, trousers and one suit later, Serena was prepared to go to the till. But Kim had fallen in love with a short black dress and wanted to try it on.

'Go on. Black suits you too.' It was Serena's turn to return the compliment.

'I want you near the changing room so I can have a second opinion. I want it for formal wear so I don't want it very short, it shouldn't flash more leg than required,' Kim requested.

'I understand. Go change and come out and show me.'

Kim was a professional model. It took her precisely two minutes to change.

God - she's looking gorgeous in the short black dress, Serena thought when she saw Kim come out.

'Wow!' That was all that came out of Serena's mouth.

'Honestly?'

'I swear.'

'Not too short then?' Kim looked for reassurance.

'Not at all; you look stunning. It reveals exactly as much as you would want in a formal setting. But, what do you need a formal dress for?' Serena asked.

'I will tell you in a minute. Let me go and change.'

Kim was out in two minutes. 'One of the creative directors, from an advertising agency I work with, has been nice and would like to promote me. He's invited me for a sit-down dinner with other guests as a friend... he's promised to help me get more contracts. I would like to look right on this occasion. Reveal a bit of leg to the crowd but without looking desperate. You know what I mean?' Kim asked.

'It's a great choice for such a party. You won't look desperate in this dress but you will create more than a ripple,' Serena said.

'That'll do, my friend.'

'All set to become a big time model?' Serena commented.

All Kim needed was a big break. She was a natural beauty with an attractive face and an incredibly shaped body and had nurtured her personality to suit her profession, resulting in great panache for what she did. She was not exactly struggling, but she was nowhere near the A-list supermodels that got the prized assignments, adulation and respect from the industry, which obviously translated into wealth. If something like that did not come her way soon, she would pass her prime and would always be considered as a 'B' grade model. The detergents and depilatory creams were good for survival, but it was certainly not something Kim would want to be remembered for, if she would be remembered at all. With no mentor in show business, beginning small was a necessity, but staying small was certainly not the plan. After a long time, one guy had seen potential in her work and she wasn't leaving it to chance. This could well be her big break.

Kim took Serena shopping for the house in the next few days and made her buy lamps, linen, pots, pans, a dinner set and even ordered new curtains.

'You need to get things that you can relate to. Or else you would keep feeling you live in someone else's house.' Kim had emphasised.

'Okay.'

The week ended very soon. Both friends knew what they had gone through in the past few weeks, though they did not discuss it, but they were glad that their relationship was intact.

The office felt alien to Serena after being away for five weeks. The people were nice and polite. One of her direct reports had managed well in her absence, so things were not pending to over burden her on her return. She met her manager GK, who was only too polite, asking her if she wanted some more time. She explained that sitting at home wasn't proving helpful any more and she would rather carry on with work to keep herself busy. It took Serena only a couple of weeks to come up to speed and then she was back in action.

10

March 1997

GK was anything but a traditional south Indian Brahmin. After completing his post graduation from the Kellogg School of Management, he had worked in the bank for over five years in America and then returned to India as the business head for retail banking. Like most Indians from the south, he had a long name that was shortened to an acronym in business school and carried on in his personal and corporate life. While in America, GK fell in love and married a girl from New York, something for which he was ostracised by his family and the Brahmin community. As for him, he never had any regrets about marrying Stella. She had always stood by him, altered her lifestyle, had become a vegetarian, wore Indian clothes when required and even spoke some Hindi. Unlike a lot of inter-cultural marriages, where the Indian spouse stayed back in the more developed and comfortable part of the world, she had decided to move to India with him. There were rumours that she was dating other young men in the banking circles. People could never stop talking about how gorgeous she was and, often, wondered how she could have fallen in love with a guy like GK.

GK had an in-depth understanding of the banking industry and how his portfolio in the growing Indian economy impacted the global corporation. Understandably, his outlook was broader than running a fiefdom for short-term gains. One of the major reasons for his meteoric rise within the organisation was his leadership skill of catching sight of opportunities early for business and providing important career breaks to competent people. He was quick to spot and nurture talent. His mantra was simple and commendable: if the people under him did not grow, he wouldn't either.

Serena had been working for GK for a little over three years now. He had always regarded her as an individual with a lot of potential and the capability to rise above the ordinary. She had delivered every project for him proficiently – on time and within budget. Moreover, he saw a glimpse of himself in her business acumen and people-handling skills. There was no way she could be content with hanging on to her current assignment for long. In the last three years, he got her to the next grade and added a new operational function to her responsibilities that made her the head of retail banking for the Western region, but that, he knew, was not enough. GK was mindful that if he did not find a good opportunity for her soon, the competition would, and he wasn't prepared to lose a valuable resource like Serena. He had offered her a big break in Singapore, a year ago, but she had declined it. She wasn't ready to move out of Mumbai as Raaj had a thriving business in the city, a dilemma every successful couple faces at some point where one has to compromise career opportunities for the other.

Circumstances had changed since then, and GK speculated on whether Serena would now be willing to take up an assignment abroad. He decided it was worth discussing the possibility again if there was a suitable opening. Fortuitously, he did not have to wait for long. GK had invited the whole department to the Juhu Gymkhana for a party to celebrate his tenth wedding anniversary. He had been considerate enough to send out the invites early, giving people time to plan ahead. The party was only a week away now and he was considering having an informal word with Serena to check if she would be interested in some project abroad.

The evening was super. Stella and GK had got the club to arrange everything on the terrace. Two marquees were set up; one for the bar stocked with all kinds of beverages, and the other with crispy bites that would later be converted into dinner buffet. Hot snacks were to be served by the club staff all through the evening. Regardless of being vegetarians themselves, the host couple had ordered food for an omnivorous crowd. GK had a large department with four direct reports and each of them had a sizeable team. With almost half of them coming with their partners, they were expecting over forty guests.

People started arriving by eight and were greeted by the couple. Serena had anticipated that Stella would wear a sari for the ceremonial occasion and decided to wear one herself. She had, however, not envisaged that both would end up wearing the same colour that evening. Pink. Only, hers was lighter than Stella's. Both women looked gorgeous. Stella, who was at least five years older and ten centimetres taller than Serena, had chosen a dark pink silk sari with a crimson and gold border that contrasted beautifully with her pale skin and blond hair. As an alternative to the traditional custom-stitched blouse that most Indian women wear, she was wearing an even darker pink halter-neck top, made of lycra, which contoured her form and somehow made her look even more glamorous. Serena had chosen a lighter shade of pink and looked extremely attractive too. Not surprisingly, all the other women were in Western outfits. If there were an award for the shortest dress that night, it would have gone to GK's secretary Maria who wore a blood-red short dress that barely covered her bottom.

'Congratulations to both of you,' Serena said, as she handed flowers to Stella.

'Thanks. How have you been, Serena?' Stella greeted Serena, meeting her for the first time since the tragedy.

'I'm fine, thanks. How are you?' Serena asked politely.

'Did you two decide on a dress code?' GK pointed out, seeing them both in pink saris. Everyone around him laughed. A boss's joke is always funny, irrespective of how perceptive or predictable it is. GK took both women's arms and walked towards the bar, like a celebrity. 'What will my darling wife have tonight?'

'Whatever Serena has.' Stella was quick.

GK looked at Serena for a response.

'Vodka with cola please,' Serena said.

'Three large vodkas, one with orange juice and two with colas please,' GK told the bartender.

The guests were getting in the party mood by nine. Someone had brought a CD with every possible remix of Toni Braxton's *Un-break*

My Heart after its recent success in the charts and a few versions prompted the crowd to get into the groove. People generally let their hair down after a few drinks making it interesting to watch, particularly, the interaction between the singles, which was ordinarily veiled in the formal office environment. With experience over the years, Serena and GK could easily predict who-will-date-whom for the next six months by the dance partner one picked, the closeness of the dance and the amount of time they stuck around as the alcohol level rose. Maria was an exception; everyone wanted a dance with her – she was pretty, single and scantily dressed that night, plus no one wanted the boss's secretary to stand alone in the corner.

Serena was also an exception. GK was dancing with Stella when he saw her standing alone in the corner with a drink. It was quite bizarre that no one had picked her up for a dance yet. In almost all the previous parties that GK had attended, Raaj could hardly ever get a chance to dance with his wife as everyone else would keep taking her away from him. GK whispered something in Stella's ear and they both walked to her as the song faded.

'Is everything okay?' Stella asked.

'Yeah, fine.'

'Why aren't you dancing?' GK joined the conversation.

'It's the sari; I wish I had worn something else,' Serena lied. She was clearly missing Raaj.

'Let's sit for a while,' said GK as he sat down.

Stella excused herself to get refills for all of them.

'Thanks to you and the good work we've done in retail banking here in India, we've got a brilliant project coming up in Dubai… would you be interested?' GK asked without warning.

'What is it about?' Serena asked.

'If you are interested…'

'Stop talking shop GK,' Stella cut him off politely as she returned.

'Let's talk on Monday,' GK told Serena, then quickly turned to Stella and said, 'Sorry darling. No more shop.'

The party was still continuing when Serena left at midnight.

May 1997

'Hi, Kim,' Serena called.

'Hi. Where have you been? I haven't seen you for ages,' Kim said with her usual enthusiasm.

'Let's meet this weekend. Have I got news for you, baby?' Serena sounded excited for the first time in a long while.

'What is it?' Kim couldn't wait.

'I'll tell you tomorrow evening. Why don't you bring a changeover? Let's catch up tomorrow.'

Kim arrived at Serena's apartment around eight. After the customary hug, they sat down with a drink and Serena told Kim about the project she had decided to take up in Dubai.

'You are leaving Mumbai?' Kim was shocked.

'Not leaving silly, it's only a short project. A maximum of six months and then I will be back.'

'When did this happen?' Kim was curious.

'GK discussed it with me in March. Initially, I had concerns, but we worked on understanding the project better before I agreed. After GK put my name up for consideration, it took a while for them to come back to let him know that I've been selected. It is a six-month secondment to the regional office in Dubai. I thought you should be the first to know.'

'I'll miss you, Serena.' Kim got sentimental.

'I will miss you too, girl, but you've been the one telling me to move on with my life for the last nine months. It would be a change of environment for me.'

'I will visit you for sure. Dubai is a great place for shopping,' Kim said with glee in her eyes.

'That reminds me, I need to shop before I go.'

'When are you going?' Kim questioned.

'In four weeks. They are processing the papers now.'

'Let's go shopping next weekend,' Kim declared, sipping her drink.

It took an awfully long time for Serena's offer letter to arrive, as they had decided to slash budgets in the bank and new launches were the worst affected. Weeks turned to months before she applied for the visa.

11

Dubai
January 1998

Dubai is a beautiful city. The new airport was still under construction but Serena could see that it would give serious competition to Changi and even to Hong Kong International Airport, in time. If she could change one thing about the place, it would be the weather; it was either hot or very hot. But someone in Serena's professional capacity hardly spent time in a non air-conditioned environment. From the residences, to the cars, to the office, to the shopping malls, everything was climate controlled.

Serena was to stay in a service apartment as getting an apartment to rent had its own complications. For one, it was difficult to find a short-term lease without paying an unnecessary premium and, secondly, finding an apartment for a single woman in Dubai was not straightforward. She was quick to understand that Dubai was a living paradox caught between conservatism and Western modernism. It wanted to portray itself as a society with high morals, but one could see all kinds of promiscuous and illicit trade happening on the streets. The semi-clad, heavily made up women who lined all neighbourhoods soon after sunset were definitely not there to provide tourists with information. As a result, most decent professional single women, like

Serena, found it impossible to find accommodation. The bank was aware of this and it was recommended that she did not even look for it to avoid an awkward situation.

Serena was fine as the bank was picking up the tab. As it was a short-term assignment it was much easier to live in a service residence, where everything would be taken care of. The apartment she finally moved into could best be described as an IKEA showroom; the sofas, the bed, the lamps and even the prints on the walls were sourced from there.

Serena's bank had been in Dubai since the early 1970s when the country formed the United Arab Emirates with six others and opted for a unified local currency: Dirham. Prior to that, like some of the other banks, even her bank had managed the region from India, because the Reserve Bank of India was the one issuing currency in Gulf-Rupees. Cab drivers and many traders, still, referred to the local money as rupees.

Until now, the sole focus of Serena's bank had been on corporate business. It now wanted to make a foray into the retail side, which was becoming immensely lucrative for competitors. Serena had proved herself in re-launching the image of retail banking in India and was therefore a logical choice. She knew retail banking and could speak the language, as a majority of the task force in Dubai spoke both Hindi and English. The reward would be grand if she could repeat her Indian success in Dubai. It wouldn't be easy but, at least, she knew where to start.

On her first day on the job, Serena met her new manager. He outlined the objective, timeline, team and budget and wished her luck. He clarified that he would not be able to provide Serena with day-to-day advice, but would like to have a fortnightly status meeting, and if something required escalating up she could contact him. Serena had known from the very beginning that this would be different from her regular job at Mumbai. This was an autonomous project: to deliver a new product in the market with all the responsibilities that go with it. She would have to work with various other departments within the bank, and outside it, to deliver results. What she needed was to be self-motivated; at all times she must lead from the front.

She had a meeting with her direct reports later in the day to oversee the status of the project so far. The five people on the team were as multicultural and colourful as one required for a Benetton commercial. Syed a senior Pakistani gentleman looked after all the marketing and communications. Ravi, an Indian, was responsible for retail – property, look and style. Recruitment was assigned to Elena from Spain. A Dutchman called Tony headed operations, and the responsibility of technology was given to Adam, an impossibly good-looking Afro-American.

This needs reorganisation, Serena thought.

She regrouped the team and made a retail report into marketing to establish a single brand identity, be it communications or customer touch points at retail. The other change was to combine operations and technology into one team under Tony. Recruitment, being a staff function, was made to report to both the groups and her. She was clear that in order for this project to succeed, it needed the right people in the right jobs. There was no ambiguity that she would be directly involved in the communications and selection of retail locations, which were the first impressions to the consumer. Ravi was not averse to the changes. In fact, he welcomed reporting to Syed who came with a vast knowledge and experience. He was young and ambitious and he understood that if they were successful in the retail-banking launch in Dubai, being part of the core team would be a boon to his career. Adam, on the other hand, was not a happy man. He did not appreciate working under Tony, but he recognised he was helpless at this point in time. The launch of retail banking was the sole focus of the team and Serena was the guardian, so he did not voice his discontentment.

The team was convinced that they could deliver a class leading retail bank. Everyone was motivated to deliver. The advertising agency was appointed and briefed. The recruitments were taking place and training plans, identified. The properties were being short-listed for final selection. Everything was progressing fine, and on time.

Two things about Dubai annoyed Serena. One was the weekends. They had Sunday as a working day and Fridays and Saturdays off. It took her some time to get used to the routine, but given the short time she had, she was working most of the weekends anyway. The other frustration was the lack of wine stores in the country. Dubai had a strange system where one registers oneself for a liquor permit to go to one of the state owned warehouse stores with a limit to how much one could buy in a month - a ration shop. To add insult to injury, she found out that the law forbade women to hold liquor permits. She had carried two bottles of vodka from the duty free at the airport when she came in, but they were all but empty now. Only restaurants in hotels had a permit to serve alcohol and since she did not have much company, she rarely went out to them.

Months went by. She had a review with her manager and he was glad at the pace the team had progressed. The whole team had worked relentlessly with a single aim, without giving themselves any personal space. Others in the team might have been active in their personal and social lives, but Serena had her head buried in work alone.

It was late Thursday evening when Adam walked into Serena's office to invite her for a night out. 'Some of us are planning to go clubbing to The Lodge tomorrow night. Do you want to join us?' He asked casually.

'Of course,' Serena responded immediately as if she had been waiting for it. It had been quite a while since she'd had a drink or danced a bit. 'What time?'

'We'll meet after dinner so let's say around half-past-nine?'

'Fine… How many of us are going?'

'I've invited about fifteen people. More than half of them should turn up.'

'Okay. See you there.' Serena closed the conversation and got back to work.

On the way back from work, Serena realised that she had nothing to wear to a dance club, but she could go shopping for it. It dawned on her that she hadn't gone out shopping without Kim for a long time.

'How are you, Kim?' She called Kim that evening.

'I am fine. How are you… haven't heard from you for quite some time now.'

'I know… just been busy. I have to go shopping tomorrow without you after so long.' Serena sounded low.

'Cheer up, girl. Any good guys around?' Kim tried to cheer up Serena.

'There's an American in my team. He's very good looking – he's of mixed race certainly, though I haven't asked. He's organised a clubbing night for us and we're meeting after dinner.'

'Just you and him?' Kim sounded excited. At last Serena was trying to live.

'No. A lot of us from the team are going.'

'Damn. Tell me more about him.' Kim was anxious.

'He is much younger.'

'That shouldn't matter.'

'That wasn't what I had called for. I wanted to know what I should wear.'

'Nothing.' Kim laughed.

'Shut up. Tell me.'

'Is he tall?'

'What should I wear?' Serena ignored Kim's question.

'That was a genuine question, Serena. If he is tall, you'd want to wear a short dress to make you look taller,' Kim advised.

'What do you want me to look like?'

'A sexy, single woman.'

'What if he…'

'Go with it, Serena. You have to move on in life after Raaj; he's gone and you haven't taken an oath of celibacy, have you?' Kim pre-empted Serena's hesitation and responded to assure her friend. There was a minute's silence before Kim continued. 'Do not let any unnecessary inhibitions or redundant morals hold you back girl.'

'Thanks for the reassurance Kim. And how are you doing? Have you found someone yet?' It was Serena's turn to question.

'No. But I am looking.'

'Keep in touch,' Serena said. 'My mobile phone is ringing. I'll talk to you later.' She disconnected the phone to take the other call.

Serena went shopping on Friday morning. Every time she liked or tried something, Kim's words echoed in her ears; *you'd want to wear a short dress.* She finally zeroed in on a short black dress, which ended about half a foot above her knees. It was a classic design with a halter neck and cut-away shoulders that had a stand-up collar with a zipper running all along the back to fasten it. As it was made of viscose and lycra, she was conscious that it would cling to her body and she was at ease with that. The next thing to buy was footwear. Calf leather knee-high boots would have looked great with this short dress, but Dubai weather does not grant someone that joy and she discarded all other shoes. As advised, she wanted to add a bit of height so she went for a sleek and stunning, strappy open-toe sandal detailed in black, with glittering crystals to shine on the club floor, and a metal-tipped heel.

'You've got very beautiful feet sweetheart,' Raaj had always pointed out.

'Are you saying that's the only beautiful thing about me?'

'You're gorgeous my precious.'

Serena wiped away her tears.

She spent the rest of the day at a hair and beauty salon, as she felt that she deserved a treat after such a long time. The little black dress snugly hugged her petite perfect body, flaunted her toned arms and showed her lovely legs that made her look exceptionally sensational. She wore a posh, but subtle make-up in a style she had learnt from Kim years ago, and enhanced it with light pink nail paint.

She hadn't partied for a long time now. It was about time.

12

The cab dropped Serena outside The Lodge, a little after nine-thirty. A few people from the office had already arrived and were waiting for others. As she got out of the cab and walked towards them, Adam stepped forward to give her a ceremonial kiss.

'You look hot, Serena,' he whispered.

'Thank you.'

A few others complimented her too. Most were equally well groomed. All the guys wore jeans and smart shirts, but the girls were definitely dressed up.

The Lodge had first opened in the eighties and had been updated a few times since then. It had very a large indoor space with a few bars with music playing. Outside there were several bars, fast food points and an enormous dance floor where the DJ mixed some great tunes. They opened a tab on the bar and ordered the first round of drinks. Serena pulled a packet of Bensons from her bag and lit up.

'Could I have one?' asked Adam and Ravi and Elena and...

'How come we don't see this glamorous side of you in the office?' Adam asked all the girls, looking directly at Serena.

'Because... it is the office so we dress formally, like you guys don't wear jeans there,' someone from the crowd responded.

'All of you look dashing.' He still hadn't removed his stare from Serena.

'Thanks,' everyone said in unison.

'Could I have a dance with you please?' Adam extended his hand to Serena.

'What's the rush? Let's get a few more drinks before we hit the floor,' Ravi intercepted, looking for approval from everyone.

'Okay.' Adam didn't sound convinced.

As Adam walked away to get the next round of drinks, Elena warned Serena, 'Watch out, he's got the hots for you tonight.'

'I have been watching him; he doesn't seem to stop staring at me. It's kind of eerie,' Serena agreed.

'I don't blame him. I am sure a lot of men here would want to dance with you and take you home tonight. You look dazzling,' Elena complimented.

'Thanks. You do, too.' Serena blushed.

Adam was back with a round of tequila.

'I haven't had a drink for some time now, Adam. If I have this, I will get drunk.' Serena tried excusing herself.

'It doesn't matter. I will take you home. Come on… You've got very sexy legs,' he whispered in her ear putting his arm around her shoulder.

Serena was aware if she didn't ward off Adam, now, it might get a bit embarrassing as the night progressed. She quickly took the tequila shot with the others. 'Excuse me. I have to go to the Ladies.'

'I'll come along,' Elena offered.

Another girl from the team joined them.

'You were right, Elena. He's getting a bit out of hand now.'

'I told you. He definitely wants to take you home tonight. Just be careful. Don't get too drunk,' Elena advised.

It was getting close to eleven now. Most of the gang were in good spirits and were beginning to feel the alcohol inside them.

'Should we have another round of drinks before we hit the dance floor?' someone asked.

'Yes,' the rest of the crowd responded.

As everyone walked outdoors to the dance floor, Adam asked Serena for a dance again. She agreed this time. It was fine for the first few minutes while they danced in the group. But Adam had other ideas. He was trying to get closer to Serena all the time and each time he advanced she moved a step backwards to avoid him breathing on her.

To break eye contact with him, she looked behind him towards the bar and spotted another amazingly handsome olive-skinned guy dressed in what looked like a dark grey, almost ash-coloured pin-striped suit. He was staring at her too. She got a bit nervous. Before she could calm herself, Adam put his arm around her and brought her tightly close to himself, his hands moving all over her back. Serena could not get away from his clasp even if she tried. Instead of making a scene there, she thought she would dance till the end of this song before excusing herself. But he got more vulgar by the minute, forcing his right leg between her legs to bring her still closer. When he put his hand on her bottom, Serena decided it was enough. 'Excuse me. I need to go to the Ladies,' she said loudly.

Adam was in no mood to lose the opportunity of holding her, so he ignored the request. Serena thumped her heel into his shoe to make him let go. He did. She turned around to see if the other guy, who was staring at her, was still around. He was gone. Elena walked back with Serena again.

'I think I should leave now,' Serena told Elena.

'Why?'

'I don't think I can take any more molestation from Adam.'

'What?'

'What else is it? He's physically mauling me - feeling me all over under the pretext of dancing. I don't want as pleasant a night as this to end in something we all might have to regret.' Serena was certainly not happy.

'Don't dance with him, but don't leave yet, please.'

'Okay,' Serena agreed.

'Thanks.'

They walked outdoors to a corner and lit up cigarettes. Ravi had bought another round of drinks and brought them over. 'You girls aren't dancing any more?' he asked innocently.

'Serena is planning to leave,' Elena announced.

'Why?'

'She's a bit upset…'

'Adam is drunk and he's being offensive now… I don't want to be treated like a ragdoll here,' Serena explained.

'You don't have to dance with him.'

Syed, who had been around all evening, drinking non-alcoholic beverages, joined the three of them and Ravi told him about Adam creating a nuisance.

It did not take Adam long to realise that his sexy dance partner wasn't coming back to the floor, so he started looking around and spotted them standing in the corner, sipping their drinks. He continued dancing and impolitely gestured to Serena to return, but she ignored it by looking the other way. Not one to easily take no for an answer, he marched towards her.

'There he comes…' Serena murmured.

'I'll take care of this. Don't worry, Serena,' Syed assured all of them.

'Why aren't you dancing with me?' Adam rudely asked, looking at Serena as he approached them.

'Adam, she's tired so let's hang around here,' Syed requested politely.

'Tired? We've only been dancing for ten minutes.' He was persistent and got really close to Serena.

'She doesn't feel like it,' Syed argued again.

'And who are you… her pimp?'

Everyone present was aghast at his choice of words for Syed and the implication it carried for Serena.

'I don't want to dance with you and be treated roughly,' Serena said loudly.

'This is not your office where you say something and I have to agree,' Adam growled. 'This is a club and I want to dance with you. Do you get that?' He caught hold of Serena's arm strongly and pulled, clearly hurting her.

'Leave me alone,' Serena screamed.

'What if I don't, you tease…'

'The lady said, LEAVE,' someone said from behind. It wasn't screamed, but was loud and clear even with the music blaring on the floor. Everyone turned around to see who it was, as it didn't sound like anyone from the office. Moving forward out of the darkness was the guy Serena had spotted in the pinstriped suit; he was a tad shorter than the six-foot Adam, but equally well built, and had piercing blue eyes that were fixed on Adam.

'Stay out of it; it's between us friends.' Adam was clearly annoyed. 'And who are you?'

'I am the Sheriff of Dubai,' the man said.

His voice was cold enough to curdle the blood with fear. Adam, instantly, left Serena's arm and let her go. 'I was only requesting that my friend have a dance.' He was suddenly offering an explanation to the sheriff.

'I don't think your friend looks interested,' the sheriff said, as he stood amongst them now, looking at Serena.

'Thank you.' Serena felt relieved.

'Good night.' Adam walked away, his plans gone awry.

'I don't think you should drive in the state you are in,' someone called.

Syed hurried after Adam.

'I didn't know they had a sheriff in Dubai.' Serena turned to the man.

'To be honest, I don't know either.' The man smiled. 'I didn't want the situation to turn nasty. Calling oneself the sheriff usually turns drunken men away from whatever they are doing.'

'Thanks again.' This time it was Ravi.

'You're welcome.' The sheriff walked away from the group to the bar.

When Syed caught up with Adam outside the club, the American was still raging. 'What does the bitch think of herself? She cannot tease me and expect me to behave like a gentleman.'

'What makes you think she was teasing you?' Syed asked politely.

'What do you know? She's been coming on to me all night.'

'Adam, she wasn't giving you any such signals.'

'I'll kill her. I'll kill that bastard – he might be the sheriff, I don't care. I will take her home tonight.' Adam was almost shouting now.

Syed understood it was unsafe standing there with a drunken Adam swearing at the top of his voice, so he coaxed him to come into the car. Once inside, Syed suggested that he could drop Adam home or call for a cab for him.

'I'm not leaving here without her; tell her to come with me.'

'She's not coming with you. And don't forget, this might be a club, but she's still your manager at work. What makes you think she'll sleep with you?' Syed tried reasoning. 'I am requesting you to leave or this will lead to something you might have to repent later. You just brushed with the sheriff and there's enough security in this place to stop you from getting near her.'

'No. I am not leaving without her.'

'Do as you want, Adam. I cannot advise you any more. I am going in.' Syed walked out of Adam's car and slammed the door.

Adam watched him go all the way back to the club. He knew well that he could not drive drunk. He could be caught and the drink driving law in Dubai was very strictly enforced.

'Has he left?' Serena asked as soon as Syed came back.

'No. He's still outside. He's not in the best state or mood, Serena. He's got some crush on you tonight. I wouldn't be surprised if he acts irresponsibly when you go out,' Syed warned.

'What should I do now?' Serena asked nervously.

'Don't worry about it. One of us will drop you home. I hope he does not know where you live.'

'I don't think so, but he can follow me.'

'We'll see what happens later. He may leave in time if he does not see us coming out. It's probably best to stay here for some time.'

'Calm down, Serena. You can come over to my place,' Elena offered.

'Where did the sheriff go?' Syed asked.

'He was no sheriff. He just said that to avoid any confrontation with Adam,' Ravi explained.

'Smart guy.'

Another round of drinks followed and they became oblivious to the fact that Adam might still be outside. Serena confided in the others she shouldn't have agreed to come for the evening, though she hadn't anticipated that events would turn ugly. Others comforted her that it wasn't her fault at all. Adam had drunk too much and obviously misread her attire as something she had worn to attract him in particular.

'It's not that I have worn anything too provocative. Looking at some of the other women here, I am well covered,' Serena said, looking around at some other women who were scantily clad.

'Of course you are well dressed. In any case, what you wear is totally your choice. He's no one to make conclusions about our dresses. We are not living here at his mercy to dress according to what he thinks is decent enough for him. Nor to treat us as some cheap pick-ups,' Elena added.

They moved back to the dance floor and chose to remain in a group this time and not fragment into pairs. Elena saw the sheriff sitting and chatting with a woman at the bar. She went to ask him for a dance and he excused himself from the lady and followed her back to where the others were sitting.

'Has your admirer gone?' The sheriff asked Serena, as Elena brought him to the group.

'I am told he is waiting outside in the car.'

'Don't let that bother you. If need be, I will drop you back.' He meant every word he said.

'Thanks, but that shouldn't be necessary.'

The sheriff danced with Elena for ten minutes before he excused himself. 'I am sorry everyone, I have to leave now. My friend is waiting for me at the bar,' he apologised.

'Thanks for intervening at the right moment,' Serena thanked him again.

'You're welcome.' He went back to the bar to the girl he was with before he had joined them.

'I wish he was alone,' Elena said.

'I do too,' Serena seconded it.

'Just the kind I like...' another one said.

'Smashing, isn't he?'

Elena kept eyeing the sheriff till his friend left him alone at the bar. She walked up to him, as he sat on the barstool.

'Can I buy you a drink, Sheriff?' she asked.

He looked up. 'I should buy you one. What would you like to have?'

'Whatever you want...' Elena wasn't in a mood to play hard to get.

'Two scotches on the rocks please...' he told the barman before turning to Elena, 'I am sorry; I didn't get your name...'

'What do you want it to be?' She was obviously flirting now.

'Excuse me...?' He winked at her.

Serena joined them at the bar to get her drink. 'Someone's got company,' she commented.

'Join us,' Elena offered.

'You know, two's company, three is a crowd...' Serena said, mischievously.

'Maybe I'm the odd one out,' the sheriff said.

'You know you're not,' Elena said almost immediately. 'Maybe I am.'

'What is your name?' Serena asked looking at the sheriff.

'What do you want it to be?' He repeated Elena's line and both of them laughed. Elena told Serena about their conversation a minute ago.

'Let's party,' Elena said.

The three of them moved to the dance floor again to join the rest, and the sheriff danced with both the girls for a while. Elena was a tall, bleached-blonde southern Spanish belle with almost the same skin colour as Serena, but she was a few years younger. Tonight she wore a striking off-shoulder dress that ended around her knees; originally the dress was worn with a grey-silver stole, which was kept somewhere that even Elena did not know now. The mood of the evening had definitely got into her and she was enjoying herself with an infectious abandon.

It was close to two in the morning now. The discothèque music had turned from loud jarring mixes to slower tracks as it got near to closing time. In a surprising move, the sheriff pulled Elena for a close dance; close enough for any stray onlooker to have mistaken them for a honeymoon couple. As the music faded into another track, Elena asked Serena if she wanted to have a close dance with the Sheriff. Serena looked sceptical at first; she was fully aware that the rest of her team was watching, but eventually gave in to the request. As she came into the arms of the sheriff, she wondered how the evening would end. She had just started getting comfortable with him when they announced that it was time to close and the lights came on. Serena's head lay against the sheriff's chest completely unmindful of the people around her.

'Time to leave, Serena.' Elena tapped on her shoulder.

'I don't want to leave.' Serena sounded slightly drunk.

'I can take care of her, you guys can carry on,' the sheriff offered.

One could noticeably see that the office crowd was hesitant in leaving Serena in this state with a guy they had only met a few hours ago. He might have been nice in fending Adam off, buying a few drinks for the girls and dancing with them, but no one knew anything about him. Serena didn't seem to care; Kim's words resonated in her ears and the vodka helped her understand them better – she hadn't been with a guy for over two years now. She recognised that she could be acting recklessly by ignoring the advice from her colleagues and staying back with a stranger to take care of her, but she insisted on continuing with her party. Elena was disappointed that Serena had swept the good-looking sheriff away from her. However, she eventually kissed her good night and started to leave. Everyone else followed.

Before she made her exit from the club, she grudgingly glanced back at the dance floor to see the sheriff and Serena kissing. She was envious it wasn't her in his arms. She was the one who had flirted with him first, but it was Serena's day, she convinced herself, and stepped out.

Serena was playing Kim's sexy single woman to the hilt tonight.

Adam woke up to someone knocking on his car window. It was the police. He didn't realise he had dozed off in the car, waiting for Serena. A quick glance at his watch told him it was three in the morning. He opened the window and explained to the police that he had drunk a bit over his limit and hence did not wish to drive. The police asked him to take a cab and go home, as he was not allowed to sleep in the car park; he could come and take the car the next day. Adam got out of the car, locked it and walked to the small queue waiting for cabs. The club had wound up some time ago and he comprehended he had missed the group and Serena coming out, and hence wasn't left with much of a choice but to leave as advised by police. He reflected that his behaviour had cost him a probable steamy night with Serena; he had an eye for her since the first time she had met the team. He hadn't made a noise, nor had he resigned when she made him report to Tony because he was certain that his good looks would melt her sooner or later. He had organised the whole club event for her to come, and he was still convinced she had come as a tease for him. Organising another one like this and expecting anyone, especially her, to turn up would be highly optimistic now.

'Damn,' he murmured as he sat in the cab. 'Bar Dubai behind the Hotel Ramada, please.'

He tried calling Serena on her mobile phone from the cab, but it was switched off.

Next day

Adam got up with a huge hangover at eleven in the morning.

If only he had had a few less drinks, he would have woken up with Serena in his bed this morning, he reckoned.

As he gulped down aspirins, he couldn't do much but be disappointed about the lost opportunity and his inappropriate, unruly conduct. It would be difficult to save face in front of his colleagues in the office the next day. He wondered if he should call Serena to apologise. He tried her mobile and it went to the voicemail after a few rings, but he did not leave a message. He made several other attempts during the afternoon, but the calls kept being diverted. It was evident that she did not wish to speak to him.

Serena reached home around noon after spending the whole night out. Sitting in her apartment in the evening and going through the events of the previous day, she wondered if she should update Kim on the sexy single woman's one night adventure with a stranger. It was no longer uncommon for singles to pick up dates in discothèques or nightclubs, but it was rare for her. After deliberating on it for some time, she couldn't resist confiding in Kim about the glorious time she had with the sheriff.

'You are such a slut,' Kim said in way of appreciation.

'Hmm…'

'It was time you looked after yourself. Was it good?'

'Very good,' Serena said timidly.

'Going out with him again tonight?'

'No.'

'Why?' Kim wanted to know.

'I am not ready for a relationship yet,' Serena explained.

'Understandable. When are you getting back here?'

'It will take a few more months.'

'Hook up with someone else next weekend.'

13

Elena walked into Serena's room on Sunday morning at ten to inform her that Adam had called to resign from the job.

'Why didn't you stop him?' Serena exclaimed.

'I tried. I think he's reluctant to even turn up here. He asked me to send the papers over to him through the local courier. He's dreading disciplinary action.'

'Sad. We're right in the middle of the project. I realise more than anyone that his behaviour was inappropriate in the club, but we were all drunk and it was out of the office, so there is no reason for anyone to take any disciplinary action. He could have simply come in, apologised and carried on,' Serena tried reasoning.

'You're right, but he's still going to be embarrassed.'

'Okay. Do we have anyone in his team who can take up his position as acting head of technology? Let me speak to Tony…' Serena picked up the phone and gestured Elena to stay put in her office.

The plan for the launch of the retail business was unconventional. Unlike other retailers or banks that inaugurate a single branch or franchise, Serena had convinced the board that they would go for three retail walk-in branches. The branches, with open-floor layouts, looked more like retail stores than offices. They had bought out spaces at a few gas stations for new ATMs, but largely purchased a local bank's ATMs and rebranded them. Serena's argument was that it made more sense to buy these rather than spend all the money for outdoor media on billboards, as this would make the brand presence felt overnight.

The August opening of the bank's retail business was more than just successful. Prime-time television and radio were booked for the advertising campaign broadcasting the launch with the PR machinery in place. To jazz up an otherwise boring banking activity, an art exhibition was organised in the retail premises to get consumers into the branches for the first time. The promotional offers on savings and current accounts, plus the rewards programme on credit cards were second to none in the market. Serena always believed that banks should behave like high-end retailers and not like the tellers they had been for centuries. She had seen to it that the consumer experience was equally upbeat by training the team not only in banking functions, but in retail discipline too. She was almost in tears when she thanked her team in the evening.

Local head-hunters started calling before the end of the day. The competition had been watching cynically right till the end. They had disbelieved the rumours of a retail bank going trendy. A bank, with no retail presence till now, had moved the bar higher. It was obvious that offers would start pouring in from existing retail banks in the city - given the small banking community - outbidding each other. Serena had expected the reaction, but not so quickly.

GK called to congratulate Serena early next morning. He had planned to be in Dubai for the launch, but had to change plans, last minute, to accommodate another meeting in America. He was on the way back and called from Heathrow before boarding for Dubai.

'Catch you in a few hours. Any plans for the evening?' he asked.

'No.'

'I would like to take you out for dinner.'

In the last seven months, Serena had lost touch with GK, primarily, because of her workload. She was conscious that she should have made an effort; GK would have expected emails or, at least, short telephone calls. He was in her office just after lunch and gave her a customary hug. 'Congratulations Serena,' he said loud enough for everyone in the office to hear. He had lost some weight and some more hair on his already balding head and he looked tired because of the long travel.

'Thanks GK. Glad to see you again.'

'You completely forgot about me,' GK quipped.

'I am sorry. I was thinking the same. The work has kept me horribly busy, but now that the launch is behind me...' Serena explained apologetically. 'How's Stella?'

GK chose, for some reason, to ignore the pleasantry. 'Come on – show me the retail branches that I have been reading about in all the local dailies since my arrival,' he said.

'Okay.'

'This is incredible work, Serena,' GK commented, as they walked into the first branch. 'I think you should return and do some more good work with our retail branches in India. Got any job offers out here?' he asked.

'Lots...'

'Not taking them, I suppose. You work for one of the best banks in business today and should take a long-term view. We can always look at the grade and money when you return. Let's talk at dinner tonight.'

The Irish Village at Dubai Aviation Club is famous for its lively and vibrant atmosphere. It has, convincingly, simulated settings of an Irish village with stores that sell traditional stuff like the Celtic crosses in stained glass or print. The whole courtyard is paved and it boasts a pond in the desert kingdom. Serena had been there once, and knew that it stocked Irish beer and cider, making it a big hit with the local Irish population who called it 'their Ireland' in Dubai. The music was live on some nights, but the food, however, was great every night. Sadly, tonight wasn't one of those live-band nights. It was late in the evening, well after sunset, and the cool breeze had set in when GK and Serena arrived. They chose to sit outside and ordered beer and food.

'Congratulations again,' GK started.

'Thank you.'

'What's your plan now? The launch is over. I am sure they would like to keep you for the expansion and I am willing to extend your stay, if you want. I cannot afford to lose you to the competition.' GK was candid.

'I am not even considering jumping ship at the moment.' Serena was frank too.

'Good. You will go a long way in this bank, I promise.'

'Thanks.'

'When do you want to return?'

'In a couple of months. I need to find a replacement for myself and hand over the portfolio.'

'Great.'

The beers had arrived.

'How's Stella?' Serena asked again, as she put the glass of beer down after a sip to light up a cigarette.

'We divorced,' GK said softly.

'What?' Serena almost choked for a moment.

'That's why I couldn't come to your launch; I was in New York for the final settlement. I found out Stella has been dating some guy in Mumbai for a few years now.'

'Who was she dating?' Serena was aghast.

'I don't know; I have never met him. He moved to New York about two years ago and they had been carrying on their affair whenever she went home. She had started doing longer trips more frequently, but I was so much involved in the work that I totally missed any clues. She finally decided to move in with him.'

'Unbelievable.'

'You're telling me.'

'Is he American?'

'No, Indian. He is much younger than her too. I am really sad, but I hope it works out for both of them.' GK was being magnanimous; he was clearly hurt. 'Another beer for you?'

'Yes.'

'That's all about me. How are you? Met anyone interesting here?' GK asked.

'Not yet.'

She hadn't lied; a one-night rendezvous could hardly be termed as meeting someone.

After dinner they ordered coffee. Serena felt sorry for GK - he was a nice guy who had sacrificed all his family and relatives by getting married, against their wishes, to an American. And, she had all too conveniently left him for another man.

'I am sorry,' Serena summoned all her courage to mutter.

'You don't have to be. I was the one who didn't have the faintest idea that my wife was in a relationship with someone else for over three years. I was a fool and this world is not made for idiots like me. Shit happens,' GK said with a shrug, controlling his emotions.

He left Dubai the next morning.

Mumbai
September 1998
In spite of all his hard and brilliant work, Senior Inspector Michael D'Cunha was still waiting for the promotion he deserved, and he had, now, got exhausted getting nowhere and accomplishing nothing. He raised the issue a few times with his superiors, but the bureaucracy, at its customary best, provided evasive responses; no concrete plans, reasons or dates.

He sat brooding over the infuriatingly slow bureaucracy of his establishment when he got called into his next investigation about a suicide in Worli. He picked up his cap, called for his driver and left immediately.

Dubai
The razzmatazz over, Serena got busy with work yet again; she also needed to find her replacement. They had to, eventually, hire externally, because there was a lack of talent with the required skill set; the new person came onboard in mid-September. The handover, the knowledge transfer, took another month without breaking for weekends before she and her Dubai line-manager were confident the replacement hired could carry on the good work.

Without being aware of it, Serena realised she had collected a substantial amount of baggage to be carried back. It took her a week to wind up before saying good-bye to Dubai. It was mid-October before she boarded the flight to Mumbai.

14

Mumbai
October 1998

Serena arrived over the weekend to unpack and relax. Kim, good friend that she was, had organised the cleaning of the apartment, some groceries in the refrigerator and sent her friend's car for servicing with the driver. She had even arranged flowers to be sent there on Serena's arrival, as she was herself out of town for a shoot. She was no longer just an up and coming model, having just been signed by L'Oreal and Nokia.

Serena was early in the office on Monday morning. GK wasn't in yet so she met with her old team. Rohan, who had replaced her when she moved to Dubai, was still around; he was certain that she would be given greater responsibility, so there wasn't a risk to his job.

GK arrived after nine. 'Welcome home Serena,' he said with loud aplomb.

'Thanks.' Serena walked beside him as he dashed towards his office. She exchanged greetings with Maria, while GK collected his mail from her desk.

'Any calls?' GK asked Maria.

'No.'

'Two strong coffees and stop all calls unless they are absolutely necessary please,' he told Maria, and politely gestured Serena towards his office.

The office had windows on two sides and a glass partition overlooking his secretary on the third. On his right side was the only wall and a large picture of Stella had adorned it for as long as Serena had known GK. The picture was missing now. The wallpaper around it had faded leaving a visible emptiness on the wall.

'Why don't you put something there, GK?' Serena asked as she entered.

'Give me a picture of yours.'

Maria brought in the coffees and left them on GK's desk. She walked out quietly closing the door behind her.

'You did a fantastic job in Dubai Serena,' GK eulogised as he raised the cup of coffee as if it were a toast.

'Thanks.' Serena did the same before taking a sip.

'You're welcome.' He pulled out a paper from a stack on his desk and handed it over to Serena. 'You are now a vice president and a director. Congratulations.'

'Thank you GK,' Serena said, taking the paper from his hand.

'Ordinarily, it does not happen this way, in this organisation, but as you are no average person, the bank has decided to give you a choice of two assignments to decide between. One is to move into corporate banking as the head of the Western region. I know you were head of the regional retail before you left this place, but the corporate business is far bigger than retail in terms of revenue. It would give you an understanding of a new business and groom you for your next move across corporate and retail banking. The other option is to head up the retail banking for the country, which is, effectively, my job.'

'What do you do then?'

'Sorry. I forgot to tell you, I have been promoted to business manager for the country, heading both retail and corporate banking,' he replied.

'Congratulations. That's really good.'

'Thank you. If you take the job of the retail head for the country, you report directly to me. On the other hand, in the regional corporate banking job you will report to Shiva, who is the head of corporate banking. I can assure you that within the next eighteen months Shiva will move up to make space for a good performer like you, so you needn't worry on those grounds.' GK stated it as if it were a matter of fact.

'What would you take, if you were me?' Serena asked the standard question most people ask their supervisors when in a quandary.

'In my mind, both of the jobs add value; one comes with a national responsibility and the other teaches more aspects of business. One makes you a specialist, the other broadens your experience,' GK answered, exactly, how supervisors respond to such questions: guarded but not evasive.

Serena sat silently.

'You don't have to decide right now,' he explained, seeing Serena in a dilemma. 'You can take a day or two, think about it, talk to people and let me know.'

'I think I know what I want...' Serena started.

'Take my job,' GK said as if he had read her mind.

'How did you guess?' Serena was surprised.

'Give me some credit Serena, this wasn't a guess. I have known you for a long time now. That is precisely why I asked you for your picture for this wall.' GK smiled, pointing towards the empty space on his right.

'I was surprised you even offered me the choice then.'

'It's your career. The final choice should be yours,' GK summed up.

'You're right, GK. Thanks.'

'I would have allocated a month of transition for the new person in my role, but if you are taking it, it shouldn't take that long. I would start handing over the work to you from today and you should be up to speed before the end of the month. In any case, I am not moving out just moving to the next office, so I am around if you need me.' He arose from his desk and put his hand out. Serena got up and shook his hand. 'I wish you all the best, Serena. I am confident you will do it to the best of your ability,' he said confidently.

'I will.' Serena turned and opened the door to walk out of his office.

Serena was happy that the high-risk retail banking launch project in Dubai had got rewarded with a national responsibility. She loved retail banking, and a specialist was what she wanted to be referred as.

November 1998

Serena was meeting up with Kim after ten months. They had decided to spend the weekend together to catch-up as it had been a long time.

'It feels so nice to see you again, darling,' Kim screamed and gave a big hug to Serena as she opened her apartment door. 'Almost a year without you in the city… let's party sweetheart.'

'Sure. How was your trip to Hong Kong?' Serena asked casually. 'How's Adi?'

'You still remember him? You know, he's a nice guy. He got me out of trouble once, I never told you about it,' Kim said, thinking of the time he had called to stop D'Cunha from harassing her. 'How about you… how was Dubai?

'Pity you couldn't make it while I was there. It is a heaven for shopping.'

'And also, I could see your Prince Charming…' Kim teased.

'Hardly...' Serena said as both of them walked to the bar to pour a drink.

'You mean you made out with someone who is less than a charming prince?'

'I meant, I just met him once; we were both drunk in the nightclub and it happened,' Serena clarified.

'What *happened*? Tell me about it… in detail.' Kim sounded anxious.

'It's entirely your fault.'

'How?'

'You pushed me into wearing a short dress to look a sexy single woman. I had one of my office guys falling all over me, calling me a tease.' Serena was reminded of Adam, suddenly.

'It wasn't a fault; it was good advice. You got laid. You needed it. You hadn't slept with a man for two years, Virgin Mary. How was it?' Kim couldn't stop probing.

'What do you mean – how was it?'

'Was he any good?'

'It was amazing. As you said I needed to make out… it had been a very long time.'

'I've never done it with a stranger like that. You're such a slut,' Kim quipped.

'I wouldn't have either, but I was drunk and I just didn't want to resist any more.' Serena offered unnecessary explanations.

'Good for you. What's his name?'

'What do you want it to be?' Serena described the whole evening in detail over drinks. She narrated how Adam had misbehaved and how the sheriff had intervened at the right time; Elena's funny story about flirting with him and he in turn repeating the words when Serena asked him his name; the close dancing and shameless kissing on the crowded dance floor and how he reassured the rest of her office crowd that he would take care of her… and care he took, very good care.

'As the club closed he asked if I wanted to have a drink in his room. He was staying in the same hotel as the discotheque, and I was expecting him to take me somewhere, so I nodded the moment he asked. As he closed the door to his room, we hugged and kissed. It was pretty clear that I would be spending the night with him then, so I asked him if he had anything I could change into to be comfortable. He responded by asking why I needed anything. That was it. The little dress that you made me buy was off and he was all over me.' Serena was hardly coy telling Kim.

'Wow… where was he from? What did he look like?'

'Don't know. He could be anything from Middle Eastern to Mediterranean descent, but he had deep ocean blue eyes and slightly greying sideburns.'

'Never met him again?'

'Like I said, I wasn't ready for a relationship. So we never exchanged any cards. But, I should have... now when I think of that hot night with him,' Serena said regretfully.

'Did you leave in the morning?'

'No. We made out again in the morning and then he called for breakfast in bed. I left after eleven.' Serena's pupils dilated reliving the episode.

'Next time you sleep with someone, at least ask him his name, just in case he makes you scream.'

'Thanks for the advice but I don't know when I'll get a chance again,' Serena moaned.

'I can introduce you to some male models.' Kim winked.

'You know how it is here in Mumbai… people won't stop talking about it if they find out.'

Serena wasn't entirely wrong. It wasn't easy for a woman of her age to find the right sort of man. She was getting to her mid thirties now. She could either meet men like Adi who had their brains between their legs, or men who were in their twenties and who were single. Serena had no inclination for either. She certainly wasn't keen on the former and wasn't sure about a long-term relationship with a younger guy. Hooking up with men of either group for mere physical intimacy wasn't her idea. Certainly not in Mumbai.

'Anyway, I have been promoted.' Serena changed the subject.

'That's great news. So what will you do now?'

'GK's job. He's got promoted too. Did I tell you that he split up with Stella - his American wife? She was two-timing poor GK. She finally dumped him to move back to America with another guy.' Serena told Kim about the unhappy conversation she had had with GK in Dubai.

'That's really sad. I thought only men left their wives for younger women.'

'Let's put on some music.' Serena walked to the CD player. 'It'll change the mood, too.'

Serena realised that in the last two years, she had not invited friends over to her place even once. She had virtually shut herself out of the whole social scene, indiscriminately declining every invitation she got. Kim had been the only friend she had met regularly. Consequently, after a few attempts, the friends had stopped inviting her, and had obviously carried on with their own lives.

'I'm thinking of organising a small get-together with old friends, Kim. Will you help me, please?' Serena requested.

'Of course I will. Why do you even ask?' Kim was nice as always. 'Who do you want to meet?'

'Everyone we used to party with. Do you have the latest telephone numbers for all? I would like to call them tomorrow.'

'Yes. I don't think a lot have changed. Only Anita has moved to Colaba and I am sure you know about Sonny…' Kim said, in a rather melancholic tone.

'What about Sonny?'

'Where have you been, girl? It was all over the news last month – he killed himself.'

'What?'

'I know, it's very sad. No one knows the bona fide cause, as he didn't leave a suicide note. He looked fine to me when we met last time. He was his usual jovial self; nothing seemed out of place for any of us to even doubt. As far as I know, he had everything going for him. When he did not turn up for work for two days, his colleagues informed the police who found his body in the apartment later. The postmortem stated the cause of his death as an overdose of sleeping pills. The police and the media have only been guessing… some tabloids even suggested he was gay and his lover walked out on him; others said he had lost all his money in the recent stock market crash last month – you know how these tabloids work. They'd write anything that sells.'

'Oh no!' Serena closed her eyes.

'And, because he was in Worli, it was Inspector Michael D'Cunha, once again, who was investigating the case. He recognised me instantly.

In fact, he even asked about you, though he struggled to remember your name,' Kim said.

'Anyone can recognise you, Kim. I am really sad about Sonny. It happened while I was still in Dubai. I must have missed the news, since the last few weeks were absolutely hectic. Sonny and Raaj were close friends and I just saw him once after Raaj...' Serena remembered her meeting with Sonny soon after she had moved into the Bandra apartment. She narrated to Kim the short early morning meeting with Sonny and how broken he was when he had come to see her. She also told Kim she had been quite shocked when Sonny had asked her if the police were investigating foul play.

'In fact, they did suspect foul play,' Kim said.

'I know. We were together when he asked me a lot of questions.'

'No. He particularly picked me up for lot of ridiculous questions later on and humiliated me like I have never been before. Don't know why, but I had a feeling he was hot on my scent for some strange reason linking Raaj romantically with me. He was downright rude and traumatising, unlike his behaviour with you.' Kim then told Serena for the first time about her ordeal with D'Cunha two years ago.

'In one of the meetings he mentioned to me that he suspected someone, but he later confirmed that his inkling had been baseless.' Serena recounted D'Cunha's telephone call saying that he had received all the reports and was closing the case.

'That inspector was, still is, such an eccentric and distrustful guy. I was shocked to see him again when I reached Sonny's place after the news. I thought he might have moved on, or got promoted to some place else. It wasn't pleasant seeing the same police inspector twice at such unnatural incidents in two years. He could have conveniently looped me into another investigation with no substantial evidence. He scared the daylights out of me,' Kim said slightly hysterically.

'I am glad all that is behind us and our friendship is intact. He almost caused a split among us, it seems. Why didn't you tell me about this before?'

'You were going through hell. I just didn't think it was fair to bother you with this. Adi helped me get him off the needless investigation.' Kim then narrated how Adi had helped her without divulging the details of the evening at the guesthouse.

15

January 1999

The year's targets were being set for retail sales and Serena had determined that the numbers to be delivered by her team were dreadfully steep. The growing competition was acquiring new customers by discounting the credit card fees and offering generous interest rates. In the past few years, GK had aggressively increased the market share by over five percentage points, making them the market leader in retail. Maintaining the leadership, as always, looked more difficult. It needed a revamped selling strategy. Putting money into variable marketing by discounting bank products wasn't an option; that would mean buying market share while making losses.

Instead, Serena presented a plan to GK requesting generosity on incentives to all outbound telesales staff and bank sales agents. Agencies worked on commission and a decimal increase in percentage could help them to employ more - and better - staff. When it came to her own employee incentives, GK wasn't comfortable dishing out cash. He influenced Serena to talk with her team and agree on a team conference and pleasure trip abroad if they surpassed the targets in the second quarter.

'The location would depend on how much you beat the target by,' he challenged. *'If you only reach your target, you only get your salaries.'*

The debate on incentives concluded. The first quarter was an enormous setback. From the current position of the sales, it didn't seem the team would recover in the second quarter to even meet the targets; exceeding them looked far-fetched.

The Member-Get-Member programme for existing customers started in April with lukewarm results. After being coaxed by their advertising agency, Serena had signed off some money for product placement in a small budget Bollywood movie. The scene was built around the lead actor, playing a struggling sales agent, trying to sell Member-Get-Member under their bank banner. Surprisingly, the movie became a blockbuster beyond expectations and the rub on credit card sales was so astonishing that no amount of bought media or advertising could have matched it. The credit card sales didn't look back after that. Given the large increase in the customer base, it was easy for the telesales and the sales agents to sell other bank products too. By early June the targets had been surpassed; the balance of the month only consolidated the position in the market.

'Where are we going for the incentive trip?' Serena asked GK, as she entered his office with the sales data.

'You are smart… and lucky,' GK complimented.

'Thanks GK.'

'Why don't you canvas some opinion from your team on the location?' GK passed a paper to Serena. 'This is the budget before you start planning for Las Vegas.'

Serena took the sheet and walked to Maria, who was now her secretary. 'Could you call up our travel agents and ask for five-day trip options overseas for thirty-five people please? It needs to be organised as a conference for the first two days and then we can add the weekend to give time off to everyone. And, you are coming along.'

The shortlist was on Serena's desk shortly after lunch. Dubai, Singapore, Thailand or Egypt were the suggested places where thirty-five people could travel and stay in the budget provided.

'First two days in Cairo and then we take a coach to Sharm El Sheikh,' Serena told GK.

'Okay by me.'

Cairo
August 24, 1999
Cairo is another Mumbai. The infrastructure, the chaos, the traffic, the dust and pollution in the atmosphere... everything reminded Serena of that city. Cairo, even, looks equally populated, although it is not. The Grand Hyatt, located in the heart of the commercial area of Cairo and overlooking the River Nile, was well placed for a conference-cum-incentive trip. The group booking had got them a good discount to board thirty-five of them comfortably.

The flight arrived Tuesday, late afternoon. After checking into the hotel by six, most in the group were at the concierge to check out their options for the remainder of the evening. The old part of the city, Khan-el-Khalili, was the consensus, as it was a touristic spot offering traditional and exotic shopping plus street-side local food. A few of them stayed back in the hotel for a relaxed evening, while some others wanted to explore the newer parts of the city near the hotel. According to the plan the conference was to start Wednesday morning and end late Thursday afternoon, leaving people time to visit the ancient Pyramids of Giza, as they were almost in the suburbs of Cairo. The coach was booked to pick them all up from the hotel early Friday and take them to Sharm El Sheikh before they made their way back to Mumbai, travelling through Cairo.

GK and Serena were among the few who stayed back in the hotel. Serena wanted to check with the banqueting staff to ensure that everything was organised for the conference the next day. After confirming the arrangements, Serena called GK and some others to check if they were in a mood for dinner in the only revolving restaurant in Egypt, which was in the hotel they were staying.

The conference the next day was more a presentation from different regions on their objectives and actual accomplishments. The Eastern region, based in Calcutta, was lagging behind their targets, but because the west and north had significantly over-achieved, the whole team had earned themselves the incentive. It was decided that the region needed a fix when they got back. Serena summed up the one and a half day event with a morale boosting speech on their success, motivating people by promising another trip if they repeated their success at the end of the year. GK was taken by surprise at the announcement but did not seem to mind.

If people delivered, they deserved it. Why not?

The Pyramids of Giza make everyone wonder how a seemingly impossible feat was accomplished without modern machinery and equipment more than five thousand years ago. Though most of the treasure in them has already been looted, or is on show in government museums around the world, the structures, themselves, are imposing. One can enter only the smallest of the three.

It was definitely dusty and a bit claustrophobic - the authorities, surely, must be spraying some disinfectant for it to smell the way it did. Serena felt queasy and nauseous halfway down the tunnel and, there being no exit till one reached the bottom before turning back, her condition deteriorated. GK, who had been inside them before had cautioned them all about the atmosphere inside, but she was primed to brave it. One cannot return from Egypt without experiencing the Pyramids, she was firm. Two of the team members played good Samaritans, and brought her out while others continued with the tour. There wasn't a doctor on site, so cold water was the only medicine. She sat on the Sphinx nearby, with a few others, to recuperate. Back at the hotel, she went straight into her room to rest before the hectic eight-hour coach journey to the Red Sea planned for the next day. Everyone, except Serena, was down with his or her baggage early next morning. After trying to call her room several times, Rohan knocked on her door to check if everything was okay, as she hadn't even come down for dinner the night before. She looked a mess. She had, obviously, had a rough night throwing up and looked in no shape to travel. Most of the team was disappointed because Serena had been so keen to go to the Red Sea for swimming, snorkelling and all the other water sports. She had been working out in the gym for the last three months to tone her body, and the guys, naturally, were excited at the prospect of seeing their lovely boss in a bikini, along with the other girls. GK decided Serena should stay back and join the rest by the evening or next day, if she felt fine, or else she could decide to fly back, whenever she chose, to Mumbai. Alternatively, she could wait and join the rest of the group in Cairo on the Monday morning flight, as planned. As the troop boarded the coach, Serena retreated into her room to relax.

She hardly stepped out of the hotel room anytime between then and Monday morning, when she took the cab to Cairo airport to rejoin her office colleagues. Everyone sympathised with her for missing so much fun at Sharm El Sheikh. One and all talked about Maria's bikinis, the great nightlife, brilliant pubs and cafes, the sea... Serena, still looking pale, was nearly in tears for missing the big party.

Mumbai
January 2000
Serena's department had repeated the mid-year achievement. She had also chaired the cross-functional initiative to effectively manage the Y2K transition. The new millennium started positively after her review with GK.

'You're a star,' GK complimented.

'Thank you GK. Nothing could have been achieved without your support and guidance through the difficult times,' Serena reciprocated.

'The bonus and pay rise shouldn't be a cause of concern for you Serena, but I am at a loss as to how we can reward you in terms of assignments?'

'I don't know. You're the boss.'

'Do you have anything in mind, besides joining the competition?' GK surprised her by the question.

'GK, I have been thinking, I need a change of scene, both for professional and personal reasons.' GK listened patiently. 'Professionally, because I am at the helm of retail banking and there seems to be nowhere else for me to go, unless of course you move. I am not sure if I want to foray into another area for now…'

'…And personally?' GK asked impatiently.

'I am the wrong side of thirty. Being a widow makes my situation even more difficult. I can't seem to meet the right guys in Mumbai. I either meet middle-aged men who are boring, or ones who aren't looking for a long-term relationship. They treat me as someone who should be willing to jump into bed with them with no commitment whatsoever...'

'I understand, though I am not sure what I can do about it?'

'Could I move oversees to a location where I can make a fresh start please? Any other place, where society is less conservative than India and men aren't blatant chauvinists trying to get into my bed if I talk casually or flirt,' Serena pleaded; she sounded like a recent victim of some hypocrite.

'That could only be Europe or the US. Unfortunately, we don't have anything in the offing but... we can look out. I know some people who I worked with, years back, in the New York office. Let's see when something comes up next,' he offered.

The objectives were set. They didn't seem so impossible to achieve after last year's success. The trip, the one to be organised for surpassing the full year objectives, got postponed due to budget cuts. It was disappointing, but it was time to get back to work.

16

New Delhi
February 2000

Deputy Superintendent of Police Michael D'Cunha walked into Delhi Police HQ to take up his new assignment. His promotion had got delayed due to red tape, but he was glad that everything had paid off in the end. His commitment to work was never in doubt; his obstinate investigations, however, put his superiors in awkward situations sometimes. He had come up the ranks successfully in the State of Maharashtra and was now promoted to the IPS cadre, with an initial two-year posting in the capital. A lot of ambitious officers in the police force who joined the state police retired there. Only a select few like D'Cunha went into the higher echelons of the police force, which was otherwise comprised of officers that had got through the tough qualification process of IPS rather than the state-run examinations. Even the training facilities for IPS were located separately at Hyderabad. Those selected in IPS cut through the ranks and joined as superintendents in various states and union territories across the country, on a range of police and peripheral functions. As they did not go through usual ranks, they tended to be much younger; hence, their chances of rising to the top were significantly higher simply because of their years of service. D'Cunha was in his late forties when he became the DSP, while an IPS graduate could have been in the same position by his early thirties.

D'Cunha was fully aware that his new supervisor, Kabir Singh, Superintendent of Police - South Delhi, was an astute IPS officer from the early 1990s batch, known for his strict discipline and regimented style of working. News on the grapevine was that he had fallen in love with a girl in his college days and having lost her to another man, he had pledged to remain a bachelor, dedicating his entire time to work. Like most extraordinary performers he missed the essential work-life balance, working over fourteen hours a day. He was also driven by a neurotic obsession to deliver exceptionally superior and quick results. With few interests besides his career, he was still in his late thirties and going by his impressive track record, he was destined to be Inspector General before retiring.

D'Cunha reasoned if he spent a couple of years on this job and managed another high profile central position (with Kabir's recommendation) he could well be back in Mumbai as the Additional Commissioner of Police – at the level his dad retired - with a good seven years of service left to rise further. Determined to succeed, he had made arrangements for his family to stay in Mumbai for a year to give him time to settle in the new job. Moreover, his elder son was in his last year of school and he and his wife had agreed that a small sacrifice to better both his own and the child's future was important at this juncture. But first, Kabir needed to be convinced that D'Cunha had the mettle to be made in-charge to demonstrate his true capabilities, and was not merely worthy of a marginal position in traffic police, which a few over-enthusiastic recruits had been sidelined into after losing their sanity in working for Kabir.

With no desire to be late on the first day of his new assignment, D'Cunha was early for his meeting with his new supervisor who walked in at the dot of nine, sat down on his oak-coloured enormous desk of simple cubist design, and looked at the stack of files in the 'in' tray. The room was much richer than any at D'Cunha's Worli office, with ritual pictures of Gandhi, Nehru and his daughter Indira Gandhi adorning the walls in glass frames. On his left side there was a credenza over which were displayed numerous awards, departmental pictures and some photographs of Kabir with various VIPs and political personalities. There was no uncertainty that the man thrived on his accomplishments.

D'Cunha walked into the office at ten. 'Good morning sir... Michael D'Cunha, Deputy Superintendent reporting on duty.'

'Good morning Michael,' Kabir said, glancing at D'Cunha's file. 'Sit down.' Despite the expectations and warnings, which had been voiced by several colleagues, Kabir was respectful. There was a five-minute silence, which felt like hours to D'Cunha, as Kabir went through his file. 'You have a very impressive professional record, Michael. Like you, I have always advocated that what goes into the work is more significant than the length of time worked, and you seem to be just the right guy. You don't have a single open, unresolved case in your entire career. I am sure you've heard all about me and my rigorous working style, but there's one more thing I tell everyone who joins my team – I trust people who work for me, completely, and if they let me down, that's where their career ends.' Kabir was polite, but he did not mince words.

'Yes sir.'

'I demand absolute dedication to the service. Police is an essential service where deadlines do not shift with changing circumstances. There cannot be any office hours, so anyone who wants a nine-to-five job shouldn't join the police force.'

'Yes sir.'

'Your phones should never be switched off, I am sure you know this.'

'Yes sir.'

'And, you don't have to say *sir* after every sentence. You don't call me *sir* off duty either. The name's Kabir.'

'Okay sir... I meant okay.'

'Are you from Goa?' Kabir looked at the family name on the file.

'Yes, but born and brought up in Mumbai.'

'Besides what's there in the file, tell me about yourself.'

'I am a second-generation police officer. My father retired as the Additional Commissioner of Police...' D'Cunha started.

'Are you ACP Ryan D'Cunha's son?' Kabir interrupted with the question.

'Yes, I am. Did you know him?'

'Oh yes. While I was training at the Police Academy at Hyderabad, he was a guest trainer on homicide investigations and one could see he didn't present other people's cases. Some of us were keen to work for him, but he retired before we completed the training,' Kabir said.

'You have very big boots to fill, then.'

'Yes.'

'Good. As I understand it, you are on a two-year secondment from Mumbai Police. I promise, if you do well here, I will push for you to get another highly visible role in the centre that can be the starting block for your return to Mumbai with another promotion.'

'That is what I endeavour to do.' D'Cunha looked around the room at all the trophies and pictures making it obvious that he wanted to be triumphant like Kabir.

'Good. Here is the file of your first assignment, beginning now. Do you have any doubts or questions?' Kabir concluded the discussion.

'Not at the moment, sir.'

'I wish you all the best, Michael.' Kabir got up like a gentleman to shake hands.

'Thank you, sir.' D'Cunha shook hands, saluted and turned to leave. Walking out of the room, one picture on the wall caught his eye. It was a group photograph from Kabir's university days that read: Faculty of Management Studies, Delhi – Class of 1987. He couldn't remember whom he had met from the same institute, but he knew this was neither the time nor the place to stop and ponder.

17

Mumbai
July 2000

'Good morning.' GK sauntered into Serena's office one Friday morning with a cup of coffee.

'Good morning, GK.'

'I've got good news for you,' he began. 'Firstly, congratulations on outdoing the mid-term objectives and, secondly, one of my past colleagues, Andrew, has just the assignment you asked for, a while back.'

'New York!' Serena was suddenly energised.

'London. He moved to London a while ago.'

'Really? What is the job?'

'Ditto – what you do here. I have spoken to him regarding you. The retail bank is in a shambles there. He is looking for international staff to head up retail for the UK. I know it would have been ideal to get a bigger assignment for you, but I guess that should come in time if you join him and deliver what's required. Interested?' GK asked.

'Yes, though New York would have been more exciting.'

'Think about it. If you are interested, send me your latest CV and I'll pass it on to Andy.'

'How long do I have?' Serena asked.

'The assignment is open now; the earlier you apply the better.'

'I'll take it.' Serena was decisive.

'Okay. Send me your CV. I'll send it across with my comments. Please do not forget to highlight your Dubai project; international successes always help. I can guarantee an interview and I am confident they won't find a better candidate than you,' he advised before he walked out of her office.

'Kim?' Serena was excited when she called her friend.

'What's the matter with you? You are all charged up, honey...'

'You bet I am. What are you doing tonight?'

'Nothing planned for the weekend. How about you?' Kim asked.

'I am driving straight from work to your place, for the weekend.'

'Are you carrying a changeover?'

'I'll sleep naked. See you in an hour.'

Serena was at Kim's place by seven. Kim opened the door dressed in a black and white floral deep V-necked, side-tied dress, which ended well above her knees. It could have been worn with jeans or tights but Kim was comfortable wearing it with nothing, especially, as it was a girlie night with Serena. 'How lovely to see you, honey,' she greeted Serena with a hug. 'Tell me…'

'In a minute, let me just have a wash first. Do you have anything I can change into?' Serena threw her bag on the sofa.

'I thought you didn't mind being naked.'

'Oi… you filthy-minded girl.' Serena smiled as she went into the guest bedroom.

'Will you have tea or coffee?' Kim asked.

'Vodka please… '

Serena was out of the guest bedroom in ten minutes, wearing a loose white cotton top with a stretch denim Capri which fitted her beautifully, with elaborate embroidery and glass beadwork on the waistband, pocket and seams. 'Thanks.' She carried her glass from the table and sank into the sofa. She picked up Kim's pack of Bensons, lit one up and started, 'I might get a new assignment abroad.'

'Dubai?' Kim asked.

'London.'

'That's too far.'

'I won't commute daily.' Serena winked.

'I know, but…'

'Look at me, Kim. I've nothing in this city anymore. I can't even find a decent guy… I have been thinking, maybe a change of place will help me get out of this lonely life...'

'I can always fix you up with someone here,' Kim offered.

'Adi?'

Over the course of the evening, Serena explained that the job in London opened up doors for her to an overseas career and, now, that Raaj was no longer in business in Mumbai, there was neither an attachment to the city nor the need to stick around. She was a businesswoman and had reached too high in the country's corporate pyramid to find any bigger roles locally. If she was seeking growth she had to move out, and London was a great place to start. She had been keener on New York, but she didn't have a choice. She also explained how GK had been a big help talking to people to get her the interview.

'So there's still time before you move.' Kim sounded relieved.

'There's still a chance of not moving. The interviewer, Andrew, might get better applications and candidates, but GK has great connections and knows him personally. That might help.'

'Don't know about others, but I will really miss you very much.' Kim sounded sad as she lit up another cigarette.

'Me too. I sure am going to miss you. But I hope you understand my situation...'

'When was the last time you got laid?'

'Two years ago, in Dubai; I told you.'

'I can understand your frustration...'

'Correct. So, have you been seeing anyone?'

'Yes. I was about to tell you. Remember the time I told you about one of the creative guys, in the agency, who wanted to help me with my career? Ron and I have been seeing each other for a couple of months now. I did not tell you earlier because of my past record of relationships never lasting more than a few months. I think the attraction has been there since the beginning, although I was a bit sceptical because of the age difference.'

'How old is he?' Serena was eager to know.

'Forty-five.'

'And you are thirty.'

'I'll be thirty one, next month,' Kim immediately corrected.

'Is the sugar daddy fully functional?'

'He's rocked me a few times. Don't know where he gets this energy from?'

'Wow... how come you are alone this weekend?'

'He's on a shoot in Jaipur,' Kim clarified.

'You mean he is on a shoot in another location with a sexy model?'

'That is professional. I shoot with other agencies too. That's what I like about him.' Happiness glowed on Kim's face.

'Any long-term plans?'

'He proposed today on the phone from Jaipur. He wants to get married now.'

'Isn't it early for him?'

'It's definitely late for me.'

GK told Serena that Andy was impressed with her during the telephonic interview and had selected her for the London job. He had sent the papers over to the US for sign-off and would let them know about the dates and formalities in a few weeks.

It was nearly the end of September before all the formalities were completed. GK was ready to release her as soon as they had found and trained a replacement. He could not let Serena go before that and run the department without a suitable head in the last quarter of the year. Everything got sorted by December. The replacement was trained and firmly in control. The work visa for Serena had been stamped.

She decided not to sell the Bandra apartment.

That's the only remaining memory of Raaj and me together, she told Kim and GK.

December 31, 2000

Kim, with Ron, planned a quiet farewell dinner for Serena at her place.

Ron was elegant; an unconventionally sober creative director. No ponytails, no tattoos, no piercing, no wacky hairstyle, no torn shorts, not even a turtleneck. Dressed in faded blue jeans and a white tucked-in shirt, he looked much younger than he was. Only the hair colour revealed his vintage. Kim, standing next to him, as he poured drinks for all three of them, was wearing a timeless little black dress with beads all over and satin trim at the neck and hem. As always, she looked gorgeous. Serena had worn the same black dress she had worn in Dubai when she had gone clubbing.

The evening was more sombre than some of Kim's earlier New Year parties. She was, perhaps, growing up with Ron. Kim and Serena discussed several memorable events they had experienced together in the last six years. Some were exhilarating; others were sad. Raaj was missed by both the women. Ron had been told about Serena's tragedy and every time the women discussed a past event, Kim gave the background to make Ron understand.

Some tears, a few smiles, funny jokes, happy and sad memories, fine jazz, a good number of drinks, and a pre-ordered dinner - an evening can only last so long. It was finally 2001.

'Not sure when we'll be together again.' Kim was choked, realising Serena would soon be gone; she was flying to London the same evening, which was, now, only hours away.

'I know but we'll meet again, soon.' Serena was on the verge of tears too.

The two women embraced for a long time, sobbing on each other's shoulder, as Ron looked on. He hadn't been part of their lives long enough to comment on some things that evening, but he had played the part of a perfect gentleman and host, making drinks and participating in the conversation whenever he could. All of them went to bed around two in the morning.

Sahar International Airport
Mumbai, January 1, 2001
Serena had decided not to carry any household possession therefore, all of her personal luggage was checked-in. She paid a ransom as excess-baggage charge and carried a small cabin bag. 'Bye Kim. All I can say is, thanks for everything. I wouldn't have survived in this city if it had not been for you.' She was in tears.

'I'll miss you.' Kim broke down like a child.

'I'll email you my numbers as soon as I can. Keep in touch. It was nice meeting you, Ron. Take care of my friend.'

'Don't worry about Kim. You take care,' Ron said, giving her a hug.

'Bye. You were right Kim – Ron does rock you hard. You should get some soundproofing done in your house before you have your next guest,' Serena uttered to lighten up the mood. Kim looked at Ron and blushed.

'Bye honey.'

The women embraced one last time before Serena, with moist eyes, walked through the security check. Kim was still crying and Ron took her in his arms to console her. He was mature enough to appreciate the pain of parting.

18

London Heathrow
London, January 2, 2001

From the aerobridge itself Serena realised that the world's busiest airport hadn't got its sobriquet for nothing. London, fittingly located between Asia and America, saw more international flights than any other airport in the world. The city had five airports sharing the load, with Heathrow being the biggest and the busiest. Terminal 4 was packed with people when the flight landed in the morning. Regardless of it being a bit dated now, Serena noticed that Heathrow offered all the facilities that major airports in India lacked. The sparkling environment, the ambience, the consistency and clarity of the signage directing her to the correct places and the visual screens all around advertising some of the best brands in the world, gave an international flavour to the whole place. It was quite a long walk from the aerobridge to the immigration desks. She saw people around her dressed in coats and winter wear.

I definitely need a change of wardrobe soon, she pondered.

At the immigration desk, she handed over the disembarkation card and passport to the officer at the counter.

'Did they make you go through any medical tests?' the officer asked.

'Yes.'

'Could I see the reports please?'

'Sure.' She unzipped her handbag and pulled out a large brown envelope containing all her medical tests and X-rays done for the visa.

'Thanks.' He looked at them for a few minutes, and then placing them neatly in the envelope, he handed them back to her. He passed the passport under the security scanner before stamping it. 'Have a nice stay in the UK.' He returned her documents to her with a smile. Serena had a lot of luggage and it took time for all the pieces to arrive. She collected them on a trolley and walked through the green channel. A middle-aged English cab driver, booked by her new office, was paging for Ms Serena.

'Good afternoon Serena. Welcome to London,' he said charmingly.

Serena hadn't realised it had taken her all morning to get out. 'Good afternoon.' She glanced at her watch. He chivalrously took the trolley from her and led her to the car park. It was cold and wet; not freezing but, nevertheless, much colder than Mumbai. Serena had heard that it always rained in London, but, for now, she didn't mind it. It wasn't like Mumbai rain where it poured; just a steady gentle shower.

The cab ride from Heathrow to Canary Wharf was exciting for Serena, as it was her first time in the city. She was upset the driver did not bring the famous London black cab, which she had seen at Singapore airport as a tourist attraction. The cab driver explained that pre-booked cab companies didn't have those in their fleets. London felt very diverse with its people, cars and shops. She admired it all… as the cab crawled in the traffic. The red telephone booths and the London buses were exactly as she had seen on postcards in her childhood.

Who uses telephone booths in this age of mobile phones?

The chirpy driver highlighted the various landmarks to Serena… Hyde Park, Harrods at Knightsbridge, Big Ben, the London Eye and then Tower Bridge as they drove by the Thames. He told a story about a Yank who bought the old London Bridge, thinking it was the Tower Bridge, and shipped it all the way to America. Serena did not believe the story one bit, but laughed with him as he told it.

'Where exactly would you like to go in Canary Wharf?' he asked as they approached the Limehouse tunnel.

'The Four Seasons Hotel at the Westferry Circus please,' Serena told him, looking at the hotel reservation papers.

'Okay.'

The valet was at the cab, in a flash, the moment it stopped in the portico of the hotel. He took the baggage while Serena paid the cabbie and thanked him for the guided tour of London. He smiled, expressed gratitude and left.

It was nearing two o'clock. Serena, already pre-booked in the hotel, checked-in at the reception, collected her keys, and went straight to the room to find a message light already flashing on her telephone. The red-eye and the extended drive from the airport to the hotel had taken a toll, and she dozed off without any lunch, having put the *Do Not Disturb* sign on the door.

Serena's office, in Canary Wharf, was a short walk from the hotel, and though it was still a bit dark for eight in the morning, she decided to walk since it wasn't raining. This office was the UK and European Headquarters of the bank and housed a lot of staff. The building was new and their bank had leased twenty floors in a single tower. She showed her Indian ID card at the reception to obtain the guest pass for day visitors, crossed the turnstile and took the elevator up to the thirtieth floor.

Andrew Harrison had been waiting for her. He must have been in his mid-forties; a tall and slim American with a receding hairline. He wore a blue well-tailored suit with a powder blue shirt and, an asymmetrical, printed matching tie. He had quite stylish rimless glasses on. He was typing something on the keyboard when she knocked on his open door. 'Welcome to London. How are you?' he said, in his American accent, when he saw her.

'I am fine, thank you. How are you?'

'Not bad at all. Come in…I've been waiting for you. How was your journey?'

'It was fine. Thanks.'

'Coffee?'

'Yes, please.' She definitely needed caffeine.

'Let's go.' Andy collected his wallet from the drawer and got up. He was certainly taking her somewhere for coffee, as the secretaries here didn't run to get one. Serena hadn't yet comprehended *how* different it would be in the UK.

They took the lift to the top floor of the building that housed a Costa Coffee. 'What will you have?' he asked approaching the counter.

'A skinny cappuccino for me, please,' she said.

'Make that two please,' he told the lady at the till.

They carried their coffees to an empty table in the café and sat down. Andy advised Serena to meet the HR department in the morning and complete the initial formalities. They – Serena and him - should meet, in the afternoon, for discussions on the job and he would introduce her to the team. He called up the HR representative to come over to his office when they returned. Serena spent the whole morning completing tedious HR formalities and returned to Andy's desk at lunch.

'Let's go for lunch.' Andy got up.

Life moves at a different pace here, Serena reflected.

The office had its own cafeteria that had choices of hot and cold food. There was a salad bar, a sandwich counter and a hot pizza grill as well as a vast choice of laid-out dishes: pasta, steak, burgers, soup, and even Indian. Serena picked up a salad and joined Andy who had picked up his food and was sitting at the table waiting for her.

'Where are you staying?' he enquired after she had sat down with her lunch.

'At the Four Seasons.'

'Has HR booked a service apartment for you?'

'Yes. Thankfully that's at the Westferry Circus too, so I shouldn't have a problem with the luggage,' she said.

'Good. Have you decided where you want to stay in London or it too soon for that?'

'I have been advised to live somewhere in Docklands, I believe it is close by.'

'Take your time in deciding. You have an eight-week allowance to stay in the guest accommodation when you move. There's no rush. Save the rent to take all of us out for a drink sometime,' he joked.

'Of course.'

Over the meal and, almost, all afternoon, Andy updated Serena on the situation of the retail business in the UK. The bank, unlike its Indian counterpart, wasn't the market leader. They had a total of seven branches in the country, and though there was ample manpower in the branches, there weren't enough resources in the central office to lead the marketing and operations. Due to various cost cuts year-on-year, the bank hadn't invested much money on marketing, for years, and was sadly a *me-too* bank in one of the richest markets in the world. As if that wasn't enough, they had been inordinately slow in terms of Internet banking. Some non-banking players were dominating the market place having launched innovative products like Internet-only banking and credit cards. Given the price of the properties in central London, the banks without brick and mortar branches had an undue advantage.

'We need an earth-shattering strategy to penetrate this market. If we had the money, we would have acquired a local player and built on that. The US Head Office does not want to invest in developed markets and hence, we must to do something different. And we need to do it soon,' Andy concluded.

'I am sure we can work on it,' Serena consoled him.

How? She didn't have a clue at this moment.

Andy called in his secretary and asked her to check if a meeting room was available. It was getting close to four now and he had organised a meeting to introduce Serena to her team, which turned out to be only three people.

I need to hire some real talent, right away, she realised.

A month had passed since Serena had moved to London. She had spent a lot of time visiting the branches, the competition, working with HR to recruit new staff, meeting the communication and PR agencies. She didn't mind working over the weekends (unlike some local staff) to get her fully up to speed. It was time, now, to start interviewing for new hires before she could think of a plan to revitalise the bank and its brand. Andy was right when he had said it needed a business strategy rather than a tactical fix.

She enquired around the office to find out if anyone else lived in Docklands, specifically on the Isle of Dogs, to get a fair idea of respectable buildings in the area and met Paul Black who lived in a riverside apartment on Westferry Road. He took Serena for a drink in a pub near the office in the evening. He explained the area in detail, highlighting the new buildings that were good. He was very friendly, a soft-spoken Englishman who sat three offices away from Serena. They became friends and had coffee or lunch together once in a while, chatting about the differences between them. He had never been to

India, but desired to. He was single and excited when he realised that Serena was too.

The estate agents showed her apartments in the area and she settled on a newly built warehouse, converted to a two-bedroom apartment. It overlooked the Thames, with a gym and swimming pool. The apartment came fully furnished, including the crockery and cutlery, and was within her budget. She signed the lease for a year to move in, in March.

'Paul, I'll buy you a drink after work today,' Serena told Paul one morning.

'Why?'

'It's Friday. I have found an apartment, which wouldn't have been possible without your help.

'It's a date. I'll be free by six.'

They went for a drink after work at the Slug and Lettuce, which was crowded with what seemed a million people, and struggled to get to the till to buy a drink. Paul enlightened her that there wasn't anything strange in that, everyone in the UK celebrated the weekends.

She took a couple of days off to move into the new apartment. Though it was furnished, she went out to buy personal stuff first.

You need to get things that you can relate to or you would keep feeling you live in someone else's house. She remembered Kim saying that when she moved into her Bandra apartment.

19

April 2001

'Coffee?' Serena asked Paul, at ten o'clock.

'I've already had one, but I can have another.' Paul cheerfully got up to leave.

'How come you have already had one so early in the morning? We usually have one around this time,' Serena asked as they came out of his room.

'I couldn't sleep last night.' He yawned.

'All okay?'

'Oh yes… I've had this new neighbour on the floor above me since last month, and he's weird. He puts on loud music at odd hours and it wakes me up. I had to knock at his door at one in the morning to ask him to lower the bloody volume,' Paul whined.

'Does he live in the penthouse?'

'Yes. How did you guess?'

'Elementary my dear Paul, you live one floor below the top. It is apparent that the one on the top should be a penthouse,' Serena replied smartly.

'Oh yes.' Paul remembered he had invited Serena over and shown his apartment when she was looking for one to rent.

'Strange. Normally people here don't do that.'

'He doesn't look like he's from here, though his accent is British,' Paul said, paying for both the coffees. 'He looks Greek to me.'

'Doesn't his family wake up to his loud music?'

'I think he is single. I have warned him not to blast his sound system at odd hours.'

'Good. Any plans for the weekend?' Serena asked, it being a Friday.

'Nothing important, I just need time to clean my place. Let's catch a movie.'

'Which one?'

'There's a good one playing – *Bridget Jones's Diary*. Do you want to come tomorrow evening?'

'That sounds good and I have nothing to do. I'll give you a call tomorrow morning,' Serena said.

Serena had gathered enough information regarding the retail banking industry in the past few months; appropriate staff had been poached from the competition for vacant positions. She regrouped her department based on her experiences in India and Dubai. She understood the nuances of a highly mature market and that the issues she faced here were different from those in the developing economies. She hired a research agency and briefed them on the challenge. Well-targeted funding, allied to some unconventional marketing with a great strategy, could bring results.

But first, she should wait for the research agency to come up with a proposal.

It was almost three in the afternoon, after the two-hour team meeting that started at ten, and Serena had only just returned to her desk when Paul came by to invite her for coffee. He was humming all the way as they took the elevator to the cafeteria.

'Haven't seen you since the movie…' Paul said when they sat down with their coffee.

'I was out visiting the branches for work the whole of last week,' Serena explained.

'You know this guy I was talking about who lives in the penthouse above me…'

'Yes, you told me. Has he bothered you again?'

'No. He's quite a cool guy. He met me in the lift on Saturday morning, as I returned with groceries and apologised for the other night once again. He invited me to his penthouse for a drink in the evening. I had no plans so I accepted. The penthouse is amazing, Serena. You've seen my house with the living room windows overlooking the Thames – the penthouse occupies two floors with a mezzanine, so his living room has double height windows opening into a terrace over the river.'

'What does he do?' Serena sounded interested.

'He lives in Greece most of the year, and comes here only in the summer.'

'And, what does he do?' Serena repeated her question.

'He told me he deals in antiques. His house is immaculate… he has incredible finesse. We even went down to the basement to see his Jaguar 'E' Type. He's even promised me a ride this coming weekend. It looks like he's a millionaire.'

'He's a millionaire... And, he is single...wow!'

'Yes.'

'So, when can I meet him?'

'Why? Don't you consider me worth dating?' Paul said flirtatiously, and both of them laughed.

'But you don't have a penthouse, or a Jaguar.'

'That's true.'

'You know what they say about men and coffee don't you?' she asked, finishing her drink.

'They are both preferred rich.' He completed the joke finishing his brew.

'You're so right. Meeting single men is good for me, but millionaire would be so much better. Isn't that right?'

'Let me get to know him a bit better. I will try to speak to him when we go for a ride this Saturday. I don't want him to feel I am introducing single women to him as soon as I figured out that he's rich.'

'I am in no hurry. It's okay even if I don't meet him. I was only teasing.'

Paul was as excited as a kid after his joyride in the 'E' type. He told everyone who was there in the office. He had plenty to tell about the trip to Cambridge and back in the car with his new friend.

'Did you ask him if he wanted to meet your friends?' Serena ragged Paul again.

'Yes, but I didn't mention your intentions.'

'I don't have any malicious ones. I just want to meet single men.'

'I know, I know. He's not free this weekend. I told him I am organising a small get together at my place with some close friends from work and he'd be welcome to join us if he cares to. He's agreed to come next weekend,' Paul told Serena.

'But you haven't invited me."

'I have now, haven't I?'

'Thank you for the invitation.'

Paul invited a few others over to his place for drinks. Serena realised she needed to shop. She did not want the first impression to be wasted. Since she had arrived, in London, she had picked up a few work clothes and was mindful her existing dresses might fall short by a huge margin. The last thing she wanted to do was to turn up in jeans. She thought about Kim but discarded the idea. Kim might not be conversant with fashion and trends in this part of the world. Before she left work on Friday, there were two personal emails. The first one was from GK.

'Hi Serena,

It's probable that by the time that you read this, I will have been marched off the premises, since this morning I have handed in my notice to inform HR that I am leaving the bank. I am sorry that I have not been able to let you know beforehand, but it's only in the past few days that I have really made up my mind to go. It might come as a shock to you, but I can assure you that I have carefully thought about it for a few weeks now. I had expected my family and relatives to accept me after Stella left, but after trying for so long, I think I should reconcile myself to the fact that that will never happen. As I have no other relations in India I have decided go back to America and start all over again, like you did.

Just let me finish by saying how much I have enjoyed working with you. Your style, philosophy and integrity will always stay in my memory. Keep up the good work.

I will send you my contact details once I settle down in the US.

Best wishes and please stay in touch.

Your friend,

GK'

Maybe Stella had broken off with the young guy, and GK being magnanimous, was planning to get back with her again. Good for him, she contemplated.

The second email was from Kim.

'Hi honey,

How are you? Why haven't been in touch since you left Mumbai? I am worried about you... please send me your numbers and I shall call you over the weekend.

Ron and I have decided to tie the knot in January (next year) and I am giving you more than a six month-advance notice, so start planning. I definitely want you to come... no excuses please or I will be very, very, very hurt.

Forgot to ask you – have you found some prince charming in London? Or, are you trying a new one every week?

Send me your number quickly, or call me.

Love xx

Kim'

Serena read both the emails twice and her eyes went moist as she remembered all the good times she had shared with GK and Kim. There seemed no point in responding to GK, as he would have left by now. She considered responding to Kim's email, then pondered a minute and decided to defer doing so till the next week.

20

May 12, 2001

Serena booked herself into the beauty salon in the morning for a facial, manicure, pedicure, a holistic body massage, a haircut and colour with highlights in bronze and professional straightening. She looked in the mirror admiring her looks before grabbing a quick bite at a salad bar at the Waitrose nearby. She got back to her apartment shortly after noon, lit some candles, put on a CD and got into the bath. The lukewarm water was extremely relaxing as she closed her eyes.

She had bought a dress that made her look attractive and relaxed after almost half a day of shopping. It was a knee length dress in olive with forest green print in silk that had a halter neck and straps attached to an *O* ring on the back, with a little fish tail. It was accentuated with a contrast lemon stitching and a full-length zip on the side. She wasn't wasting her pedicure knowing she had good feet. She opted for peep-toe shoes.

'You've got very beautiful feet, sweetheart,' Raaj would have said.

'Are you saying that's the only beautiful thing about me?'

'You're gorgeous my precious.'

Serena remembered Raaj's words and wiped away the tears. She matched accessories and a handbag with her dress and spent a lifetime putting on subtle make-up, but was ready by seven. Considering it was a short walk down the road to Paul's apartment, she switched on the television to catch some of last season's *Friends* and made herself a sandwich – a bite before drinks to ensure she did not get drunk too soon.

She set off at eight.

'Hi Serena,' Paul greeted her as he opened the door.

'Hi!'

He introduced her to the two guests who had already arrived. She knew Rob as he worked for Paul, while Lisa worked in some insurance company in the city. Lisa looked stunning – she was a tall and slender brunette wearing a short polka dot dress in black, flaunting her long, tanned legs.

'Competition?' Paul whispered in Serena's ear and both of them smiled. 'What will you drink?'

'A glass of red should be fine. Thanks.'

'Okay,' he said and looked around to see if any of the other guests needed a refill.

Next to arrive were Mike and Gina, old friends of Paul who had driven down from somewhere in Essex. A tote bag on Mike's shoulder publicised the fact that they were geared up to stay the night at Paul's place.

'I am stepping out for a smoke,' Lisa announced, picking up her cigarettes to go to the small deck.

'May I join you?' Serena asked.

'I didn't know you smoked.' Paul appeared surprised.

'Sometimes…' Serena started chatting with Lisa and found out that she used to work for Paul till about a year ago before she moved to the insurance company. They had dated in the past and taken a brief relationship-break when she switched jobs. Paul, surprisingly, hadn't told Serena about it.

'Paul and I are getting back together again,' Lisa suddenly said when Paul joined them.

'That's good news.'

'Congratulations, Paul,' Rob chipped in.

The girls were still out on the deck and Paul went in to get drinks for the newly arrived guests. As they made conversation, Serena heard someone being introduced to the three guests inside. It must be *him*. Her heart skipped a beat. When they stepped inside, they saw the new guy, standing with his back towards them, talking to Rob and Mike.

'Serena, Lisa… meet Nikos,' Paul said, once the girls came closer.

'Hi.' Nikos turned around.

The English dictionary might describe coincidence and miracle as separate words but for Serena, at this point, the boundaries undoubtedly got distorted as she struggled to articulate. Standing in front of her, in a black shirt and jeans, was the guy with the deepest pair of blue eyes she had ever seen. And, she had seen those eyes before. In Dubai. The ground beneath her shook for a moment when she saw the sheriff.

'Hello,' he said to both of them, kissing their cheeks.

'Hi, Nikos.'

'Hello.'

Both Serena and Nikos, without any discussion, decided to avoid mentioning the Dubai incident, and their ad hoc tryst. They understood there would be other opportunities, when they would be alone, during the course of the evening or, maybe, later. The look in both their eyes, their expressions, reassured one another that they certainly hadn't forgotten about that hot August night, even though they weren't acknowledging it publicly.

Paul was an excellent host. He saw to it that the glasses were refilled at all times. He relentlessly ran between the living room and the oven in the kitchen to keep his guests' plates full of hot finger food.

'Paul told me that you have a vintage car, Nikos.' Lisa started the conversation.

'It's only a 60's Jaguar 'E' Type.' He attempted to be modest.

'Is that a collectible, or do you use it to drive to work daily?' It was Rob this time.

'It's the only car I have here, but I don't drive it to work daily.'

'He doesn't go to work daily,' Paul enlightened his guests as they sat chatting across the living room. 'Nikos is an antique dealer and only spends the summers in the UK.'

'Where do you live for the rest of the year?'

'Greece. My mother was Greek, so I have both family and business there.'

'So, when you are away, why don't you leave the car with me?' Mike joked.

'It's not a bad idea if you have a covered garage. I could get you insured as an additional driver rather than paying for the garage I use and also save me some money on its commissioning every time I come back.' Nikos sounded serious.

'That's really nice of you. Do you live somewhere around here?'

'Right on top of this apartment,' Nikos said, pointing towards the ceiling. 'That's how I met Paul.'

Serena and Lisa stepped out for a smoke again. Paul kept refilling the glasses and the discussions continued. It was apparent that Lisa was staying the night with Paul, Mike and Gina weren't driving back and with Nikos and Serena living close by, Rob was the only one who had to go far, so he made everyone else aware of the time by declaring that he should be leaving soon. It was past eleven and the tube did not run all night.

'I think I, too, should be leaving soon,' Serena said, finishing her wine.

'Where do you live?' Nikos asked.

'She's lives only a few buildings away.' Paul pointed east.

'Don't worry, I'll walk you back… you can have another glass.' Nikos assured Serena.

'May I?' Paul carried the carafe around to her.

'Thanks.' She took some more wine. Nikos had taken care of her before; she could trust him.

Rob left. The rest carried on for some time till everyone slowed down, refusing refills. Serena said goodbye to all and got up. As promised, Nikos was ready to walk her home. They hadn't spoken about their Dubai episode, all evening.

'Care to join me for a drink at my apartment?' he asked, the moment they stepped out and approached the lift.

'I don't see why not…'

'Great.'

He turned the key to open the door and gestured for her to step into the penthouse.

'I need a smoke,' she said, and headed straight to the terrace.

'I'll bring your drink there.' He switched on the terrace lights.

A few minutes later, he came to the deck holding two champagne flutes with a bottle of Moët and put them on the table. She threw away the cigarette and came into his arms. The kiss lasted forever. As they parted, Nikos moved back a step to have a good, long look at her…

'You've got very beautiful feet sweetheart,' he said.

'Are you saying that's the only beautiful thing about me?' How could she have missed this opportunity?

'You're gorgeous my precious.'

She came into his arms again. 'I've missed you so much, Raaj.'

'I have missed you too, sweetheart.'

'I love you.'

'I love you too,' he responded and they kissed again.

Serena had tears in her eyes reminiscing on the last five years she had spent waiting for this moment. It had been long enough for the ordinary and vulnerable to give up hope, but they were different – their plan had been invincible. Nikos popped open the bottle of champagne, poured it for both of them and handed a glass to Serena.

'We did it!' He raised the toast.

'You are a genius, my love.'

'Only half a genius without you… it was our plan, remember?'

'Yes, Raaj.'

'Just remember one more thing sweetheart.'

'What's that?' Serena asked.

'Raaj is dead; long live Raaj.'

'Make love to me, Nikos. Now,' Serena demanded. She unzipped and took off her dress in one motion, standing in her lacy lingerie which did not take long to join the dress, lying in a heap, on the ground. Raaj pulled a sheet from the bedroom, put it on the terrace floor and switched off the lights. They made love on the open terrace with the summer wind cooling their bodies.

'Now that we have met and started dating, where do we go from here?' Serena asked.

'Six months of dating should be enough to get married, then you quit your job and we move to a beachside villa in Spain.' He took her in his arms again and kissed her. The two lay undressed on the terrace against the backdrop of lights from the Canary Wharf offices.

'I thought you said Greece.'

'That was for everybody else's ears.'

'You don't smoke anymore?' Serena asked, as she lit up.

'I had a very nasty accident in my past life sweetheart. I almost burnt down the whole apartment and just about managed to escape… so I quit.' He smiled. 'It's time you quit smoking too.'

They couldn't contain their laughter.

PART TWO

'You only have to do a very few things right in your life so long as you don't do too many things wrong'

— Warren Buffett

21

Faculty of Management Studies (FMS), Delhi
July 1985

Admission into FMS Delhi was anything but easy. With ninety seats contested by over thirty thousand applicants from all over the country, it was a vain hope to assume that anyone without serious merit could slip through the meticulous selection process. On the first day at the business school young women and men sat in the auditorium listening to the dean's address. Raaj, sitting at the back of the class, perused his classmates and mentally counted the number of girls in the batch. His count was not far from the guesstimate of thirty that he had before the start of the session. Twenty-eight. He was on a second round of perusing to look for pretty ones when he heard the dean summarising the address…

'*…the only limitation is your imagination.*'

Powerful words but, so apt, he thought. Raaj came from a humble working class family; it was not even a full family, since his parents were divorced and he had never even seen his father, only heard about him from his mother who had worked painstakingly to provide him with the best education she possibly could. He remembered his mother telling him once:

'*Even if I need to sell everything I have, I will do so gladly to fund your studies in the best schools, Raaj.'*

'You don't have to do that Mum. Once I pass my bachelor's I can easily find a good job,' Raaj had tried arguing.

'Nothing in later life can compensate for the lack of a good education. Do not be in a hurry and repent for the rest of your life.'

'But, why do we need to strive for anything more... we have everything now.'

'There is a big difference between living your dreams and existing in denial,' she had said, mindful of the financial humiliation she had endured after the bitter separation from her husband.

He did not have any argument to counter that and he never dared to open the debate again.

Raaj's father was born in the frontier region of Afghanistan, and the family had moved to India before the partition in 1947. Raaj had inherited a finely chiselled face, a frame that was a hair shorter than six feet and a pale skin colour that meant he was often mistaken for someone Arabic or Mediterranean. He represented college in the tennis tournaments and there was little excess weight to detract from his good looks. Like most of the youths in the class, he dressed casually, wearing a knitted white T-shirt and a pair of faded blue jeans with comfortable trainers.

The dean finished his address and invited everyone for a luncheon that was organised by one of the companies that regularly recruited from the business school. One of the reasons for this inaugural lunch was to give everybody a chance to meet the faculty and classmates. The moment the dean left the room everyone collected their papers and bags and started walking towards the cafeteria; all ninety of them. As the young men and women present came from a wide geographical spectrum, only a few of them knew each other. Raaj waited till a large part of the class was out of the room before he got up to leave. Everyone in the dining hall was introducing themselves to others. The women appeared to be doing a better job of blending with each other than the men; maybe it was the smaller numbers working for them or just that the women knew how to bond better, and faster. And, as was perhaps inevitable, whenever there is a mixed group of this nature, the men congregated around the women. The dean, professors and some of the administrative staff joined them soon, and the buffet lunch was served. For the next hour or so, the students networked with the professors and the rest of the staff to get a true understanding of the course and placement avenues. All of the new students understood that the learning experience at the business school would be way beyond whatever they had so far and they were willing to put in two laborious years into the course for the final reward - the high paying assignment in their chosen field and industry. The faculty members retreated to their offices leaving the new entrants to mingle. Raaj circulated calmly, patted arms, introduced himself, and murmured pleasantries till his eyes spotted a head-turner. She was standing with four other women, mesmerising them with her conversation.

It is futile to approach her with all of them around, a voice in his mind warned.

Standing in one corner, with a glass of water in his hand and unbeknown to Raaj, another young man was eyeing the same subject. The girl in both the young men's sight was simply the most startling girl in the class, unless some were still to join later. But that hadn't been mentioned in any communication or the dean's address, making it clear that everyone who was on this course was present. The girl was absolutely gorgeous. Marginally shorter than five and a half feet with a petite frame, she had long straight coffee-brown hair, ending just below her shoulders, which allowed a few strands, every so often, to stray across her flawless face. Her thin and perfectly shaped lips had a slight pout, nurtured to look natural, that made her look even more attractive. She had thick, arched eyebrows over unusual deep black eyes. She was dressed in blue jeans with a black top with extremely striking sequin buttons and gathering on the V-neck, which enhanced her bust without looking provocative. She didn't have much make-up on and it didn't look like she needed any.

The two young men did not have to wait long before they saw her walking away from the small group towards the table that had glasses of water on. Raaj moved forward under the guise of picking up a glass for himself.

'Hi. I am Raaj,' he introduced himself, handing a glass of water to the pretty girl like a well-mannered gentleman.

'Thanks. I am Serena,' she responded.

'Hello, both of you, I am Kabir.' The other guy just walked up to the table to put down the tumbler from which he had been sipping.

'Hi.'

'Hello.'

Kabir Singh was a touch taller than Raaj and equally well built. His father was a colonel in the army, which had given Kabir an all-round education in various schools across the country, since the family moved every time the colonel had a new posting. He was obviously from a more privileged background than Raaj, but was nowhere near as fortunate as Serena, whose father had a thriving garment export business. Her family even owned an expensive South Delhi farmhouse, which was more luxury than Raaj, or even Kabir, could possibly dream of.

The three were joined by a few more students after a while and the threesome split before any bond was established. They met again the next day, during the second lecture of the morning. Raaj and Kabir saw Serena sitting alone. Not wanting to lose a chance, they each sat down next to her...

The trio, eventually, became friends.

Raaj fell in love with Serena; there wasn't any question about that. Kabir enjoyed her company, but could not decide if it was love or simply attraction. He was cautious and did not want to jump into a long-term relationship since he was still nursing a hurt from the past. Serena was attracted to both the guys and she loved the attention she got from two of the most attractive boys in the class. The three of them started hanging out together on the campus during the day till Serena left the premises in the evenings. Sometimes on their own, at other times with a few classmates, they organised regular outings, and due to their mutual desire for Serena's company, the two guys, too, became inseparable friends.

Raaj proposed to Serena in October. It was another regular day and she was looking as gorgeous as ever, sipping tea at the nearby stall outside the campus, with some girlfriends. He walked right up to the table, pulled out a chair and sat down amongst them.

'Serena, I think I have fallen in love with you,' he announced in the most outrageously unromantic tone of voice she could have imagined.

'Are you proposing to me?' she asked, looking at him, aware of all the girls sitting around. And if that was not enough of an audience, Kabir walked in as well.

'No. At this moment, I am only declaring my love for you,' Raaj clarified.

No red roses, no kisses, not even a commitment, just a declaration? Weird, Serena thought.

Not many around were taken by surprise at Raaj's declaration. A lot of the other students suspected that Serena was dating either Raaj or Kabir; this helped them put the right picture in the frame. The mood at the tea stall turned jubilant with one couple in the class declaring their love, well – only one half, but still. As some of the students cheered and ordered another round of teas, Kabir's face turned red with regret. He had taken far too long to make any such declaration or proposal to Serena and it was, now, stupid to pursue his interest as it would lead to a pointless rivalry between him and Raaj. Hence he joined the crowd in cheering and kept his latent intentions to himself rather than fuel any complication or controversy. He stepped forward and gave Raaj a big friendly hug. Encouraged by the crowd and reassured by his friend Kabir, Raaj went down on one knee to propose to Serena. She accepted gladly. The tea stall owner, who had seen endless students every year in the college, had witnessed all this before, and as his token of being part of the fraternity, announced free teas for everyone present.

'Congratulations.' Kabir was the first to applaud.

'Thanks.'

'If it wasn't for him, I would have proposed,' he said humourously as they sat with tea in their hands. Everyone laughed it off.

Too late.

The trio of Serena, Raaj and Kabir was now reduced to a pair. Kabir found it wrong to tag along with the lovebirds, therefore declined a lot of outings to let the two carry on with their plans. He used to be around with them at the campus in the beginning, but by the end of the year he withdrew himself totally from them. Raaj and Serena were engrossed in dating and did not realise that Kabir was pulling out from most of their plans, perhaps, because he always seemed to have a practical reason rather than a pathetic excuse.

Kabir found respite in January when his father retired and moved to Delhi. He left the hostel and moved in with his parents, giving him a reason to completely disassociate himself from the couple. The initial comradeship, which had been on the decline since Serena and Raaj started dating, was now almost over. The three were hardly ever seen together for the rest of the term unless it was in a larger group or college event. There wasn't any apparent incident or confrontation, it wasn't even planned, but Kabir decided to stay away as he thought any closeness with Serena might trouble him more than anyone else. The lovebirds, eventually, realised that Kabir had purposely distanced himself from them, though they never figured out why. They had initially thought he wanted to give them time together but, in time, became aware that he avoided them at every given opportunity.

Raaj and Serena went for their internship to Bombay, in the summer, while Kabir stayed on in Delhi. The second year began, a fresh batch of students joined, and if one had asked them, they would have never believed that Kabir was once a close friend of Raaj and Serena. Whenever he was asked about Raaj or Serena, he was careful with his words and complimented the pair; the favour was also duly returned.

The final term was rigorous, with no time for friends and socialising although some people studied in pairs or groups. The corporations had started coming to campus for recruitments and, as in past years, most of the final year students who were looking for work had been snapped up. Raaj, being a numerical genius, got pulled into investment banking and wealth management while Serena kept to the retail side of the banking business.

It was the last day at FMS and everyone was in formal attire for the group picture. As the group got rearranged, based on their heights, Raaj and Kabir were relegated to the back row, standing next to each other. Serena wasn't short, but she was in the second row. Once the picture had been taken, the classmates stood there for some time reflecting on the past two years and the memories they would carry for the rest of their lives. Three couples were, now, dating in the class, which was a good statistic compared to last year's two.

'Kabir…' Raaj called after the congregation. Kabir turned back and smiled. 'You're not leaving without saying bye to us, are you?'

'I thought you guys were busy,' Kabir responded.

'It's the last day Kabir. Who knows if, and when, we will meet again?' Serena chipped in.

'It's a long life Serena. I am sure we will see each other again,'

'Is that something you wish for, or a prophecy?' Serena asked.

'Both, actually.' Kabir hugged Serena and Raaj. 'Wish you both all the best. Do not forget to send me your wedding card,' Kabir said, and walked away.

Serena initially got an assignment in Delhi so she stayed back. Raaj received an offer from a UK bank, but the proposed to move abroad encountered difficulties with the authorities who had declined his mother's visa, hence he was re-assigned to Mumbai. Before he moved, Serena insisted that he meet her father and tell them about their relationship and plans. Serena's father was not initially happy with Raaj's family background, but he could see that the young man was promising. The businessman had never refused anything his only daughter had ever wanted in life, and he wasn't going to start now by interfering in her choice of life partner. His only request was that they worked for a few years before tying the knot so that it gave them some time to establish their careers before adjusting to married life. Raaj and Serena weren't planning to get married anytime soon in any case, therefore the suggestion suited everyone. They parted on a promise that they would meet every couple of months and agreed that as Raaj would travel north, to Jaipur, to see his mother, he would come – or go - via Delhi and see Serena and her family.

Raaj had a few tragic years. His mother died in January 1990. He was at her bedside and she told him about his father and his family. One of her last wishes was that he should speak to his father and reconnect with the rest of the family, but when he called after her death, he was told that his father had also passed away only a month back, and no one from his father's family had cared to inform him, or his mother. As for the rest of his father's family, they were not free to come down for the cremation, but they promised to stay in touch with Raaj.

Raaj was a broken man. He had lost the one person he loved more than anything else in his life. Brought up by a single parent he had been exceedingly attached to her. Mindful of not shedding tears in public, he went through some excruciating times. Everything seemed to remind him of her – the time she had got him admitted into the primary school, the time she explained to him that being fatherless was not any kind of a handicap to be embarrassed about. He remembered all the important lessons in life she had given him. And how, regardless of all their financial problems, she had provided the best upbringing and education she could manage.

In Mumbai, Raaj made friends with Sonny, a professional chef at the Sheraton. They had met at a party and clicked from the start. Sonny was looking for a temporary place to stay and Raaj offered to share lodgings for a couple of months before Sonny found his own accommodation. The solidarity remained long after Sonny had moved out of Raaj's apartment. Sonny, coming from an incredibly affluent background, always took Raaj's advice before investing money, and Raaj was an ardent food lover; their friendship had the all the right ingredients. Whenever Sonny wasn't working on weekends, he always prepared a new dish for Raaj.

Raaj quit his job in early 1993 and intended to set up his own finance consultancy. It was also time to take a break and get married. He insisted on doing the ceremonies in Jaipur because of the memories he had of his childhood, and he thought Serena, too, should have some relationship with the city. As agreed between Raaj and Serena, the wedding was a low-key affair in March with Serena's parents, a few relatives and only Sonny attending from Bombay.

22

Taj Coral Reef Resort
Male, Indian Ocean
March 1993

Raaj was deep in thought, sitting on the deck, when he saw Serena emerging from the water and coming up the steps of the lagoon villa they were staying in. She wore a halter neck, tropical-print bikini in red with a clasp fitting at the back and a low-slung bikini bottom that moulded to her body beautifully. The sunlight falling on the droplets of water on her skin shone like pearls and her wet tresses clung to her body. His mind went blank as he took her in his arms and kissed her.

'If I wasn't in love with you yet, I would be falling in love with you now,' he murmured after disengaging from the kiss.

'Promise me, whatever happens, you will never leave me.'

'Promise my precious.'

They went in and made love; again and again.

'Common sense tells me that rich people are happier than their poor counterparts and I am sure all research could provide evidence for that. People find various ways of getting wealthy...' Raaj started when they lay exhausted after endless rounds of lovemaking.

'We have enough money...'

'Describe what "enough" is,' Raaj politely interjected. 'I want to be rich. My job was well paying but my dreams are far bigger. I hope I am successful in my business.' He had always aspired to be rich. A large part of the deep-rooted inspiration came from the financial difficulties he had seen his mother face, knowing well that his father amassed enormous wealth and she hardly got any of it. When he had spoken to his father's family after his mother's death, he was infuriated to know that they had lived a life of luxury and with that came a complete abhorrence for people who did little but inherit.

'So, do you have any ideas of growing rich?' Serena questioned nonchalantly.

'Yes, I do … but I need you to complete the plan,' Raaj responded, driven by enormous ambition and great determination.

Serena realised that she needed to pay more attention. 'I am up for anything you say darling. I don't want to work for ever, either.'

'We're a team then.'

'We always were. What is the plan?'

'Counterfeiting.'

'You're joking?'

'I am serious sweetheart,' Raaj asserted.

'What if we get caught?'

'You haven't even heard the plan.'

'Okay… I'm all ears, my love.'

'I have shared this information with you before but let me start again. There is almost a parallel economy in our country. A lot of businessmen never declare their actual incomes for fear of heavy taxation and hence they have wealth that's unaccounted for. You might be forgiven for thinking it's a small amount…'

Serena nodded as she listened patiently.

'…Most of these people who hide their wealth, are by definition, wealthy. They could potentially be sitting on stock piles of cash and that's where it gets interesting.' Raaj smiled.

'How?'

Raaj paused for a moment and lit up a cigarette.

'These shrewd businessmen - and women - know if they keep cash as such, they lose money due to inflation, so they make investments.'

Serena lit up a cigarette too.

'They invest in property under bogus names, they have bank accounts all over the place in fictitious names, and they buy and sell shares in companies, without giving a whiff, of what is going on, to the government authorities or companies that actually issue them. They do not send these share certificates over to the companies for transfer to their names because that would mean that they would have to declare these assets. What's more, I know a lot of such people through my contacts in my last job.'

'I am still not clear how we fit into the picture,' Serena asked naively.

'Simple. If the certificates do not go to the company, that issued them, for years, no one spots if they are genuine or counterfeit.'

'And how long could this cycle last?'

'Two, three or four years... who knows? And one certificate might change hands ten times before the company registrar receives them.'

'It sounds like a highly ambitious plan. We'd certainly be caught one day.'

'Not likely.' Raaj sounded confident.

Serena didn't believe him in the beginning. Naturally, she had concerns about the whole plan, the repercussions. There was always the possibility of something going wrong and then they could have to face calamitous consequences. It was one thing to dream about counterfeiting, but entirely another to carry it out in reality. It would be difficult and markedly dangerous. But Raaj with his silky verbal skills made even a remarkable counterfeiting plan of this kind sound like a routine operation. Knowing Raaj well by now, she knew he had thought of everything and this idea hadn't sprung in his mind in the last few minutes. He would have, unquestionably, been planning this for months, probably years.

'I get it now.' She gave in, as she found herself being infected by the highly ambitious plan.

'And the best part is when the shares are sent to the company the officials they will not, in all probability, be able to detect a genuine from a counterfeit.'

'Really?' she was even more enthused now.

'Unless they receive two certificates of the same serial number and details concurrently, in which case, they undoubtedly would.' Raaj stopped and looked at his watch. 'Should we go to the bar for a drink?' It was now almost seven in the evening.

Serena kissed him and disappeared into the bathroom. She came out putting on the shortest skirt on the face of the earth. She had purposefully bought it for her honeymoon knowing she wanted to look coquettish and desirable. It was dark, almost bottle green with some mirror work that shone and drew attention to contrast with her pale, toned legs. She also wore a leaf-green tank top that didn't cover much either.

'You've got very beautiful feet sweetheart,' Raaj commented, as he looked down her bare legs.

'Are you saying that's the only beautiful thing about me?' She did not want to miss the chance when she revealed more than she concealed.

'You're gorgeous my precious.' He took her in his arms. 'But please don't tease me any more or we will be late for drinks.'

'Come on then. Let's go.'

Raaj had got into a beige vest and khaki coloured cotton cargo trousers with pockets bulging with keys, camera, lighter and cigarettes, et al.

'Get me drunk tonight. I've never been drunk before.' Serena said as they sat on the bar stools. She was really coy about her rather short skirt and made it a point to face either the bar counter or Raaj. She wanted Raaj to know that she was only being desirable for him, and not for the rest of the crowd there. Though with the hotel full of honeymooners, from all around the world, there did not seem to be many guys interested in other people's wives when they were only recently married themselves.

'Drunk?'

'Yes. I have never been "blown off my head." I want to experience it.' She was adamant.

'Okay. That should not take long.'

The bartender had finished serving drinks to another couple and was waiting for their orders.

'Could we have two large vodkas with colas?' Raaj said and added, '...and two shots of tequila please.'

The bartender nodded and retreated to make drinks for them.

'So, tell me more about the plan,' Serena started.

'Not here sweetheart... we shall speak later.' Raaj was quick to warn her, knowing well that they could be overheard in the bar. They sat there for about an hour cuddling and romancing like every other newly wed couple around them. An hour of mixed drinks was enough for Serena to get drunk. Raaj walked her to the restaurant holding her arm with her head against his shoulders till they sat down on comfortable sofas. He ordered a lobster in mustard sauce topped with cheese and sweet potatoes and peppers on the side. Serena, being a paltry eater, ordered mussels in Thai green sauce from the starters menu.

'So what's on your mind?' Serena started again, hinting at the conversation they had had a while ago in bed.

'With what you're wearing, or rather not wearing now, I have only one thing on my mind, sweetheart.' Raaj tried sounding as lecherous as possible.

They went for a short walk on the beach after the dinner to watch the crab race that was organised for the hotel guests once a week. It was a big novelty factor for most of the guests and it became even more interesting as Raaj and a few other men started betting on them. Serena enjoyed the cool sea breeze, which helped her feel a bit better after the drinking session. She had taken off her beach sandals to enjoy the night-time cool white sands under her feet. By the time everyone retreated to their rooms, it was around ten. As they reached the room, Raaj suggested that they go down their lagoon for a dip in the water. Serena did not need much persuasion.

'How about skinny-dipping?' she asked teasingly, almost pulling off her tank top.

'We've got neighbours, sweetheart.'

Serena was drunk and tired so she slept like a log within moments of hitting the bed. Raaj tried reading under the bedside lamp, but his mind was busy making plans. He had been thinking of this grand scheme for quite some time now, and was happy that Serena had shown some initial interest in it. He knew there would be a lot of planning and hard work required, but it should not be impossible.

Raaj got up late to find Serena missing from his bedside. She had got up early and was playing in the water close to their villa wearing another teasing minimalist bikini. After a while she came into the room and without making any efforts to cover herself, put the kettle on for some tea for both of them. 'So will you tell me the whole plan now?' she asked as she stood drying her hair with the towel.

'Yes… where were we?' Raaj paused to think.

'You were telling me that it would be virtually impossible for company registrars to tell the difference between the genuine and counterfeit share certificates…'

'That is, if they do not get two with matching numbers simultaneously.' Raaj was inspired again.

Serena's raised eyebrows told him that she was wondering about serial numbers.

'There is no cipher to be decoded here. They are just alpha-numerical serial numbers and a hologram of the company in some cases that is not difficult to copy.'

'How will you… er… we... ensure that the company does not receive the same serial numbered certificates simultaneously?'

'Simple. We only duplicate the ones we have access to.'

'We don't have much money to buy enough to make it worthwhile then.' She sounded disappointed.

'We don't need to own them all, we can duplicate all the ones we have access to.'

'I'm not sure I understand.'

Raaj explained to Serena in great detail that physical share certificates were treated as another form of currency at their market value. They were traded through a stock trader and wealth manager, like him, who advises his business clients to pick up high-value blue-chip stocks. As the share certificate must pass through him, to his clients, he could keep the original certificates and deliver the counterfeit ones. He would only duplicate if a particular one had not been recently transferred - in the last one year or so – and had not been reassigned to the latest seller. Hence, there should be no conclusive evidence of who replaced the original certificate with the counterfeited one in the chain.

'How do we make the money?' Serena couldn't stop herself asking.

'We charge the clients for fake certificates and we keep the originals to offload them when the stock market is on a high, plus don't forget we could reproduce one certificate several times. Since I know these people well, I would sell only to clients where there's more than a fifty percent probability that the person buying from us would not send it to the company for transfer before changing hands a few more times. It would be unfeasible to trace back such certificates, and even if they try, it would take years and still not prove anything categorically.'

'How much will we make?'

'More than a few million dollars, I guess. Depends on how big a window we get before we have to sell and then we leave India and settle in some place like... Canada.'

'More than a few million *dollars*?' Serena couldn't believe what she was hearing.

'Yes sweetheart.'

'You've thought about everything, haven't you?' Serena lit up a cigarette.

'Yes sweetheart.'

'How do we get started?' Serena asked eagerly, now appearing even more motivated than Raaj.

'Let's see how many clients I get. I will speak to Sonny - he already invests on my advice and does not seem to be in any haste to sell. If I get his portfolio, it could be a good beginning. I shall contact others once I set up the company when we return.'

'One last question... where would you get these counterfeits printed?'

'Somewhere they don't speak English,' Raaj responded pulling her into bed.

On the flight back to Bombay, Raaj asked Serena not to speak about the whole thing to anyone, ever. 'Two traits are common across all successful people - they never stop thinking of being successful and they don't disclose their plans to anyone,' he said as the flight landed at Sahar International Airport.

23

Bombay
1993

Sonny couldn't wait to see Raaj and Serena when they invited him over for a few drinks, dinner and some initial discussions around setting up the new business. He felt privileged that Raaj wanted him to be the first client and consequently he carried his entire portfolio for an evaluation by the financial expert. 'Hello, Raaj.' He arrived fifteen minutes earlier than the invited hour of seven, threw his bag carelessly, and slumped on the sofa.

'Hi,' Raaj said shutting the door.

Sonny was the perfect guinea pig for this experiment. Firstly, Raaj would have been hard pressed to find a more staggeringly inept client than him. Secondly, the kind of trust he had in Raaj made him extremely vulnerable, and lastly, being born to a rich father, and inheriting all the money and investments, he would be less likely to notice the difference between certificates - something Raaj had always despised about such dumb and fortunate people.

'Where's Serena?' Sonny asked, looking around the living room.

'She's still getting ready.'

'You've got a very beautiful wife, I must say.'

'Thank you.'

'Want to have a look at my portfolio?' Sonny pointed towards his sloppily dropped camel leather bag.

'What's the need to dash into it, we've got all evening.'

Serena came out of her room a few minutes later wearing a dark pink knee length dress with a corset-style waist in viscose that gripped her narrow waistline to highlight her petite frame. It had flared sleeves and the wrap over the front provided a provocatively high slit, in case it was required to impinge on Sonny's attention. 'There you are gorgeous,' Sonny said getting up to welcome her.

'Hello Sonny.'

Raaj was sitting on the sofa opposite Sonny. Serena leisurely walked over and sat on its arm paying special attention to flash just a little bit of leg for Sonny to notice.

Raaj looked at Sonny. 'Do you want to come to my makeshift office or would you have a drink first?'

'Let's have a drink and forget the office. We can see these papers over a drink. I don't mind Serena being around. There's nothing professional between you and me.'

'As you wish, but remember I don't want you to trust me blindly. All decisions should be yours, though I will guide you like before – however, for a fee from now onwards.' Raaj smiled as he got up to make the drinks. 'What will you have?'

'I'll have some Bacardi please.'

Raaj returned with the drinks for all three of them.

'Cheers to you and Serena. I wish you all the success in the new business.'

'Cheers.'

Sonny got up and opened his bag to show the contents. The business card on the file showed him as one of the directors in his father's business, signifying where the money came from, and not as the professional chef that he was.

'That's a great card. I like the embossed hologram on it,' Raaj complimented the moment he saw it, suddenly realising that this careless goldmine could be helpful in more ways than one.

'It's unique. Not many printers do this kind of stuff in the country yet.'

'I haven't yet thought of a logo for my new company and this gives me an idea.' Raaj's mind was racing miles ahead now.

'My dad's company gets it printed in Bombay, I can introduce the printer to you.'

'Great. Thanks. I don't want to get too creative with a logo that cannot be printed. I would like to visit him first to understand the printing technologies and jargon.'

'Of course; my dad gives him so much business in a year that he would provide you with all the time and information you want if I gave him a call.'

'Thanks.'

Sonny's portfolio was in a glorious mess. He had some good blue-chip stocks bought on Raaj's advice, but a large accumulation consisted of relatively unknown and scarcely traded companies. Raaj looked at the share certificates and saw that over ninety percent of the portfolio hadn't been transferred, yet, to Sonny's name. Serena, who gazed at the papers, instantaneously understood what Raaj had explained to her on their honeymoon.

'May I suggest that you sell some of this junk to consolidate into a few good stocks?' Raaj commented after a quick browse through Sonny's entire portfolio.

'Anything you say. I can leave them with you.'

'I cannot give you a receipt since my company is not registered and I don't even have any stationery at the moment...'

'Don't embarrass me Raaj,' Sonny said, stealing a glance at Serena who moved a bit. He thought he saw a little more skin.

The evening was good. They agreed to sort out Sonny's portfolio with Raaj tasked to sell the identified, useless shares and buy some great performing ones that should provide good returns in a few years. Sonny was pleased that he wouldn't have to run around for all his work since, for a moderate fee, Raaj would, henceforth, take care of all his investments. They had a few drinks and Sonny helped the hosts by providing the final garnish to the dinner. He was too drunk to ride his motorcycle by the end of the evening and hence the hosts gladly offered him the spare bedroom in their apartment.

'I told you he would be the best to start with. Did you notice he didn't have a large part of his high value shares transferred to him and he's been holding them for years now? Who knows how many hands those certificates have passed through before they've ended in this thickhead's portfolio?' Raaj told Serena after Sonny left in the morning.

'I saw that when you looked at them.'

'I knew you would.'

'How much is he worth?'

'Quite a lot, though I will have to run some numbers to estimate them better, sweetheart.'

'You're a genius,' she complimented.

'Thanks sweetheart.' Raaj accepted the compliment and blew a kiss to his wife.

'I love you.'

Sonny fixed an appointment for Raaj with the printer for the next week. Raaj visited the site and spent an entire day asking questions on logos, holograms, embossing, serial numbers for receipts and other stationery, different kinds of papers, inks, colours, kinds of printing and timelines required for complicated tasks. By the time he left he could write a white paper on printing. All it required, now, was to find the precise printing press for the plan to progress.

Bangkok
End-1993

The Bangkok vacation at the end of the year was also a business trip for Raaj and Serena. He had scouted for printers in non-English speaking counties and zeroed in on Thailand. He took Serena along with him so that it seemed like another honeymoon for the newlyweds. They parked themselves in Menam Riverside Hotel and wandered in the market for a printer – he had shortlisted a few already – till he found Mr Chalong who struggled to say a word, after *hello,* in English. Raaj pretended he was working on a confidential case, with some important documents, and he ought to be present on site when the printing went on, and hence it would be ideal if Mr Chalong could run his printing operation for a couple of nights. It was quite a conversation, with Raaj carrying an English-Thai dictionary, to convey that he would be around to help choose the paper and type the actual words on the page and Mr Chalong would need to focus on managing the layout, the designing, colours and the technology. Two nights of hard work and Raaj had more script printed than he could possibly use in a decade. He had already noted from his visit to the Bombay printer that the serial numbers were, stamped later and, not a print job.

'All done sweetheart,' he announced walking into the hotel room with the loaded bag.

'Let's do something different tonight,' Serena said excitedly.

'Heard of Patpong?'

'You mean the notorious place?'

'Adult entertainment is a better description.'

'Will I be comfortable watching that?'

'You're the one who asked for something different.'

'What should I wear?'

'Nothing. Most of the women who perform there wear nothing,' he said it with a smile keeping the bag securely in the corner.

Patpong had some really vibrant market streets, with stalls that spilled on to the pavement, trying to sell anything from cheap souvenirs to adult toys to fake electronics.

'Buy me a fancy watch please,' Serena urged, as they passed one of the street vendors.

'You know I hate fakes,' Raaj quipped.

'You are such a convincing liar.'

'I'll buy you an original soon, sweetheart. Very soon.'

Bombay
1994
Back in Bombay, Raaj started his counterfeiting operation with gusto. He found larger and more imprudent fishes in addition to Sonny, and they all looked comfortable when they received the counterfeit certificates. Meeting Kim in early 1994 was a bonus. She came with a large circle of financially-illiterate, cash-rich friends and friends of friends. When Kim met Raaj for the first time she was surprised to learn that he ran a successful finance company. 'If I did not know Raaj, and had met him at the local brassiere, I might have exhausted all my guesses and never thought he was a finance guru,' she had told Serena later. 'My friends would love to grow their wealth with someone like Raaj, who is so untypical of a finance broker… I mean he is so much like any of us.'

'Thank you Kim,' Serena smiled accepting the compliment on her choice of guy.

The prices of the stocks that Raaj recommended to his clients soared in the next eighteen months and his commissions rolled in, that was all in addition to building his own portfolio of original share certificates that he could sell later. With money coming in and their investments growing, they bought a sea-facing apartment in Worli that symbolised their success, and rented out the one they were staying in. The new place was in an older building, but large enough to house both their home and Raaj's office. It had three en-suite bedrooms, and a study that lay between the master bedroom and the huge living and large dining area, this opened into a small balcony with sea views. They allowed some time for a reputable builder to plaster the walls and paint them in an ivory matte finish and change the ancient lighting to recessed halogens in the ceilings that could be directed at the paintings and other *objet d'art* in the house as well as carry out modifications to make the study room into a working office.

Serena was thrilled at the whole idea of a new place to decorate, since they had left the old apartment with the furniture and fittings to be rented out. They constituted the only inheritance Raaj had from his father's side - an old family Persian carpet in an uncommon earth and pale blue colour that he had carried to Bombay after his mother's death. He had done this because she had lovingly displayed and taken care of it for over three decades, not because of any attachment he had to his father. The carpet was handmade of silk and wool with tassles on all four sides' The natural dyes had aged beautifully, making it worth a small fortune. Kim was a great help in taking Serena around to shop for antique furniture and new furnishings. Raaj selected all the electronics without any help from anyone. It took them a while, but both of them enjoyed setting up their new home.

The Worli residence brought them closer to the more financially sound-but-ignorant crowd.

24

Mumbai
January 1996

Bombay changed to Mumbai in 1995 but there was another big, unforeseen change coming. 'What happened?' Serena asked as she saw Raaj looking dour when she walked into the house after being at the office.

'We're done.' Raaj sounded ominous.

Serena hadn't seen Raaj so dejected since his mother's death. He pointed towards the newspaper kept at his office desk. She scanned through the headlines.

The Securities & Exchange Board of India (SEBI) announced the dematerialisation of physical (paper) share certificates to bring all the shares - and the holding individuals or organisations - to book. Every individual that held shares would now have to dematerialise these holdings and trade through *Demat* bank accounts, which would record all transactions. As in the developed Western economies, people could no longer hold and trade paper shares without the companies knowing who the actual owners were. Every time a deal took place, it would be recorded in the books through the banks. SEBI gave a window of two years for the companies and banks to work out the modalities.

'This means…' she started.

'This means we are headed towards the end. We're finished, ruined.'

'What do we do now?' She was shaking dreadfully.

'I can't think of anything.'

Raaj lit up in desperation. The omens certainly did not look good. Serena had already started shuddering at the sheer thought of the people around them – in fact everywhere – getting to know about the fraud. Nothing spells doom more than being a target for schadenfreude at parties or the office. Then, prison...

'You said they would never be able to trace the source.' It was more a question than a statement from Serena.

'But I didn't know we would have to rush things. If I had more time, I could have made some more deals to distance myself from the counterfeit certificates. Two years is all I've got, and too frequent transactions would raise eyebrows. There's a limit to how fast I can run.' He belligerently hit his fist on the desk.

'Calm down. Let's have a drink. I'm sure we can think of something.' Serena tried comforting him.

All the recent success in which Raaj had revelled appeared to be heading towards a grotesque end at high speed. His magnificent plan had turned into a terrible disaster, a nightmare. He lost his balance totally by the evening, having too many drinks, too quickly. The couple sat in Raaj's home-office drinking till midnight, without much communication, absolutely unmindful of the time or anything around them. The evening had passed like a wrist slashing session as a dangerous uncertainty hovered all around. Serena, eventually, convinced him that they sleep on the problem and that might help figure out some approach.

'Promise me one thing, sweetheart,' Raaj expressed as they got into bed.

'What?'

'If something happens to me, do not ever admit to anyone that you had been a part of it or, even, knew about it. It was totally my plan and as I am the sole owner…'

'Don't be a nitwit, Raaj… and you promise me that you will not do anything brainless. It was our plan, we will think of a way to get out of it,' Serena said in a very stern tone.

She took the rest of the week off from work to be with Raaj. She felt uncomfortable in leaving him alone, given his current state of mind and the kind of conversations he had with her the night before.

'There is no way out,' Raaj told Serena when she got tea for them in the morning.

'You are more intelligent than this, Raaj. You cannot give up so easily.'

'Let me think.' For all his bravado, he knew that the chances to succeed in getting out of the mess he had created were very slim, almost nonexistent. 'Aren't you going to the office?' he asked.

'I have taken a few days off.'

'Don't do that. We must not show any signs of this blow to anyone.'

'I told them you weren't well, so its okay, I'll go back to work from Monday. Let's relax.'

They stayed home for the rest of the week but could not think of any solution.

'What if we admit what we've done and inform the police?' Serena suggested.

'Will they forgive us? Have you lost your mind?'

'What if we buy all the fake ones back?' Another one.

'How can we do that? Some of them might have changed countless hands by now. Besides, where's the cash?'

The spectrum of serious possibilities was decreasing with every idea falling short. Raaj was fazed, beset by the problem. He couldn't decide whether he had been overconfident, foolhardy or a complete idiot by rushing into his plan a couple of years ago. He certainly hadn't foreseen this catastrophic development and could not think of any escape from the dreadful consequences. The thought of devastation and dark clouds led him into a self-evoked trance for a while. Faced with the need for a bail-out to cover his disastrous bet, Raaj needed an idea. There was no simple answer.

Sadly, there was *no* answer.

Kim invited them to a party as she had got herself a new painting in lieu of a big contract. It wasn't a big brand name to endorse, but visibility in her profession was paramount. She had started getting offers after the assignment with Serena's bank, and she wanted to show her gratitude. Raaj and Serena considered opting out, but Kim wouldn't budge. She was willing to change the day and date to suit their schedules. They accepted the invite fearing that their absence could send unwarranted signals. 'Let's go. It will take our minds off this mess for a while but remember to remain calm. No one should even get a whiff of it,' Raaj advised.

'I agree. I'm sure we will find a way out.' Serena comforted him by coming close and putting her head on his chest.

How? Raaj thought.

'I'll think of something. Sometimes one has to find a new way to look at the same problem, to find a solution. Let's not lose hope, sweetheart.' He put his arms round her trying his best to sound undaunted.

Kim had received a signature piece of art – it was a true beauty. Moreover, she had completed the furnishing of her pretty house. She paired the new painting with her own skimpily clad photograph on the opposite wall. Women at the party were awed by the painting. Men drooled over her photograph.

'Kim, why don't you wear something like that when you invite us over?'

'You mean wear something or not wear much?'

'Whatever. With a body like hers…'

Raaj hit the bar. Sonny was there to match his drinks so it looked more like the guys were bonding rather than Raaj drinking due to any stress. Serena warned him a few times during the evening until Kim told her to stop nagging. Listening to some of his conversation, with the other guys, Serena realised that Raaj was still advising them on the financial markets and recommending stocks, which was a solace, as it was an indication that he was coming out of the depression she had seen him in since the alarming news. She had immense faith in his capabilities and was very confident that he could work his way out, of the most terrible mess of their lives, if he applied himself. When they left after dinner at midnight, Serena drove, as Raaj had been drinking all evening. Being a party animal, he had done it a few times in the past so this was not any disclosure of their troubles. But he seemed especially down at the moment. 'Everything could be sorted, if I die...' he started.

Serena screeched to a halt on the side of the road. 'You say that one more time and I will kill myself,' she yelled at him and burst into tears. Serena had hardly ever raised her voice before this. She was more the sulking kind if things went wrong, or they had split hairs over something in the past. This was a totally new version of Serena that he saw; frustration combined with fear, forgery and misfortune had fired her up. 'Raaj, we got into this together. Why are you being so diffident?

You are not a weak man...I know you can think of a way out.'

'I'm sorry, sweetheart.' Raaj realised his mutterings had been insensitive. 'I cannot think of any other solution.'

'You will. It's not like you have to do something today. Two years is not a small period of time.'

Mumbai
March 1996

'I have a plan,' Raaj called Serena at her office.

'I'm relieved,' she said. 'What is it?'

'It's a little too detailed for a phone call. We'll discuss it when you get home, sweetheart.'

Serena was home by seven after her driver waded successfully through the Mumbai traffic. 'Tell me now, love?' she asked as soon as she entered the apartment.

'It's still nascent, but the outline of the solution is clear in my mind and we just need to work out the details.' Raaj pointed towards the chair in his office, requesting her to sit down.

'Let's go to the living room.'

'Good idea; let's have a drink first.'

'Let me change and come while you fix the drinks,' she said before disappearing into the bedroom.

Raaj was nervous. He, nevertheless, tried to look optimistic for Serena. She came out of the room dressed in white spandex shorts with a wide elastic waistband that had a metallic drawstring and a screen-printed *hot* adorned in red. They hugged her tightly, showing off her bare legs, under the tight white T-shirt that ended over her belly button.'

So you want to play?'

'It's been a while. Let's hear the plan first.' She hinted at a total lack of intimacy in the past few months.

Raaj handed her a drink, lit two cigarettes, passed one to her and sank into the black leather sofa. When she accepted her drink and turned towards him, he realised that her shorts were more abbreviated than he initially thought. 'When did you buy these?' he salivated.

'Last time I went shopping with Kim when you didn't come along.'

'Did she buy a pair as well?' he smirked.

'Stop imagining and tell me your plan.'

Raaj composed himself for a brief moment. 'I need to die…' he started.

'Not again. Please don't start this thing all over again,' Serena snapped back.

'Let me complete. I need to die for the world.'

'I am not sure I understand.'

'Let me rephrase it for you, sweetheart. I need to disappear like I am dead, but I don't, truly, die. So, when the shit hits the fan and - if and when – I am exposed, I would be long gone from memory. They cannot possibly come after a dead guy, can they?' Raaj took a long sip as he finished the sentence. He went on to detail that if he faked his death in the next few months, the police and public would forget about him by the time the bubble burst, the enquiry took place and they would never suspect or pinpoint him. He would need to separate from Serena for some time. She would have to mourn him, but continue to work, and after enough time had elapsed, she could take a posting abroad to join him.

'And how would you disappear from the face of the earth? Wouldn't the police need a body to confirm you're dead?'

'It would have to be a finely choreographed spectacle. The police would find a dead body, my dead body,' he said.

'Is this the second part of your plan?'

'The first one was a plan sweetheart. This will be a performance,' he buoyantly said, seeing Serena unconvinced.

'How will we produce a dead body?'

'We will dig a grave and get a body out if need be.'

'We can't do that.' She was aghast at the whole idea shaking her head in distress, almost on the verge of breaking down.

'There is no other way out unless you can think of something better. But before that, I need to offload all my stocks in the market, collect all the cash and transfer it abroad,' Raaj carried on.

'How and where?' She seemed to buy the idea now.

'I will make arrangements for one of the big money launderers to deliver me hard cash, in US dollars, in Switzerland. Let me speak to a few people first.'

'Who is going to Switzerland?'

'We will go for another honeymoon so that I can pull off your sexy shorts, sweetheart.' He got up, lifted her and took her into the bedroom.

'Thank God for that.'

25

Zürich, Switzerland
June 1996

Surrounded by five countries, Switzerland is a banking haven. All information on clients and their assets is protected by law, and some of the banks, consequently, go a step further to issue the fabled, numbered account rather than opening one in the name of the customers to give absolute privacy and peace of mind, since the disclosure and access of such accounts are highly restricted to a few senior employees only. Raaj had spoken to a few of the banks prior to travelling to know the exact documentation requirements for identification and account opening. The amount of cash, though significant for him and Serena, was tiny for the big banks, and they would hardly suspect any money laundering that could instigate investigations.

As the couple flew into Zurich, they saw the beautiful and picturesque Alps, which they had seen only in films and in posters. The temperature was around twenty degrees when they got down, a welcome relief from Mumbai's hot and humid June. They checked into a lesser-known hotel in District One, on the bank of the River Limmat and discovered, after checking-in, Lake Zurich was visible from the balcony of their room. As the cash was expected the next day, they went for an evening stroll on the promenade. Both of them were awe-struck by the panoramic view of the city with a number of churches beautifully filling the skyline. They wandered into the old city as the clock on St. Peter's church struck nine. Serena, filled with fear and remorse, recognised this was their last holiday together, for a long time to come, and stood outside the church praying for a long time.

'What did you ask for?' Raaj asked when she finished praying.

'I hope all goes well after this. I am very nervous.'

'You worry too much, sweetheart.' They kissed in front of the church. Despite the brave front, he was scared too, this being a large punt; the biggest gamble of his life. It was a scary prospect, and the chances of succeeding were only marginally greater than zero.

But, they weren't zero, he convinced himself.

Raaj set out early next morning for the neighbouring District Six to receive the cash. It filled a suitcase even after shrinking the rupees into dollars. He had asked Serena to meet him at the bank around eleven in order to avoid coming back to the hotel with the baggage. Serena knew her job well. She wore the finest blue pin-stripe pencil-skirt suit that made her look like a senior director of some significant private firm, although the shirt was unbuttoned quite low down in case she needed to distract some bank manger. She waited for him, around the corner, with a cigarette in her hand.

'You look real corporate.' He was dressed in a matching blue Armani suit.

'I can be a tease too.' She pushed her chest out to show Raaj her cleavage.

'Let's go in.' Raaj opened the door for her.

Dirk, the bank manager with whom Raaj had fixed the appointment, was waiting for them. He took them to a discreet private banking lounge and made them comfortable. It took a good part of the day to complete all the formalities and deposit the cash. They insisted on a numbered account, to ensure total privacy, and got one.

'Keep this card.' Dirk handed over a plain card with no emblem, logo or name; just a telephone number. Raaj and Serena looked at it for a while but did not quite fathom how it worked.

'All you need to do is call this number and punch in a few details to establish your identity. Once that's confirmed, whoever comes on line would have your details and would carry out your instructions. You don't need to mention your name and details every time you call on us,' Dirk explained. 'Could I help you with anything else?'

'That should be enough for the day. Thanks.' Raaj shook hands with Dirk. It was almost two in the afternoon.

'One less thing to worry about,' Raaj said as they went down the steps in the bank. 'Let's do some shopping now.'

As they ambled aimlessly, holding hands, Raaj spotted a jeweller and got reminded of Serena's desire for an expensive watch. 'Let me buy you an original.'

'I don't need it.' Serena, surprisingly, wasn't in a shopping mood.

'Let's see some at least.'

Once in, Serena fell in love with en expensive Omega she tried on herself. 'It's too expensive,' she said, looking at the price tag.

'But you like it.'

'We don't have to buy everything I like.'

'You only live once sweetheart.' He finished the argument and asked the sales attendant to bill the same.

They were back at the hotel by six to get ready to go out for dinner. Both of them changed out of the formal attires they had donned since the morning. Raaj wore a pair of denims with a white shirt and a navy cotton jacket. Serena, as usual, took time to dress up. She looked stunning, when she was finally ready, in a great looking knee length plain black tunic dress with a chiffon overlay. Going with bare legs wasn't an option here so she matched her dress with black calf leather boots that also added a bit of height.

'Are we seeing someone?' she asked as Raaj looked at the time in her watch.

'Yes.'

'Who?'

'Me.'

'And…'

'More of me,' he said. 'I was only admiring your new watch, sweetheart.' He smiled, took her arm and walked out of the hotel room.

On the way back around midnight, Raaj fell down in the hotel lobby and twisted his left ankle. The hotel staff wanted to call in the emergency services, but Raaj did not agree it was required. The first-aider on site helped him limp to the room after they were certain that it wasn't a fracture or something serious. They gave him some pain killers and asked Serena to inform the hotel front staff if the pain persisted.

Raaj got up with excruciating pain in the morning and seemed unable to move. Serena called in the hotel staff who immediately phoned for help from the nearby private hospital, and they quickly sent an ambulance. They were told that the hospitals are not keenly priced in the country, but the couple did not mind that at all. The Hirslanden-International hospital ran quite a few tests to figure out if there was anything serious, but it looked more like cramp. During some of the tests, whilst Raaj was under sedatives, Serena caught up with the consultant, Dr. Bernhard, a large German doctor, who must have been in his late fifties. 'I hope it is nothing serious,' she asked.

'Nothing to worry at all,' Dr. Bernhard comforted.

'Could we have a DNA test done? Raaj never met his father so he would be pleased to know about his origins,' Serena requested.

'Why not? I will ask the nurse to get your signature on the forms… I am sure you know it will cost you extra…?'

'That's okay. Thanks.'

'We now know where you come from,' Serena informed Raaj that she had got his DNA test done while he was out.

'I don't believe it.' He looked at Dr. Bernhard.

'It's true. We used your blood sample to determine the same,' Dr. Bernhard explained.

'What if my hairs do not agree with my blood?' Raaj shocked Dr. Bernhard with his question.

'What do you mean?'

'Could you do DNA analysis from my hair and prove it has the same origin as my blood?' Raaj asked innocently.

'I can. But there's no point as I already know the result. It's only going to cost you an additional test,' Dr. Bernhard argued.

'Let's see.' Raaj gave a hair or two to the nurse when she came to collect the sample. As Dr. Bernhard had mentioned, the test results were identical. Raaj's pain subsided by the afternoon and, after a consultation with Dr. Bernhard, he was discharged from the place by four o'clock. Both of them were quite happy with the treatment and the reports.

'I am glad everything is fine,' Raaj said as they walked out of the hospital.

At the Zurich duty free Serena was fascinated by lingerie in one of the shops, while Raaj looked around, sipping a coffee, till he saw a convenience store. He walked into it to buy a cigarette lighter.

'What did you buy?' he asked Serena when they boarded the flight.

'You will see all when I wear them,' she teased. 'Did you buy anything?'

'Yes.' He pulled out a bottle of anti-freeze liquid for car windscreens.

'Why do you need that? It doesn't snow in Mumbai.' She looked at him, baffled.

'Read the contents, sweetheart,' he said and requested the flight attendant for some drinks. 'We have to add creativity to logic for a perfect recipe. Success never just *happens*'.

Serena noticed that the anti-freeze contained roughly twice the amount of alcohol than any regular drinking spirit.

26

Dubai
August 1998

'Keep in touch,' Serena said to Kim, who she was on the phone to. 'My mobile phone is ringing; I'll talk to you later.' And she disconnected the call to pick up her mobile.

'Hi!' She knew who the caller was.

'Hello sweetheart. You left a voicemail for me.'

'Yes. We're going out partying tomorrow night. Why don't you come over please?' she requested.

'It's very risky. What if someone recognises me?'

'There is no way anyone here will know you. I have checked out the entire team and no one who works here could possibly know you from Mumbai or your earlier banking days,' she insisted.

'Serena, please don't be irresponsible. It could endanger our plan and lives,' Raaj said.

'I haven't seen you for two years now. Please... I have pined for you every single day. I have been living with old memories. Please come once to give me a chance to make new ones, with you, to live by for some more time... p l e a s e...' She was almost choking.

'Please don't get emotional. Let me check the flights and come back to you, but you have to promise me that you will not repeat this request.'

'I promise.'

'Where are you guys going?'

'To a place called The Lodge.'

'I'll try.'

'What do you want me to wear?' she asked cheekily.

'Nothing.'

She was over the moon when she had seen him staring at her dancing with Adam with envy, and the manner in which he had come forward to manage the whole situation, wearing blue lenses as if anyone, who knew him, would not recognise him. She had got a bit jittery when Elena had started flirting with him openly at the bar, and wondered how he would manage to evade her for Serena. But he did. When they lay in bed panting after making love, he explained to her that it was risky calling him to Dubai, as all their hard work could be wasted if someone familiar to them, from their past, saw him.

'And I got this last minute flight with great difficulty. I don't even have a direct flight tomorrow; it transits via Frankfurt and I would have to wait for a couple of hours to catch the connecting flight,' he said.

'Wasn't it worth the effort?' she teased.

PART THREE

'The game isn't over until it's over.'

— Lawrence Peter 'Yogi' Berra

27

Mumbai
July 1998

In the aftermath of the SEBI announcement (a few years earlier) decreeing that all shareholders had to swap their paper-based shares for dematerialised online versions, the capitalists figured they did not have an alternative. With no one contesting the rule, the time had come to start opening *Demat* accounts and begin registering their investments with companies through various banks that provided the service.

In the process of dematerialising stocks, it was unearthed that there were a few counterfeit share certificates. Some miscreants, it seemed, had printed bogus share certificates of a few high trading companies and floated them in the market. The buyers and sellers traded on these for years without any authentication by the issuing companies. Now, when the counterfeit certificates were sent to the respective companies for dematerialisation, the reality was stark. The companies refused to honour them, and the individuals who owned them were not ready to lose all their wealth they had invested in these papers for years. There was a passive majority who had put large sums of unaccounted wealth into these and made little more noise than a whimper, but there was also a vocal minority whose hard-earned life-savings had got wiped off in the scam, and they couldn't stop screaming.

Politics being an epitome of rhetoric pageantry, a local political party came up with an agenda to accommodate the aggrieved by clearing the chaos and providing justice to the affected investors. The support was never meant to be more than cosmetic, but it soon became the pretext of the upcoming local elections. The zealot party took up the gauntlet to bring the condemned outlaws to book. As was customary, a committee was set up to look into the whole case, and one of the local politicians, known for all the wrong reasons, was appointed as its head. With no record of how many hands a particular counterfeited certificate had passed through, it was acknowledged that it would be an uphill task to go through humongous paperwork, dating back many years, to trace the person, or persons who, initially, floated them on the market. An enquiry like this could easily take a couple of years, at least, before any report could be published. Nevertheless, it provided some respite to the situation for the time being, for the investors were relieved that the government was looking into their grievance.

As the days passed, it was revealed that there was almost a parallel market of counterfeit share certificates. It became apparent to the investigating committee that there could well be more than one source, as this would have led to more money than one individual could hide or escape with. Or, it could well be that a group jointly floated these fake certificates, and distributed the unaccounted money later to avoid any unnecessary attention. Where all the money had ended up was a further mystery for everyone.

If there were any positive news from the whole meltdown it was that some investors who had planned not to dematerialise their shares till the last minute, declared their investments early, to check if they were victims of the con.

Sonny lost practically everything. When he sent his certificates for transfer to various companies, each one turned out to be a fake. His entire inherited wealth, which he had planned his life around, got wiped out. His profession as a chef, which was a pastime, could never bridge the gap between his expensive socialite lifestyle and the money required to maintain it. To make matters worse, he had unsecured debts all over the place that he had incurred knowing he had investments as his insurance, if need be. When his investments become junk overnight, Raaj was long gone and he had no one to turn to. He wanted to warn Serena that Raaj had been taken for a ride but she was not in India.

Maybe Raaj had foreseen all this, and what appeared to be an accident was actually a suicide, he deliberated.

He contemplated telling the police about Raaj, but gave up the idea since he knew it would hurt Serena very much. She had barely shown signs of moving on with her life, and any news like that could break her again and bring her back into mourning. His father had always objected to the idea of him becoming a chef and declining to join the family business. He knew going back to his father to ask for money, to bail him out of this catastrophe, would be the biggest disgrace he could bestow on himself. If he declared bankruptcy, the loan-vultures wouldn't relax till they got the last pound of his flesh - his property, his expensive Ducati and every other personal belonging. Life, he reckoned, would be far from worth living.

He couldn't imagine how Raaj could have let himself get fooled like this.

He tried putting up a bold front for his colleagues, by attending the office and working in the kitchen as normal, but his mind was far away, trying to work out his losses and an escape route from reality. Since he had become a senior chef he no longer worked the night shifts and weekends. He came back, from the office, every weekend to hit the bottle and stay locked in his pad until Monday morning, avoiding company as much as possible. But he knew that wasn't a solution; he was only behaving like a rabbit trapped in the headlights.

On that fateful Friday at work, he got a call from one of his debtors demanding the money back, since the loan they had provided him with had run its due course. He needed to pay the money off with interest by the following week. He knew from experience that individuals and non-banking outfits, which gave unsecured loans, had ways and means to recover them by twisting arms - or worse - if required. Panic set in as he left the office that evening. He stopped at three separate chemists to pick up as many sleeping pills as he could without a prescription. Once at home, he considered writing a note but decided against it. The last thing he needed was to give financial defeat as the reason for his terrible action, for it would only give his dad a chance to blame it all on his mum for allowing him to pursue his hopeless career, and not joining the promising family business. To remove all trace of his lost fortune he tore all the letters from the companies that explained why his junk portfolio could not be redeemed and flushed them down the drain. He, then, bolted and locked the door firmly from the inside, popped more pills than his body could handle and gulped them down with half a bottle of Bacardi.

He didn't see the Saturday sunrise.

On Monday evening, his office reported him missing to the local police station after they had called and left messages for him throughout the day.

Senior Inspector of Police, Michael D'Cunha, asked his staff to get a local locksmith. He did his job, but the door was bolted from the inside. With no options left, he gave the order to break the door open. Sonny's body was found in his bed smelling horribly of alcohol and whatever he threw up before his end. The biological cause of his death was revealed by the postmortem, but the real motive baffled the police, neighbours - who had always known him as a happy-go-lucky chap - and his office colleagues whom he had never failed to awe, even at his end.

D'Cunha's brain went into overdrive when he saw Kim at Sonny's place with some other friends. He made the connection that the couple in the fire-accident case at Worli, which he had solved in the last few years, knew the chef. All his investigations proved that Sonny had picked up the pills on his own, and no one had visited him in the last few weeks. Kim had never visited him at his place before this, although she could plausibly provide some information if the two cases were linked, but he deliberately did not allow himself to follow his train of thought. He was now incredibly close to his promotion, and upsetting his supervisor for a second time about the same suspect was certainly not sensible. Moreover, taking Kim in for questioning would mean a few more aggressive calls and he would have to drop the enquiry anyway.

Why initiate something that I cannot follow up, he thought, and closed the case. Self-annihilation.

Sonny's suicide generated a variety of stories by the local tabloids that labelled him as a jilted gay lover, another spoilt son of a rich industrialist, or a drug addict. One of the regular dailies raised a question about his financial state after the recent stock market bubble burst, but it was too dreary a story to attract any attention.

By January of 1999, the committee had established that the present value of all the bogus certificates was well over a few million dollars. It could be far greater depending on when they were issued, sold, and how many times each had been turned around, but no one knew that for now. It was made explicit that some counterfeit certificates, which were owned by overseas investors and others held by dubious account holders who might not have sent their holdings for dematerialisation as yet, were not included in this amount. After a few more months of analysis and probing, the committee concluded, quite logically, that the money received from these was certainly not in one of the banks in the country, as they could not find large unexplained amounts of money in any of the bank accounts they had suspected. It had either left the country through several money launderers, or was still stacked in mattresses, which would be extremely difficult, if not impossible, to trace. The committee handed the enquiry to the Central Bureau of Investigation (CBI), as the ugly scam was turning out to be more macroscopic than they had initially anticipated. It looked like the work of an organised crime ring, which had carefully planned this over a period of time, and cunningly got away with the loot, at least for now.

28

Cairo, Egypt
August 26 1999

Serena's, brilliantly feigned, claustrophobic sickness attack at the pyramids had helped her pull out from the Sharm el Sheikh trip with the rest of her office colleagues. An hour after the coach had left the hotel, Raaj, dressed in full white robe and headgear like a sheikh, got down from the cab and took the elevator without checking at the front desk. He knocked on the door of Serena's room.

'Who is it?' she asked to confirm no one had returned from her office crowd.

'It's room service madam,' he said.

She recognised the voice and rushed to the door, looked through the eyehole to check and opened it just enough for him to enter, to avoid anyone else watching if there was someone around.

'Wow…!' he exclaimed the moment he shut the door behind him and turned around to see her.

Serena had started making efforts for this trip back in Mumbai, when she knew Raaj could make it to Cairo, according to their plan. She had joined a gym to tone up, and standing in the room's entrance passage, against the sun from the blinds that pierced through her sheer satin black silk slip with floral lace in the right places (she had even worn garters to support her black seamed fishnet knickers), she looked gorgeous.

'Oh my God! You look ravishing.' He whistled.

'Then why don't you ravish me, Sheikh?' she said, commenting on his attire. 'And please keep your voice low as everyone around thinks I am not well.'

'It would be difficult for you to keep your screams down,' he muttered before he took his robe off and threw her on the bed.

'Where did you get this lingerie from?'

'Remember when I went shopping at Zurich airport? I told you I'd show you what I bought. This was one of unfortunate ones that I couldn't sport for you back then.'

'So it's new?'

'Yes, but worn by your old wife.'

'Okay… I'll be careful in taking it off.'

'Tear it off, damn it.'

He strictly followed orders.

Serena had put a *Do Not Disturb* sign on the room even before Raaj had arrived. With no one else in town, who knew them, it was a good opportunity to make up for all the lost time. She frequently kept ordering small portions of food so that no one got suspicious of two people staying in her room. In any case food was the last thing on their minds.

'What next?' she asked pulling a bottle of beer from the mini bar in the room.

'How're things in Mumbai now?'

'I told you about Sonny… he killed himself.'

'I know. I always knew he was spineless, a jellyfish. He simply wanted to enjoy what he inherited from his father. He had no courage or backbone to stand up and face the reality when the time came. All he had lost was inherited wealth. He still had his career and salary to manage his life, but the king of diamonds collapsed like a pack of cards.' Raaj almost lost his temper talking about Sonny.

'I know. Maybe he didn't have a choice.'

'In life, there is always a choice. It may be a difficult option, and people might prefer not to exercise it, but there is always choice. I hope you don't feel, in any way, that we are responsible for his death?'

'No.' Serena's doubts, if any, evaporated when she heard Raaj talk about Sonny.

'I'm sure they never linked Sonny's suicide with anything financial?'

'His death didn't make much news.'

'Was there much news about counterfeit shares? I read on the Internet about a few politicians making a fuss about catching the culprits.' He wanted to know what had happened.

'As always, they make all the right noises initially to divert the crowd's attention, but then forget about it... you know such plotters.'

'I am sure they have forgotten about the whole thing by now.' He reassured her and took the bottle from her hand to finish off its content in one large gulp.

'How long before I can join you?' she asked.

'If the dust has settled, I think you should ask for a foreign assignment by the end of the year. It might take a while before there is one that suits you.'

'Where should that be?'

'The UK, the US, or Canada.'

'Do you want some beer?' she asked, getting up to get one for herself.

'Yes please and come back to bed quickly.' If she had to live another year with the memories, as she had said, he wanted to make the most of his time in making them.

The two-day honeymoon finished with drinking out of the mini bar and eating the room service sandwiches.

'When do we meet again?' Serena asked in the morning when she was getting ready to catch her flight back, with the rest of her office colleagues, to Mumbai.

'I don't think we should meet till you move.'

'Why?'

'What if they have uncovered something that links back to me? I am sure they would start following you around,' he explained.

'Okay. I will ask for a move soon.'

'Ask by the end of the year sweetheart,' he said, and kissed her goodbye.

29

New Delhi
August 2001

A minor investigation on some counterfeit share certificates began because of a superficial intervention by a local political party, for its own political mileage, in Mumbai three years ago. This had turned its fortune in the 1999 general elections and, should have been in history's wastebasket by now. But the issue, accidentally, ended up in the recycle bin and got picked up by the party - now in opposition - at the local assembly by-elections, as they wanted to restore the confidence of the electorate in their party by promising to take the inquest to the finishing line. Propaganda, being a powerful political tool, the new guardians advocated that the investigation that had gone cold should be picked up again by the CBI to compensate the investors or, at least, convict the culprits. The victims of the scam hadn't forgotten their financial wounds yet and were boisterous at the very mention of the same. Demonstrations started by the party got support from all over the country, and as it gathered momentum, the resulting furore eventually rocked New Delhi. As expected, it was found that the earlier investigation had slowed after being passed down to a powerless sub-inspector because of the lack of a custodian.

The files were dusted off and pulled out to start afresh, but no one knew where to begin. Officers in the Civil Services knew, and knew well, that a high profile investigation like this one could make or mar their careers, with evidence heavily tipping towards the latter. Experience with the bureaucracy had taught them to stay away from controversial cases like these, as one surmised that something of this nature, and scale, would either have a godfather in the local mafia, or someone very powerful in the political system itself. They were damned if they didn't close the case on time and equally damned if they did.

What relief would the affected shareholders get, or what punishment would be meted out to the guilty was a secondary objective for the political leaders. A new committee was formed and, in a brilliant PR spin, Mr Gill, a highly respected septuagenarian freedom fighter, was appointed as the chairman, rather than a disgraced politician, like last time. Mr Gill had worked with Gandhi in the struggle for freedom and there was no bigger endorsement than that achievable in a country that still revered the Mahatma. In all fairness, Mr Gill had followed the simplistic regime in the last fifty years after independence and won every single election from his constituency that regarded him as the patriarch. Now that he had retired from active politics and with no real family, it was time for the political party on the bench to make the most of his image for the good of the nation. And, of course, their own benefit.

Mr Gill was on national television, revelling in the glory of being recognised as one of the few remaining apostles of the legendary Mahatma, assuring the nation that he would fight till the very end to finish the incomplete task handed over to him by the trusting citizens of the country.

'... I did not fight for the freedom of my country to let it go into the hands of criminals. I pledge to you that I will get to the bottom of this scam... and as some of my critics have raised doubts about my agility – referring to my age, I promise I will not even die before the enquiry brings the culprits to justice...' He declared, without any hesitation.

As the chairman, the first thing Mr Gill decreed was that the media be divorced from the investigation. He was of the opinion that the more the media flared the whole episode, the more chance it gave the culprits to get far away, and to cover their tracks, if any were left. He understood the enquiry was high profile, but it needed to be kept for internal consumption until they had uncovered everything and made any arrests. He asked for all the files relating to the case to be sent across to him, at his office, to go through the material gathered and the search undertaken so far. There was a plethora of information on what had happened, but embarrassing follow-ups, and no results whatsoever. The earlier investigation had not revealed a slightest clue.

This could only mean one of two things: either, the enquiry pointed towards some extremely influential individual or group, or the accused had meticulously planned everything to the utmost, he thought.

Disappointed by the files but not discouraged, he called for the list of the most competent senior officers in the police force and CBI. In normal circumstances, the establishment would have taken weeks to compile such a list, but this time the file listing the top ten officers was provided to him in two days. He went through the files and records of ten of the best brains in the business and shortlisted two that he wanted more information about before he met any of them. As he reflected on the given details of these two senior officers, one stood out appearing to be of the mettle that could make pigs fly.

'I want Kabir Singh for this investigation,' Mr Gill told the parliamentarian he was directly reporting to on the case.

'Kabir is granted. Do you need anything else?' The parliamentarian agreed without any persuasion.

'Not at the moment,' Mr Gill replied.

'Okay. I wish you all the very best,' said the voice, concluding the conversation.

Kabir thrived on challenges; the bigger and riskier, the better. When he got the news through his superior that he was being transferred, overnight, to the CBI - the most prestigious intelligence agency in the country - to work on a specific top-secret case, he couldn't wait to get his briefing. He was up early and went for his morning run before getting ready to meet Mr Gill at the latter's small office in the annexe of Parliament House.

'Good morning, sir,' Kabir said politely, knocking lightly on the older man's door.

'Good morning, Kabir. Come in and take a seat.'

Kabir walked up and shook hands with Mr Gill before he pulled a chair to sit down. Unlike the other government offices that had a large customary picture of Gandhi adorning the wall, his office had an original black and white framed picture of Mr Gill sitting with the Mahatma on the desk. It was the only personal asset Mr Gill had brought to the room with him when he took up this top job. The room had the bare essentials and could be summed up like Mr Gill's personality in one word. Simple. He did not even have a computer on his desk.

'How are you this morning, Kabir?' he asked seeing Kabir settled in his chair.

'I am fine, sir. Thanks.'

'Congratulations on your promotion.'

Kabir was surprised. His superior had positioned his move more as a parallel transfer than a promotion. 'I didn't know it was a promotion.'

'It will be. Going by your records, you wouldn't fall short in clearing the amethyst mist from this case to earn yourself one. In any case the move from the Indian Police Force to the CBI is a big step forward, isn't it?'

'Yes, sir.'

'I hope you know what this meeting is all about?'

'I know what it is about, but I have not been given any details yet,' Kabir responded.

'That is why you are here son…' Mr Gill slipped in the word *son* to establish his father figure status as early as possible. He handed a file over to Kabir and carried on. 'This is just the gist of the case… do you see over there?' he pointed towards a mountain of files kept in one corner. 'Those files contain all the information you need to begin.'

Kabir looked at the recently dusted-off files and raised his eyebrows in acknowledgement.

'It's a pity that the people following this enquiry, earlier, did not find a single lead. All these files contain is what happened, how many shares were counterfeited, which companies were affected, how much the scandal could be worth… I would classify this more as a piece of research than an investigation,' Mr Gill explained in disgust.

Kabir thought for a moment before he spoke. 'So we have to begin all over again, after time has elapsed, which always makes it a little more difficult.'

'Yes but that's our job. The size or complexity of the task should not deter us,' Mr Gill said.

'You're absolutely right sir.'

Mr Gill explained the whole case to Kabir in brief. 'There are a few important things I need to tell you before you take on this case. One, you will move out of your office to a smaller place here in one of the wings. I will initiate the process for getting a pass for you.

'Second, you will work exclusively on this case and report solely to me... not entertaining any calls from anyone, however important, and no statements to the media. You only take orders from me.

'To maintain absolute secrecy, I don't want to involve a lot of people. You need to identify one person who will assist you. Do you have someone in mind for this case?'

Kabir hadn't thought about that.

'I would like to meet him or her,' Mr Gill said.

'Okay. Let me look at the case files before deciding who fits the role.'

'That's good. When can you let me know?'

'Give me a day or two,' Kabir requested.

'Okay... and one more thing,' Mr Gill said as an afterthought.

'What is it?' Kabir asked.

'For the purpose of discretion, till you handle this investigation, no uniforms please. I don't want you going around like a policeman. You can keep your arms, but you have to work more like a detective.'

Kabir understood the rationale.

'Do you have any questions?' Mr Gill asked.

'Just one. Why did you select me for this case?' Kabir wanted to know the reason for getting picked for this assignment.

'Because you are the best. Your past records tell me that you have the capability, coupled with unselfishness. And I knew you would be passionate about this job.'

'Thanks for the honour.'

'I wish you all the best. All my contact details are on the first page of the file I just gave you. If you need to reach me urgently, do not bother what time of the day - or night - it is. I would like to meet you and your chosen candidate by...'

'We'll be here before the end of the week sir.' Kabir filled in the blanks.

D'Cunha had outperformed everyone, who had ever worked for Kabir before, and maintained his record in solving cases as suitably and quickly as he always had. As a matter of fact, he had exceeded his own expectations. In the last eighteen months DSP Michael D'Cunha, with his new team, had resolved two homicides, busted an unauthorised gambling den and illicit liquor supplier and arrested a money launderer, besides taking a lot of small time cases off Kabir's back. The men did not agree on everything, but Kabir always carefully considered D'Cunha's views before making decisions.

Contrary to the hearsay, D'Cunha appreciated working for a supervisor like Kabir who did not believe in being politically correct while working in the police force. Kabir had made it clear from day one that the duty of the police department was to protect citizens, and likewise, that citizens also had a responsibility to help police by providing any information that was required. It did not matter who the suspect was. If required, the person would be brought in for investigation and no amount of external pressure could stop him while Kabir was around.

The police could only do their job if everyone cooperated. Questioning someone is different from convicting. If we don't probe, how will we ever get to the truth? Kabir had articulated to his team on every occasion.

D'Cunha understood that from experience. On many occasions, like the time he wanted to probe Kim, his boss had blocked the investigation due to pressure from an influential person. As he sat there at his desk looking into a file, he heard footsteps approaching him. It was Kabir, in plain clothes.

'Keep sitting,' Kabir said seeing D'Cunha immediately drop the file to rise and greet his boss.

'Good morning sir. You could have called me…'

'I thought if I need you, I should come to you,' Kabir said and pulled a chair. 'How long have you been in this job now?'

'About eighteen months.'

'And you think you're doing a good job?'

D'Cunha's face dropped. He promptly tried to recall all the recent cases he had handled to check, in his mind, if he had gone wrong somewhere and upset Kabir. An open-ended question like the one he had just been asked did not sound very promising. He couldn't recall anything that he might have done wrong, in any case, in the last six months or so. 'I think so,' he replied.

'You think or you know?' Kabir was, somehow, enjoying making him anxious; he had noticed D'Cunha becoming disturbed with the conversation. There was a silence in the room. 'You don't even offer tea to visitors now?'

'My apologies…' D'Cunha confessed, picked up the intercom phone and asked for two teas to be rushed to his room.

'Thank you.'

'You're welcome sir.'

The teas arrived in a flash as if someone had pre-empted the request, seeing Kabir walk into D'Cunha's room a moment ago.

'Remember I told you in our first meeting, I believe in putting the utmost trust in the people who work for me…' Kabir started again.

D'Cunha had done all he could for the department. The initial arrangement he had with his family had continued for longer than he had thought. His family was still in Mumbai, he was utterly dedicated to his work, but Kabir's demeanour did not reflect any of that.

'I have been assessing your work and I think you should not be in that uniform.' Kabir carried on the onslaught.

D'Cunha wanted to close his eyes and think that it was a nightmare. He opened his mouth, but failed to get any words out in his defence. Years of service seemed like coming to an end, with all plans of a prize posting or promotion appearing to suddenly rush out of the window. He couldn't understand the reason for Kabir's behaviour because he couldn't think of anything that had gone so terribly wrong in his work that could have upset his boss to this extent. Taking a police officer out of his uniform was nothing less than suspension.

'Come into my room, I need to discuss something confidential with you.' Kabir realised that he should stop the banter and put D'Cunha out of the misery now. He finished the remaining tea in the cup in one long gulp and swiftly walked out. D'Cunha got up with his legs trembling like he had just finished running the marathon. Each step to Kabir's office felt like a mile.

'Sit down,' Kabir said with a smile as if he was a different person than the one who had just delivered the devastating message a minute ago in D'Cunha's room. D'Cunha's heartbeat was still racing after the marathon.

'Relax Michael, I was just checking your nerves. My assessment of you is that you are one of the most knowledgeable, comprehensive, capable and realistic officers in my team.' Kabir put all the adjectives he could conjure up in one sentence. And he wasn't exaggerating. 'I promised you a high profile assignment if you performed well in two years. I think you have outperformed and therefore the reward has come in eighteen months. I know I can completely trust you now. My comment about taking off your uniform was right though… even I have given that up. It's a discreet assignment and I have been temporarily moved into CBI. I need only one capable officer and I am convinced that you fit the bill.'

D'Cunha took a long breath of relief. 'Anything you say,' he said knowing well that a posting in CBI was beyond his wildest dreams just a few minutes ago.

'You understand that this job that I am offering you can bounce you into a different league if we are successful. On the flip side, if we fail…'

'We will not fail sir.' D'Cunha found it hard to hide his excitement.

'I like your confidence, Michael. That's the kind of man I like.' Kabir paused to let D'Cunha breathe for a minute. 'It's an old case, which should have been solved years ago but got sidelined due to lack of leadership. It got picked up in the recent political agenda and hence we have to reopen it. I have been through the files now.'

'When do I begin?' D'Cunha asked.

'As of now. Tomorrow I need to take you to Mr Gill, who is the chief of this enquiry – his office is in Parliament House and both of us will be working from there as well.'

'What is the case about?'

'Way back in the early or mid-nineties or so it appears for now, someone - or a syndicate - printed counterfeit share certificates and floated them on the market. It only came out in the open when the SEBI mandated the dematerialisation of paper-based shares in the late-nineties. I am sure you would have heard about it then and there has also been coverage on the news recently, but it will not get any more media coverage till we investigate and uncover the truth,' Kabir explained.

'I know… I heard about it when I was in Mumbai. It started there.'

'It got unearthed in Mumbai. But we don't know where it originated from, do we?'

'No sir.'

'Okay. You will get the files tomorrow. I shall see you there,' Kabir said handing over the address of Mr Gill's office to D'Cunha. 'And it's worth emphasising that you should not speak to anyone about this assignment, not even to your family.'

'You have my word sir,' D'Cunha assured.

'Kabir… Remember, there are no uniforms,' Kabir corrected D'Cunha, pointing towards his shirt.

D'Cunha nodded. 'You almost took my breath away,' he said after a minute of silence.

'It's all a question of nerves. I could have given you this news in a normal way, too, but the impact would have been inferior. Don't you agree?'

No, I don't agree, D'Cunha wanted to bark.

'Of course, it would have been too boring,' he said.

'I'll see you tomorrow at nine.'

'Thank you, Kabir.' D'Cunha got up to leave.

30

London
August 2001

Nikos and Serena had been officially dating for the last three months and everyone, who knew Serena in the bank, had heard about how it all started with a steamy night after Paul's party. She had kept her apartment, but had moved in with her Greek Adonis, in his penthouse, for practical purposes.

Riding the victorious wave, thinking, imprudently, that the dust had settled back in India, they assumed they were invincible and that, in itself, has many a time made people seriously vulnerable. They had taken their eyes off the ball, and hence utterly missed the news that another referee had been appointed in the game they thought was long over.

Missing one news item was probable, but if the media picked up the news regularly, the odds were that those involved would get vigilant; it would be far easier to find the void if no one was filling it all the time, Mr Gill had thought.

Serena lost her commitment to work. There were no more late hours and no additional responsibilities undertaken, and she showed a lack of initiative and drive for any new projects. She was having a good time with Nikos, knowing well she would be renouncing the dreary working life to start a new one on a swish beachside villa in Spain in a few months time. The wedding date wasn't decided, but both of them acknowledged they didn't need to have a ceremony. They could easily take a break, go somewhere in Europe without inviting anyone, and come back a fortnight later with new rings. No one would check the million churches in Europe if they ever got married.

And why would anyone, they had asked each other a few times.

'*Hola hermosa,*' Nikos said, when Serena entered his penthouse after work on Friday.

'What's that?'

'Spanish for *hello gorgeous…*'

'So you're practising your Spanish on me?'

'I think you should learn it too. And learn it fast. If we plan to move to Spain by early next year, knowing the language will be an advantage. We can make new local friends and pass off as Southern Spaniards or North Africans, so it raises fewer eyebrows in local cafes or supermarkets,' Nikos explained.

'You're right.'

'I have seen some properties on the Costa Tropical, in the Mediterranean, and have spoken to an estate agent there. Should we go to see some next weekend?'

'Why not?' She went up the stairs to the bedroom on the mezzanine.

Marbella, on the Costa del Sol, was still an upcoming beachside area with construction happening all around, which would make it popular – and expensive – in the future. Nikos and Serena talked about the place while driving, in the car rented from Malaga Airport, to view the first villa the estate agent had called them about. The magnificent villa stood on a little hill that sloped down to the sea. Alfredo, the estate agent, met them as they got down from the car.

'Hello!' he said cheerfully to his clients.

'*Hola mi amigo. ¿Cómo estás?*' Nikos shook his hand.

'*Es usted Español?*'

'*No. Greek,*' Nikos responded in fluent Spanish.

'And madam?'

It was clear from Serena's expression that she did not understand the language. However, she had started looking around the grand villa - freshly painted white - with great interest.

'She's Indian,' Nikos told Alfredo.

'Indian women are beautiful,' Alfredo complimented Serena, shook her hand and smiled. 'Hello madam, I am Alfredo.'

'Hello. I'm Serena.'

'You are Mr Nikos, obviously.' Alfredo pulled a bunch of keys from a bulging pocket.

'You're right.'

'How was your flight from Athens?' He assumed they had flown in from Greece.

'We came from London and the flight was on time.'

Alfredo tried a copious number of keys till he established the right one for this villa, but he chirped continuously, asking questions about irrelevant things as all sales people do. Nikos and Serena felt greatly relieved when he finally found the key to the front door. The villa was worth all the irritating questions. It looked even better in bricks and mortar than in had in the pictures that Nikos had shown Serena on the estate agent's website. Partly furnished, it was airy and boasted unrestricted panoramic views from large windows with low hills on one side and the Mediterranean beachfront on the other. The entrance hall was pretty and round and it opened into an enormous living room that connected to the dining room, a small cloakroom and kitchen on the same floor. The rear of the living space was all glass that opened on to a deck on stilts that could be used for al fresco dining, while one enjoyed the beach below. There were ten wooden stairs from the deck to take one down to the beach.

'Is that a private beach?' Serena asked excitedly.

'No madam. But, as you can see there isn't any other residence in the vicinity so you can consider it your own till another villa comes up in the neighbourhood, which would be at least five hundred meters away,' Alfredo explained.

'We can go skinny dipping in the night,' Serena whispered to Nikos.

'I would love to see that, madam.' Alfredo smiled to communicate he had heard her suggestion.

The first floor had four en-suite bedrooms and two of them had large balconies facing the sea. The three of them walked out to view the villa from the outdoors once again. It had three garages detached from the main villa and enough space for another dozen cars on the driveway.

'This is beautiful.' Nikos broke the silence, looking at Serena for approval.

'Amazing villa, I must say,' she agreed. 'And the view is breathtaking.'

'Are you viewing some more properties with other agents?' Alfredo asked, as the husband and wife enjoyed the panorama.

'Yes,' Serena said.

'If you want to view this again, you have my number. You just have to give me a few hours notice,' Alfredo suggested like a typical sales agent.

'We will. I wish I could live in this now,' Serena said it in a complimentary manner.

'Of course you can, madam. There are no more viewings this weekend so, if you want, you can stay here.' Alfredo tried to make sure that his extra services clinched the deal, knowing well that it would be impossible to find any other property in the area that matched its beauty and privacy and it was the perfect place for skinny-dipping, too.

'Thanks. But we are already booked in a resort.' Nikos quickly turned down the offer, while remaining polite.

But Alfredo knew how to sell. 'You can cancel that. Even if they refund fifty percent, it's a saving. And you can enjoy the villa with madam. It is very romantic here, totally remote and yet so accessible from the town. It's barely three kilometres from the nearby village that has excellent facilities, including shopping.'

'Are you sure?' Serena pitched in before Nikos could refuse again.

'Yes madam, don't worry about it. I wouldn't have offered if I was unsure.'

'Okay, we'll take the offer.' Nikos succumbed seeing his wife's keenness.

'That's good. Let me show you around a few things.' Alfredo took them on another short tour of the villa, showing them how to operate the kitchen, the alarms and the locks…

'What do you think is a good offer for this property?' Nikos started negotiating, as they came back to the living room.

'It has a listed price of fifty million pesetas, so less than a million of the new Euro currency coming from next year.'

'And what do you think should we offer?' Nikos repeated his

question, as Alfredo's chatter had given no real answer.

'Properties like these don't come to the market often, so there is no comparison that I can draw, but if you are interested I can ask the owner and come back to you. Do you have a figure in mind?'

'No.' Nikos knew the negotiation game; never quote your price first.

'I will check and let you know.'

'Thanks.'

Alfredo showed them the nearby village on the map, in case they needed to buy some groceries or essentials. Nikos was definite neither of them had any inclination to cook on a holiday, so he only briefly looked at the map, but let Alfredo go on with his speech, uninterrupted, without any questions.

'And if you need anything, please do not hesitate to give me a call anytime.' Alfredo finally decided to leave.

'When do we see you again?'

'I shall see you tomorrow evening. Till then, I leave you two alone to enjoy doing what madam wanted…' He mentioned with a mischievous smile on his face. 'And I wish you all the best for viewing other properties.'

'He's quite a character,' Serena uttered, as he drove off.

'Just be careful… he might hide himself in the bushes to watch you skinny dipping.'

'Would you like that?' She, like a tease, unbuttoned her shirt.

'Like what – him watching you?'

'I meant… would you like to go skinny dipping?' She pulled off her shirt.

'You mean now?'

'Yes honey. Let's do it now.'

'Its daylight… what if someone is around?' Nikos sounded stunned.

'I don't care. Are you coming with me, or would you rather watch me naked from the deck?' She was unfastening her belt now.

'Hold on sweetheart. What is the rush… we can do it in the evening after dusk.'

'We can do it again after dusk, my love. We've got to make up for five years.' She was out of her jeans and standing in her lingerie now.

'You are turning me on…'

'So, why don't you get started?' She unashamedly walked out on the deck stark naked.

Serena was very happy with the villa, and as it was well within their budget, even if the owner was not willing to negotiate, Nikos called and cancelled all other viewings. The other places they had seen on the websites were not even half as beautiful. They went out only in the evening for some Tapas, using the map Alfredo had left behind to find the nearby village, and they brought back bread, eggs and milk for breakfast and some wine for the rest of the evening.

'What will we do with six bottles of wine in one night?' Nikos asked when he saw Serena picking them up.

'Get drunk.'

Alfredo called to check if everything was okay and how the other viewings went during the day.

'We liked another one,' Nikos lied.

'Where exactly is that?'

'I will tell you when we meet. Did you speak to the owner about the price?'

'I wanted to check with you on that. Would you make all the payment by cheque, or is it possible to pay some part in cash?'

'We can do part-cash too.'

'Then we can do this deal for forty five.'

'Forty five million pesetas, you mean?

'Yes.'

'Let's talk tomorrow.' Nikos wanted to tell Serena that the deal for this property would go through for sure now.

'How is madam?'

She's waiting for me, naked in bed, Nikos wanted to respond.

'She's fine. Thank you and good night, Alfredo.'

'Good night, Mr Nikos.'

'What did he say?' Serena jumped on Nikos when he finished the call, though his expression had given away the suspense.

'I think we've got it.'

'Wow… let's celebrate…' She came into his arms and they kissed.

'Let me open a bottle of wine.'

'Let me take off my clothes.'

'Red or white?'

'White with lace, actually,' she said looking down at her lingerie and pulling off her powder blue T-shirt over her head.

'I meant the wine.'

'I thought you were referring to…' she murmured coquettishly.

They looked much more contented on the flight back. The offer for the villa had been accepted, and they were promised possession of the property in eight to ten weeks, which meant October. If they planned to fake a marriage in November - or December - Serena could quit her job by the end of the year, and they would finally live the life they had dreamt about on their honeymoon.

31

New Delhi
August 31, 2001

The meeting introducing D'Cunha to Mr Gill went well. D'Cunha's record and Kabir's recommendation gave Mr Gill all the confidence he needed to appoint him as Kabir's deputy on the case.

Kabir and D'Cunha had read the files a few times by now, going through the details; it was a chaotic investigation, expensive and ostentatious, but ultimately leading nowhere.

'Where do we begin, Kabir?' D'Cunha asked, later when they sat in Kabir's small and sparse office in the Parliament House annexe.

'I quite like not being called sir.'

'Really?'

'There is only one thing clear from this research.' Kabir was careful not to describe the previous work as an investigation. 'There were only five companies whose share certificates were counterfeited and hence we start by visiting their offices and checking the counterfeit certificates. The companies should have stacks of them. That should give us some clue to, perhaps, where - or what - we investigate next. So, the answer to your question is Mumbai. We begin in Mumbai.'

'Should I get the tickets organised?'

'Get two tickets for tomorrow morning please. And keep the return tickets open. Do you know of a good hotel in south Mumbai?'

'The Taj…'

'Book it for a week at least. We'll see if we have to extend our stay.'

September 2001

D'Cunha was at the IG International airport before his boss. Knowing well that Kabir would be travelling light, he checked-in for both of them with the bag of papers he was carrying. Then, picking up a coffee and the morning newspaper, he found himself a seat to savour both. He was halfway through the front-page news when he heard a *hello* from someone near him. It was Kabir.

'Good morning, Michael.' Kabir, pulling his stroller baggage and holding a coffee in his other hand, approached D'Cunha. He was casually, but sharply dressed in jeans and a white button-down cotton shirt with the sleeves rolled up. D'Cunha noticed that he had matching shoes, belt and watch strap in tan leather.

'Good morning.' D'Cunha removed some of his things from the next seat without getting up. Kabir had been clear that for this case they would work together as friends rather than two investigative police officers. 'I've checked you in, Kabir. Here's your boarding card.'

'Thanks.' Kabir took the boarding card from D'Cunha.

'You look better in casuals.'

'Thanks again. You look great too.' Kabir returned the compliment looking at D'Cunha who had discarded his frumpy image to wear a blue Polo T-shirt over jeans and trainers.

They finished their coffee and went through security.

'I like Jet Airways. They have pretty airhostesses, not like the ones they have in Indian Airlines,' Kabir said, all of a sudden, as he took breakfast from one of them.

'You're right, they are pretty.' D'Cunha echoed Kabir's opinion. 'I have been meaning to ask you for some time, but never got the chance. Now that we're friends, at least for this case, I think I can ask, but feel free to tell me to shut up…'

'Go ahead and ask.' Kabir did not want to put on a bureaucratic façade when D'Cunha was trying to break the ice. He understood that if they had to travel and stay together for extended periods of time, on this case, it would be better to know each other's interests and develop a personal relationship rather than to discuss work all the time.

'Why haven't you got married... yet?' D'Cunha carefully added the *yet* at the end to highlight that he wasn't confirming Kabir as a bachelor for life.

'I am married to my job.' Kabir replied without hesitation. D'Cunha smiled; he understood such humour, which was common in the police service. 'No one liked me enough to tie the knot, or let's just say I didn't find anyone... yet.' He made sure that the *yet* remained in the conversation.

'The latter is more like it.'

'Are you not seeing your family in Mumbai?' Kabir asked, realising that D'Cunha's family was still in Mumbai. 'Why aren't you staying with them?'

'My house is far from south Mumbai and it would be a problem commuting every day. Plus, I don't know how late we might have to work, so I thought it would be better to focus on this. If we stay the weekend, I will go over there.'

'You are a very committed man, Michael.'

'Duty always comes before self.' D'Cunha couldn't resist vocalising his clichéd motto.

'I couldn't agree more.'

Mumbai
September 2001

The two men checked into the Taj in South Mumbai, left their bags in the rooms and were back at the reception within ten minutes. D'Cunha hailed a cab once they were out of the hotel as Kabir gazed at the beauty of the monumental Gateway of India overlooking the Arabian Sea.

'Maker Towers please,' D'Cunha told the cabbie getting into the cab. As the car drove through the old streets of south Mumbai, Kabir noticed how different the business capital was from the political one that they had flown out from in the morning. This part of Mumbai still had the buildings of Victorian Bombay, though many had not been well maintained.

If someone put money into conserving the place, it would be one of the greatest cities in the world. But money was the one thing that was scarce in the country, which explained why some people did unscrupulous things like counterfeiting. He smiled, inwardly, at the thought.

Cuffe Parade in South Mumbai housed the five companies they had set out to meet. D'Cunha paid the cabbie and the two men walked into Maker Towers and asked for their key contact there. The two officers had already informed the company directors about the enquiry and their visit. Victoria, the PR director of the company, was down in a moment instead of sending a secretary or assistant.

'Good afternoon gentleman. I am Victoria.'

The two men found it extremely hard to concentrate while shaking hands with Victoria, as she was nothing short of a Vogue model; tall, slender with light eyes, her hair tidy in a bun and dressed in a pinstriped suit with a white shirt neatly tucked, into her trousers, over her flat stomach.

'Good afternoon, Victoria.' Both of them said this as if reciting a nursery rhyme for their teacher.

'I hope you had a good flight this morning.' She pointed towards the lift and the two men followed her like puppies on a leash.

'Yes. Thanks,' Kabir said. D'Cunha walked quietly, making sure they didn't repeat the recitation.

As they came out on the seventeenth floor office, she took them into a conference room stacked with papers already sorted out for their task. The building might have looked three decades old from the outside, but the conference room was plush, with state of the art communications and display equipment. Kabir, for a brief moment, got lost in his thoughts. If he had pursued a career in private enterprise, after his management degree from FMS, he would have been a company director of a medium or large corporation by now. But he had chosen to join the civil service and most of the government offices, he had worked for, were nowhere close to all these lavish rooms and facilities.

'Could I ask someone to get you tea or coffee?' Victoria asked.

'Coffee would be fine. Thanks Victoria.' Kabir said.

'Make that two please,' D'Cunha said.

'You think she will date me?' Kabir asked as soon as Victoria left the two guys alone in the room.

'If she doesn't have a boyfriend or a husband, I don't see why not.'

'Why do you always make it conditional?' Kabir quipped. Both of them understood the humour and smiled as the coffees arrived.

Even the coffee was served in bone china cups here, unlike the dirty glass tumblers they would have got in a public sector office.

The room had four piles of certificates arranged in chronological order of their receipt by the company. Each one of them, fortunately, had a copy of the covering letter attached that was sent back to the client it had come from. This gave them contact details of every single person who had been directly affected by the scam, and the broker who had been involved in the last deal. The first thing both the guys looked for was any sign of the printing press, but they realised, promptly, it was like looking for fingerprints on a murder weapon. This was neither an amateur job nor an unplanned one.

'There's got to be something that leads us to the perpetrators,' Kabir uttered scanning through a few of the papers, which obviously gave away nothing about the originator of these counterfeits.

'It's more our trial than theirs…'

'Before theirs Michael, before theirs... Failing the second time on the same case would be an epic embarrassment for the government and our department.'

'You're right.'

They spent quite a while going through the documents and did not realise that it was four till Victoria came into the room. 'Anything we could help you with?'

Give me a hug, honey, Kabir wanted to say.

'Yes please. Could you ask someone to arrange these into the order of the previous transfer dates please? I know that they are counterfeits and therefore, never actually came to your company for the same, but they have the date of last transfer in any case,' Kabir said.

'That will be done before you arrive tomorrow morning.'

'And we might need to use your office for a little longer than we originally planned. I would rather have all the other companies send their papers and files here than us visiting them. I hope that is fine with you…'

'That should be fine too.' She gladly agreed, knowing well that it might not be in the company's best interests to refuse two detectives a simple request like this. Both the requests confused D'Cunha, given that Kabir hadn't discussed any of this before, but he knew that there must be a good reason.

'Could I drop you somewhere as I'll be leaving soon?' Victoria offered.

'Only, if you have dinner with us.'

Only dinner? No dance? D'Cunha smiled.

'I can't do that today as I have a prior engagement, but we can do that some other time,' Victoria apologised.

'We are at the Taj so if that is not too much of a bother, we'll come with you.'

'Okay. I'll be leaving here around six.' She closed the door on the way out of the conference room.

Kabir turned towards D'Cunha and, finding him still bewildered about the requests, realised he needed to clarify. 'Let me explain, Michael. You would appreciate that such a large and fine-tuned counterfeit operation like this must have been thought out meticulously. It would be churlish not to admire the planning and childish to believe that someone did not have access to the originals.'

D'Cunha looked blank.

'The counterfeits were not printed at random, Michael. It is fairly evident that the miscreants only faked limited certificates in great quantities and not the whole lot. That is precisely why you have so many repeated serial numbers and names on these.' He pointed towards the pile of papers lying on the desk.

'I get that.' D'Cunha nodded and flipped through some of the certificates again to see what Kabir had just said. Kabir's cogent analysis impressed him, for he had seen the same peculiarity but hadn't considered it.

'The second request was *not* merely to stay in Victoria's office for some more time, it is to get all these papers into one place rather than doing a piecemeal investigation in offices scattered all around Mumbai. We are more likely to see trends if all the pieces are together. And I thought you would be more comfortable in Victoria's lovely company rather than in any other place that we haven't yet seen. If that wasn't enough reason, she's also promised to have dinner with you...' Kabir had a sly smile on his face as he palmed off all his flirtatious intentions onto D'Cunha.

'Am I the one interested in Victoria now?'

'Married men like you should ideally not flirt with other women, however good-looking they are. But that's my opinion. You are free to do, and flirt, as you please.'

'Hello gentlemen.' Victoria peeped into the room at six. 'Are you ready to leave?'

'Yes. Could we leave all this securely in here, please?'

'No problem.'

Victoria's driver had already collected her bag and was waiting with the car outside when they stepped out of the building. 'I have asked the staff to rearrange the papers as you asked,' she mentioned, as Kabir opened the car door for her. D'Cunha was smart enough to get into the front seat with the driver, leaving his boss and Victoria in the back seat.

'Where do you live?' Kabir asked, as they sat in the car.

'Bandra.'

'That would be quite a distance from here?' Kabir chatted on.

'Yes, but with the driver I normally sit in the back and read or make calls, so it's not that tiring. I would be worried if I had to drive the distance in this traffic myself.'

They were at the hotel soon. 'It was really nice to meet you and thank you for all the help.' The men got out of the car.

'You're very welcome. I would have stayed back for dinner, but I had promised to take my daughter for a birthday party tonight, so...' Victoria apologetically explained.

'It's okay. We can do that some other time.'

'She's got a guy,' D'Cunha murmured as they waved to her.

'All she said was that she had a daughter... you're assuming the rest, Michael.' Kabir wasn't giving up the chase, not as yet it seemed. 'On another note, could you give the other four companies a call and ask them to arrange all the papers, in the order we want, and send them over to Maker Towers please?'

'It will be done.'

'Any plans for the evening?'

'No.'

'Aren't you visiting your family? It's not late.' Kabir asked glancing at his watch.

'That's a long way off. It'll take me around an hour and a half to get there. I spoke to my wife and she's expecting me over the weekend.'

'So you will leave me alone for the weekend?'

'You can spend time with Victoria...and her daughter.' D'Cunha couldn't hold himself back. 'You're more than welcome to come along to my place.'

'I was only joking, but thanks for the offer.' Kabir expressed gratitude for the invite. They checked if they had any message from Mr Gill, as he was the only one who knew about their plans and accommodation arrangements. There wasn't any. Both of them went to their rooms, and as decided met in the hotel foyer in half an hour.

'There is a nice bar nearby called Geoffrey's. It's a short walk along the seafront, do you want to walk or should I ask for a cab?' D'Cunha asked when they met at eight.

'Let's walk. If we get drunk we'll take a cab back.' Kabir smiled, his intentions for the evening quite clear.

'Okay.'

Geoffrey's, located on the famous Marine Drive, is as English a pub as one can get in Mumbai. The dark wood panelled walls and comfortable seating made the customers stay a little bit longer for that extra drink. The food was a fusion of Indian and European continental, with the prices kept deliberately a little high to keep the unwanted crowd out. Both the police officers, now detectives, were smartly dressed like any other business travellers.

'A large Jack Daniels with Diet Coke and lots of ice please,' Kabir requested, as the waitress came along for their orders.

'I'll start with a chilled Fosters please.'

The waitress was quick.

'Cheers.' D'Cunha raised his glass.

'Cheers.'

'Looking at the files and numbers in just one company, it remains unclear how much money was made, though that is not our goal,' D'Cunha started.

'It could be quite a while before we can put an approximate figure to that.'

'What happens after all the files reach us tomorrow?'

'It might not take us to the correct answer right away, however, it should surely make us ask the right questions to the right people, and perhaps expand our logic of the probable.'

'How?'

'As I told you earlier, whoever did such a methodical job as this, had access to the original certificates, so the dates, names and serial numbers on the counterfeits should match the ones on the originals. I could put money on it that the counterfeiters were not brainless enough to have picked up freshly transferred shares to make copies. Surely, they wouldn't be the first broker to buy or sell these certificates – and risk being first amongst the accused should the police ever get hold of the whole list of dealers who were in the chain. So, they would have picked up the ones that were in the market for quite some time before duplicating the dates and other details. By the same logic they must have ensured that they were not the last in the chain either,' Kabir elaborated, taking intermittent sips from his drink.

'I agree with the first part, but how can one ensure that they were not the last brokers. Someone who bought from them could have sent them to the companies for transfer immediately.' Despite finding the first deduction blisteringly impressive, D'Cunha sounded unconvinced about Kabir's second one.

'It must be a syndicate that dealt with large investors with questionable wealth who invest in dubious names, and were, to a certain extent, confident that the counterfeit script would not be sent to companies right away. There could have been an odd case or two, but the likelihood of the original and the counterfeit reaching the company simultaneously, was almost zero.'

'What if it's a double-bluff?' D'Cunha smartly asked.

'Double-bluffs are played by pranksters, not by criminals, and certainly not on a scale of this magnitude. But, we're not ruling it out. The investigation ought to catch that anyway.' Kabir was confident.

'Working with you, I am convinced we will solve this case.'

'We've had enough discussion about work. Let's talk about something else.'

'Victoria is gorgeous,' D'Cunha said, after he had given repeat orders to the waitress.

'There's nothing wrong with this girl.' Kabir smiled looking at the waitress as she walked away from their table to the bar to get drinks for them.

'You're not serious?'

'I am not serious about Victoria either. I mean both of them are beautiful, but I have no intention to date either of them.' Kabir finished his drink and waited for the next round to be brought to the table. 'Most of the time I only practise flirting to become perfect for whenever I need it. The fact that the subject is beautiful or interesting makes my task easier.'

D'Cunha, no doubt, did not understand the reasoning. The two guys discussed things other than work the whole evening, had dinner and marched back to their hotel instead of taking a cab. They were reasonably drunk, but still had enough sense to find their way back to their rooms.

'Good night,' Kabir said unlocking his room door.

'Good night Kabir.'

D'Cunha got up with a headache. He had certainly had more beers than usual, but with some strong coffee and alternating between cold and hot showers he managed to get dressed to see Kabir at breakfast. When he got to Maker Tower, he made the few calls Kabir had requested on the previous evening, and asked for the files to be sent across from the other companies. 'The files will be arranged in chronological order, as requested, and sent to us before close of business today,' he announced, as soon as he was off the phone.

'Thanks Michael. Once they are here we can do some more digging, but till then let's play with these.'

Victoria came to see her guests around lunchtime. She offered to take them with her to the small company canteen rather than send some sandwiches into the conference room. She was as formally dressed today, as the day before, in a grey suit. The only difference was she had replaced her trousers with a long pencil skirt, which made her look even more feminine and attractive.

'How was your daughter's party?' Kabir started the conversation at lunch.

'It was great. Thank you. She had told me about it a month ago, so it would have been a big disappointment if I didn't get there on time for her.'

'That's perfectly understandable… there's a time for work and there's a time to show your children the rainbow,' Kabir wisely commented.

'You must be a great dad to your kids,' Victoria complimented.

He could be a great dad to your kid if you want, D'Cunha wanted to say.

'I don't have kids.'

'I am sorry…' Victoria tried apologising for her earlier comment.

'Why should you be sorry if I don't have kids? You should be sorry that I am not married…' Kabir furnished the, unasked, information.

'Oh I see…so you are a single guy.'

'Yes.'

'That makes two of us. I am single too. I am a single parent,' she pointed out.

Kabir looked at D'Cunha whose expression suggested, without

exchanging words, that he bowed down to the superior gut-feeling of Kabir for prophesying her single status the day before. They finished their lunch and got back to work shortly after one to find three of the companies had already delivered the material and there was a message that the fourth one was on its way already.

'This work is more than just the two of us can handle. We need more hands on deck. I will have to ask Mr Gill to provide us some local staff in Mumbai.' Kabir told D'Cunha.

'That will be good.'

The plan for the initial investigation did not require them going around questioning people, since some junior staff in uniform could handle that without giving any information regarding the big picture. The immediate plan was to begin questioning the first broker after a particular share got transferred, those details were in the company records - and hence replicated on the fake scrip - and then follow the trail probing each broker en route till it was sent for transfer to the company.

'I am sure some of the brokers would have faded away by now, some would have closed shop, some might not have old records and others might not be at the same addresses, but even if we run the whole course with half of these, we should be able to pick out some common brokers in all of them.' Kabir summed up the line of enquiry for D'Cunha.

'We need, at least, eight or ten people.'

'It will be done. I should be leaving by the weekend and you will head the whole enquiry. Be careful only to give enough information to your team to carry out what is required,' Kabir reiterated.

'No problem Kabir.'

'Thanks Michael. I'll speak to Mr Gill tonight.'

Kabir sought more resources from Mr Gill, explaining the magnitude of the work involved. He also gave an update that the realistic timelines for the initial search would take no less than a few months, before which there didn't seem much point in him being in Mumbai for any investigations. 'Michael can move in with his family and continue to head the search, sir - that will also save us the hotel expense. We don't know how long we will have to search to identify the guilty before we start looking for them. There is no quick fix for this.'

'Is Michael competent enough to lead?'

'He is very capable, sir, and I trust him completely,' Kabir clarified.

'In any case, he would be in touch with me every other day. I'd steer the whole inquiry remotely, and if need be, I'd be off to Mumbai at short notice.'

'Would this require some specialised people?'

'No sir. Junior sub-inspectors in the Mumbai police should be able to carry out this simple questioning. Once they come back with their findings, Michael would short-list those required for a second round of investigation, and I would personally attend that with Michael,' Kabir explained.

'Okay,' Mr Gill agreed. 'Ask him not to leave any stone unturned.'

'Don't worry on that account at all,' assured Kabir.

'Keep up the good work.'

'Thank you, sir.'

32

Mumbai
Mid-December, 2001

It had been more than three months now, and D'Cunha's team had laboured hard to finish the initial search. As estimated, some of the leads went cold for various reasons, while a few could not be followed up due to geography. D'Cunha consulted Kabir and decided the team should focus on Mumbai for the first round. If they didn't uncover some offenders - or even a pattern - they would go beyond Mumbai. Subsequently, D'Cunha set himself the task of sifting and scrutinising these extensive lists to spot one or more individuals or firms that was the most common link. 'I've got the lists now.' He sounded ecstatic on the phone.

'Good work, Michael. Do you want to stay in Mumbai and work on the case till you identify suspects, or would you rather come back to Delhi?' Kabir asked.

'I am fine either way.' D'Cunha would have preferred to stay back in Mumbai, with his family, but he did not want to appear to be taking his job lightly.

'Stay back in Mumbai then, be with your family and come over as soon as you've been through the lists or identified some culprits.' Kabir was considerate. He knew D'Cunha had been staying away from his family for more than eighteen months, and this particular case did not mandate where one stayed to investigate. Not at this stage for sure. He had absolute faith in D'Cunha and knew well that his DSP would not squander time unnecessarily because he was left without supervision in Mumbai. On the contrary, D'Cunha was more likely to work extra efficiently to prove himself.

New Delhi
Mid-December, 2001

'The boys have completed the first half of the search, sir,' Kabir proudly told Mr Gill the next day.

'Good. Do you suspect anyone yet?'

'Not yet, but I am sure we should be able to find them in a few weeks.'

'I can't wait.' Mr Gill showed his eagerness for the results.

'I am sure we'll get to the bottom of this soon,' Kabir assured.

Kabir knew that though he had reassured Mr Gill, it could, however, take several weeks - maybe months - to identify suspects, and then search for them. He was reasonably confident the suspects might not be trading genuine or counterfeited shares any more.

Somebody would be an idiot to be in the same line of business or trade, or even be in the country, he reflected.

London
Mid-December, 2001

'I'm getting married.' Serena announced to her team showing off the large solitaire she sported on her finger.

'Fantastic.'

'Congratulations.'

'So you've convinced him to tie the knot.' Paul came forward to give her a hug. He had seen her quite a few times with Nikos in his building, and knew that the love affair had continued from the time they had first met.

'When's the big day?' Andy asked.

'January.'

'Where is it?'

'It's in Greece,' Serena said. They had planned it to be right after the Christmas holiday period so that no one would take time off to travel to attend it.

'Why don't you get married over the Christmas break? We would like to come along…' Paul humoured her.

Because we don't want anyone to come along.

'I would have wanted you guys to attend too, but sorry…' Serena apologised.

'It's okay. We will have a party before you leave and another one when you come back,' Andy said.

'I am not coming back. I am putting in my papers today Andy.'

'What?'

'Why does she need to work anymore?' Paul chipped in.

'That's true.'

'Hello Kim.' Serena called Kim, advised by Nikos.

Just in case there's anything going on in Mumbai that we should know, Nikos had reasoned.

'Serena? Where have you been, honey? I sent you so many emails. You just forgot about me after you left Mumbai…' Kim complained, on and on.

'I am sorry Kim. Just got totally involved in the work and then fell in love…'

'You started dating someone without telling me?'

'It's not that… I wasn't sure…'

'Who is it?' Kim cut her off in excitement.

'He's a Greek guy I met at a party a while ago and we have been dating since. He proposed to me last week and I accepted.'

'What is his name?'

'Nikos.'

'Is he good?' Kim asked.

'Very good… I know what you mean.'

'Send me a picture?'

'I haven't got any here. I'll send one in a day or two.' Serena wiggled out of it.

'When's the wedding?'

'When are you getting married?' Serena remembered Kim's email earlier in the year stating that she and Ron were getting married sometime in December.

'January 7th.'

'We're getting married on the same day. What a coincidence.' Serena had fixed the impromptu date, as planned, so that there was no chance of them attending each other's wedding.

'What a coincidence, honey.'

'Yes… I am so excited, but I feel sad that you won't attend my wedding then.' Serena tried making a fuss.

'Why? Where are you getting married?'

'Greece.'

'How about planning our honeymoon together? I can't wait to meet Nikos.' Kim was as excited as a child.

'I can understand. Do you think I am doing the right thing?'

'Are you kidding? What kind of stupid question is that?' Kim comforted Serena. 'It's been five years since…'

'Five years and four months almost, but I still miss him.'

'That's because you've left it for so long that you've got used to a vacuum. I am sure everything will change after you get married, honey.'

'Coming back to the honeymoon, we are planning one in February. Nikos has some work in January… not sure what your plans are?' Serena asked.

'I can check with Ron. Where are you going?'

'I am going into his bed.'

'I know that slut, where would his bed be?'

'Why don't you check with Ron if the timing suits you guys? We can always firm up the location later,' Serena suggested.

'That's a good idea.'

'I wish we could do the wedding shopping together.'

'Why don't you come over to Mumbai and we could do it here.'

'I don't think I can.' Serena sounded disappointed.

'Don't worry, we'll catch up with each other on the honeymoon.' Kim once again comforted her friend.

'Keep in touch. You have my number now.' Serena knew her number would have been displayed on Kim's mobile.

'Thanks for calling, honey.'

'I called Kim.' Serena told Nikos when she got back. 'I told her we're getting married in Greece on January 7th.'

'Let me guess… she's getting married the same day.' He gave a wicked smile. 'Did she have any news?'

'None at all, though I didn't specifically ask about anything,' Serena replied.

'That's okay. If she had heard about anyone looking for me, for whatever reason, she would have mentioned it anyway, I am sure.'

'When do we start packing?' Serena asked.

'Most of what you see in this penthouse is not ours… we just need to carry our personal belongings…'

'Even the antiques?' Serena looked around.

'None of them are genuine. We can leave them here.'

'You lied to me all this while?'

'You never asked, sweetheart. I only lied to your friend Paul, in the beginning,' Nikos responded.

'And the Jaguar?'

'That's genuine. But I'll sell it here before I go. I don't want to transfer it to the new address so that we can be traced to Spain. I want everyone to believe we've moved to Greece.'

'You've planned everything,' Serena complimented him.

'Yes sweetheart.' He took her in his arms and kissed her forehead.

The villa deal in Spain had come through. The money had been transferred from Switzerland, and the balance paid in cash by Nikos who had made a trip alone during the week when Serena was at work. He had taken possession of the villa and collected the keys from Alfredo. All that was left was faking the wedding in Greece, which had already been announced by Serena in the bank to her colleagues, and even to Kim, back in India. Once they left the UK, they had no reason to return.

If anyone ever came looking for us, they would definitely be misguided to look further in Greece, though there was hardly a chance someone would come looking after six years, they had decided.

'Here's to us.' Nikos had poured wine for both of them.

'Cheers.' Serena picked up her glass.

'We fly to Athens and spend a few days there, before moving to Spain.'

'Anything you say.'

'There's a lot of work to do. We need to sell the car, pack our stuff in, only, as much baggage as we can carry on the flight… leave this penthouse and your apartment.'

'I have asked the estate agent to come down and take the inventory tomorrow morning, so I should be out of that apartment before the end of the week to move in with you,' Serena said with a smile.

'That's great. Let's make a comprehensive list of tasks we need to do before we say goodbye to this country.' Nikos got up to get his computer.

Mumbai
Late December 2001
D'Cunha had been through almost all of the papers collected so far. There were a few common names in the counterfeit share deals, and though the list of possible culprits was long enough, the gyre tightened every time one of them got eliminated from a search. In the end, one company – Savvy Consultants - was common throughout the reports. This company had traded all the said shares at some point in time, and since it was no more in existence, the search went cold, every time, after they had bought, because no one could uncover to whom this company had sold. The address given on the documents was a residential one in Worli. He called up his old office, in Worli, to check out the apartment before he arrived. He was told that a company that owned the apartment used it as its guesthouse. 'No one lives there except for an old caretaker,' one of the junior officers told him.

'Did he tell you who lived or worked there before?'

'No one has lived there for a long time. It is considered an inauspicious apartment sir.'

'Why?' D'Cunha got curious.

'It seems there was a fire in the apartment, some years ago, and the young owner died in the accident. No family wanted to buy it after that, so a company bought it for its guests.'

It all came back to D'Cunha in a flash. The fire, the accident, the death of the young owner who was a financial consultant, the young widow…

He obviously owned Savvy Consultants and knew what was coming his way and therefore committed suicide. And I was naïve enough to think that it was an accident, D'Cunha thought.

To confirm this, D'Cunha went over to the apartment; sure enough, it was the same one. He remembered the whole episode like it was only yesterday. He tried recollecting the name of the beautiful young wife to whom he had finally given a clearance for the insurance payout, but he couldn't. It had been over five years. He felt certain that the culprit in the counterfeiting case had known the end was nigh, and hence, to escape the naked fear of getting exposed, had been driven to the dire step of ending his life. He realised that although his investigation had been comprehensive, the end result was surely wrong. Back at his office, he went through a lot of old files to get the information he required.

Mr Raaj Kumar, owner of Savvy Consultants, died in an accidental fire at his Worli residence on August 18th, 1996. D'Cunha remembered he was the one who first attended the case and had called the wife while she was in Singapore... Kumar's burnt passport was still in the files. As part of the protocol, he couldn't take any papers out of the office and he left, disgruntled, after a few hours. He made one last attempt to look through the records of all other traders, but no one seemed to be out of order except Savvy Consultants. There were a few other brokers, but they had only dealt with these shares once or twice. Implicating them into this scam did not feel right at this point. He was absolutely convinced before he called Kabir, and said, 'I think I know who it is.'

'Do not say anything on the phone and don't mention it to anyone in Mumbai. Please take the next flight to New Delhi with all the relevant papers. I shall see you in the office on Monday.'

'Okay.'

'Carry everything, even if means booking extra baggage. We don't know what we could require for evidence.'

'Yes Kabir.'

'And say *hi* to Victoria,' Kabir gagged.

'You still haven't forgotten her?'

'I don't forget easily.' Kabir remarked before he put the phone down.

What will happen when he knows that I blew up on such a serious case. He's not known to tolerate mediocrity, D'Cunha thought as he disconnected the call.

33

New Delhi
January 2, 2002

D'Cunha prepared, organised and reorganised to ensure his confidence did not falter when he presented the case to Kabir. He had always been extremely proud of his career record, but the solitary instance in which he had bungled turned out to be the one that had got reopened because of another high profile case he was investigating for Kabir. The files in Mumbai police station clearly mentioned that the case investigated by Senior Inspector Michael D'Cunha had been closed as an "A*ccident.*"

Kabir had demonstrated immense confidence in D'Cunha, but he rarely forgot and seldom forgave. A blunder such as this could well mean the beginning of the end of D'Cunha's career.

I might end up as a traffic police officer. He almost cried thinking of it.

D'Cunha struggled to think how he would explain the five year-old case he had closed as an accident without charging anyone. Nevertheless, he was up early in the morning and carried all the papers to the office in a cab. Kabir was already at his desk with a coffee.

'Welcome, Michael. What is it?' Kabir figured D'Cunha was under undue stress.

'Nothing…I mean I have the files here that provide evidence that all the shares connect to one source, after which all tracks go missing because the company that traded them is closed now.' D'Cunha made an effort not to sound stressed.

'Could we not find the owner or manager?'

'The company closed in 1996,' D'Cunha clarified.

'Oh. Why am I not surprised?'

'What is disturbing is that the owner - and sole proprietor - of the company died in a mysterious fire in his apartment in August the same year,' D'Cunha said softly.

'And?' Kabir prompted D'Cunha to complete the story quickly.

'I was the inspector heading the investigation and it was stopped half-way because of certain people who did not want me to question a girl…'

Kabir was listening.

'Eventually, after weeks of investigation, I found no evidence of foul play and closed the case as an accident, rather than the suicide which it looks like now. I gave a *No Objection Certificate* to his wife to claim insurances. I can assure you that given the circumstances, I had left no line of enquiry unattended.' D'Cunha was almost pleading now.

Kabir's face changed colour faster than a chameleon could keep pace with. It first showed anger, changed into disgust and - in a matter of minutes - to despair. He did not know what to say at this point and decided to stay quiet for a few minutes. D'Cunha could sense the silent anger in Kabir's eyes. 'That's okay, Michael, we all make mistakes. Who was the guy?' he asked after the news of D'Cunha's failure had sunk in.

'Mr Raaj Kumar.'

'And where is his wife now?'

'She works in a bank in Mumbai, so we can contact her if you say so,' D'Cunha offered, feeling a bit better that Kabir hadn't taken the news as unfavourably as he had anticipated.

'What's her name?'

'Serena.'

Kabir closed his eyes for a few moments. The names sounded too familiar to be true. 'What was the name you said?' he asked to confirm.

'Serena Kumar.'

'You mean Raaj Kumar and Serena?' Kabir confirmed.

'Yes.'

'I had two classmates in my college days with the same names…' He laughed it off.

'Was it at the Faculty of Management Studies?' D'Cunha's suspicion grew as he suddenly remembered that he had seen the *Class of 1987* group photograph in Kabir's old office but, at the time, hadn't dared to ask about it.

'Yes... how do you know?'

'I remember it all now, Kabir. It might have been the same couple.'

'It cannot be.' Kabir sounded sure and wagged his head.

'You sound very confident...'

'When did you say all this happened; in 1996?'

'Yes.'

'I was in Germany in 1998, travelling through Frankfurt. I saw Raaj and waved. He was in a rush – must have been doing the same as me - but he waved back at me. He obviously recognised me.'

'1998, did you say?'

'Yes, I was involved in the security arrangements for the tourism minister and we had travelled to Cologne for a fair. So it's got to be 1998 for sure.'

'But… Raaj died in 1996. How can that be possible?'

'It cannot be, that's why I am sure it cannot be the same couple,' Kabir said. 'If he died in a fire in 1996, how could he be in Frankfurt in 1998?'

'Do you have that group photograph here?' D'Cunha asked.

'No. But we can always get that. Are you certain about the year, Michael?'

'I am confident Raaj died in 1996. I am not sure the year they finished college. It could have been two different years and two different men.' D'Cunha comforted himself. He surely didn't want a case that he had closed as an accident turn out to be even more mystifying than a suicide.

'My appetite for truth has suddenly increased, Michael. Let's go and check out the photograph now.' Kabir got up from his chair and collected his phone. They locked the office and came out to go to his home, since he had vacated his old office when he moved. As the driver was present in the car they decided not to talk about the case. 'Raaj and Serena…' Kabir said closing his eyes to drown in his past.

'Was he the kind to do anything like this?' D'Cunha could not hide his inquisitiveness.

'Raaj exhibited a joie de vivre I had never seen in a human being before or since, in my life, so I can rule out suicide without going into the details of the enquiry… if it is the same Raaj we are talking about.' Kabir summarised Raaj's character.

'I have a feeling we are talking about two different individuals,'

D'Cunha murmured.

'I hope we are, Michael. I sincerely hope we are...'

They were in Kabir's large bungalow in GKII that he had inherited from his parents. It had a similar feel to Kabir's office, with trophies of his late father, the Colonel, all over the place. On one of the main walls of the room there was a large portrait of his parents proudly looking at their son accomplishing his dream and career. There were leather sofas, and one could tell by the feel of the material that they were a bit old. It looked like Kabir had not bothered to buy or change much in the house since his parents passed away. He lived alone in the large house and had no tenants. On one corner of the enormous living and dining room was a well-stocked bar. D'Cunha had always known, through the grapevine, about Kabir and his love of whisky.

'Have a seat. I'll go and open the cartons that came from the office when we moved. I didn't open them thinking I'd have to move again when the current case is over,' Kabir told D'Cunha.

'Do you need any help?'

'I'll manage, don't worry. Why don't you fix yourself a drink in the meantime?'

'It's only three in the afternoon.' D'Cunha glanced at his watch.

'Suit yourself, Michael. None of the bottles, here, come with the warning that you cannot drink in the afternoon,' Kabir chuckled and disappeared into the house.

'Here it is.' He was out in five minutes holding the large photograph. 'Can you spot *your* Raaj?'

D'Cunha took the photograph and looked at it for a minute while Kabir, standing near him, made drinks for both of them. 'He's the one standing next to you... and this is Serena, his wife.' D'Cunha confidently identified the two in the picture.

The tumbler full of alcohol fell from Kabir's hand and shattered on the marble floor, as he stood there shocked. He had, until the last minute, believed that this could be a comedy of erring names, but with D'Cunha spotting both Raaj and Serena in the photograph, the truth he didn't want to face hit him hard. He glanced to see if D'Cunha had recognised the right faces and saw the truth. It felt like a close friend had betrayed him. 'The culprit is obvious now, Michael. The crime and the motive are clear enough, but the explanation is less so,' he said, the moment he could gather himself again.

'I know you might not like me asking you this, but are you sure you saw him and not someone else?' D'Cunha asked softly.

'Michael, I spent two years in college with this guy. We were really close friends for the first three months… I mean there was no bad blood after that...and though we drifted apart, I saw him virtually every day. I recognised him instantly when I saw him after eleven years. He hadn't changed,' confirmed Kabir.

'I can vouch for that too. The person I saw in the morgue was *this* Raaj,' D'Cunha looked at the photograph again.

'How can it be true Michael?' Kabir wasn't actually questioning. It was more an expression of his disbelief.

'I'm equally intrigued.'

'Let me fix another drink before we discuss this in detail. I cannot believe how intertwined these two cases have become.' Kabir quickly poured two large drinks.

D'Cunha felt like he had a new shot of adrenaline injected into him, as Kabir did not seem to blame him for some substandard investigation done five years ago any more. In his mind, he had done everything he could and if he had been allowed to question the model… 'There was a famous model I was interviewing when I was pressured to stop the proceedings,' he suddenly erupted in disgust, shaking his head as an apology.

'I want you to tell me everything about the case from the beginning, please.'

'I had received a call at home around midnight regarding a fire in an apartment in my jurisdiction and I rushed to it. Being midnight, I drove myself and remember being at the incident in forty-five minutes. The fire brigade was already there and had broken the door open to find Raaj drunk and unconscious in his bed. When I reached there, the ambulance had arrived too, and pronounced him dead at the site itself. The neighbours gave me information on the residents and I called a few friends of theirs. One of them told me that Serena had gone for a business trip to Singapore, the day before, so I called her up in her hotel around half-past one. She took the next flight and was back the same day by the afternoon flight.

'I interviewed Serena and there was nothing suspicious about the couple's relationship, they had the usual husband and wife quibbles but no rancourous disputes. She had genuinely travelled on work, which her office confirmed. At that time, the only reason to doubt anyone was the high value insurance policies, which might have been annulled if it was a suicide, but no one, I spoke to, would support my theory of Raaj committing suicide. This scam was not known to anyone back then. The only person I suspected was an up and coming model, Kim…'

'You mean Kim, the face of L'Oreal?' Kabir asked seeing D'Cunha pause for breath.

'Yes, but she was not as prominent back then.'

'Why did you suspect her?'

'She was a close friend of the couple and she knew all about their net worth and insurances and was a witness to the will.'

'So?' asked Kabir since he wasn't convinced that was enough reason to investigate someone.

'The funny thing is that after Raaj dropped Serena at the airport that fateful day… or night, he made a number of calls to Kim asking her to sleep with him. According to her, she declined all advances, but decided not to tell Serena anything about them. Contrary to her statement to the police, the investigation revealed that Raaj was in her apartment for a few hours before he went home from the airport, which made me think that it could be a devious understanding between the two of them designed to throw dust in Serena's eyes. Or maybe their extramarital affair had gone sour and that had led to manslaughter. But she had a strong alibi and political connections, so I was reprimanded and told to drop her from the investigations. The case was on the wane at that point, though I kept a watch on both of them for a while but…' D'Cunha tried furnishing every detail from memory and what he had recently seen in the file at Mumbai police station.

Kabir took a large sip to finish his drink. 'I know it is an oxymoron, if ever there was one, but you never thought that Raaj could have killed himself and escaped?'

'No.'

'How did you know that the person who died was Raaj? Who identified him?' Kabir questioned.

'Serena,' said D'Cunha, and then after a brief pause added. 'And Kim.'

'Any neighbours?' Kabir got up to fix another drink for both of them.

'They obviously saw the body being carried out of the residence and recognised him. His passport was also recovered from the apartment and it had his photograph on. As the house was burnt, Kim provided more photographs of Raaj from her albums…' D'Cunha temporarily halted as if his slip-up was coming to light.

'Are you telling me that someone with your intelligence believed the identification by two individuals whom you suspected the most, Michael?' Kabir asked assertively.

Was there anything else that I did to complete the identification? D'Cunha thought hard.

'No. I didn't rely on their identification alone. My suspicious mind led me into that direction of enquiry too, and therefore I sent the samples for DNA matching to the Metropolitan Police in London. We did not have that facility in Mumbai back then.' D'Cunha suddenly remembered the DNA report, which he had seen in the files when he was in Mumbai.

'You sent it for DNA matching? That's interesting… and the results matched?'

'Yes.'

'Where did you get the samples from?'

'They were all over the un-burnt part of the house, Kabir. A forensic expert got them for us so there was no question of doubting that.'

'Michael, our scintillating case rests on a bevy of unusual circumstances, inconclusive evidences and unbelievable reports. How, in heaven's name, can anyone fake DNA? One can only fake the results…' Kabir became aware of what he had said after he had spoken.

'He didn't know I would send the samples for DNA matching, let alone to London.'

'But he knew that you could. And he may have known that you did not have the facility in India and hence, you would send them somewhere. There could be an accomplice who either collected the sample or analysed it, or perhaps, an influential interceptor.' Kabir was building up a theory as he spoke. 'Did you get the results straight from the laboratory in the UK?'

'No. You know how it works. I had to put in a formal request asking for the analysis, which was routed via the head office in Delhi. The same protocol was maintained to deliver the results back to me, as I was handling the case,' clarified Michael.

'So you were sent a copy?'

'I got a fax in the office.'

'Even better – the thermal paper would have faded by now?'

'There was nothing legible on it when I saw it in the file, this time,' D'Cunha confirmed.

'I need to see the original.'

Both men went into a silent reverie for quite some time and then had another drink. The grotesque mystery only deepened with each passing minute and with every new discovery.

'You said that you saw his passport. And the photographs handed over to you by Kim were of Raaj, the Raaj that you have seen in this?' Kabir pointed at the group photograph he had pulled out of the box.

'Yes, I am certain.' D'Cunha was confident. 'The postmortem report would have revealed if it were plastic surgery.'

'And I am equally certain that I saw Raaj at Frankfurt in August 1998.' Kabir let out an audible sigh. 'The evidence is compelling that his death and this fraud are closely linked, but the mystery behind the whole sequence of events remains incomprehensible.'

'In retrospect, it all looks so simple. Raaj got into counterfeiting, realised early enough that his game wouldn't last forever and escaped the consequences by forging his own death.' D'Cunha complemented Kabir's unspoken words.

'One forgery led to another. The chronology of the discovery of crimes is in reverse – the death came to light first and the scam later, though they happened in the opposite order,' summarised Kabir.

'But… why would someone with such good qualifications and a flourishing business stoop to a criminal activity like this, knowing full well that the law would ultimately catch up with him?' D'Cunha was plainly perplexed.

Kabir realised that D'Cunha needed some insight into Raaj's crime. 'That hunger or poverty lead to crime is an overrated aphorism, Michael. Greed is the real offender. Greed is inversely proportional to fear… when it becomes strong, people shut themselves off to the cost of risks but the risks don't go away. Myopia blinds them to the risks. What I know of Raaj is that he was an emotionally insecure person, his behaviour was obsessive at times, almost daunting, but he knew what he wanted and seemed to know how to get it, always. He aspired to be a poster boy and he finally made it, sadly the wrong way. He was a mastermind with numbers to the extent that some of the professors in the university thought it was a stroke of luck, as no one could be so numerically gifted. I knew he was a born genius rather than having to work for it.

'Raaj was a financial ace, his education and business experience only honed his skills to exploit the loophole in the system. Given his economic background, at the time and the fact that his business was also thriving, no one would have doubted him, no one could imagine he'd stoop so low for money, to add to his already swelling bank balance. With no history of crime, why would anyone suspect him? In the end, I guess, he was too good for his own good,' Kabir reasoned.

If D'Cunha was puzzled without the explanation, he was even more bemused with it. Kabir noticed that the expression on his face was distinctly nonplussed.

'The world detests rats, but loves watching squirrels in the park, Michael. The truth is that squirrels are just another kind of rodent with thicker fur and bushier tails, however only a fraction of humans consider them pests. People trap and kill rats all the time and squirrels get away with murder, admirably.' Kabir's analogy helped D'Cunha to understand Raaj's game of getting away with his pretence. Raaj had used his bushy tail with absolute finesse. It was clear to both men what had happened. 'The question is, whose body was it that you found in the apartment?' Kabir was still trying to remove the haze. There was a brief silence in the room. 'No one else went missing the same night?'

'Not that I know about.'

'Any graves found dug up in Mumbai around the same time?'

'It is virtually impossible to know about that in Mumbai.' D'Cunha was correct;. With an endless number of cemeteries in Mumbai it would have been next to impossible to identify any such activity.

'I need to see the complete file,' Kabir requested.

'I wasn't authorised to carry or photocopy them, but I am sure you can, given your position.' D'Cunha sounded apologetic.

'Let's not get them out. Let's go to Mumbai once again. I would also like to meet Kim.'

'I'll arrange the tickets.'

'For as early as possible, please. I think tomorrow morning you should make the travel bookings straight away while I brief Mr Gill about the situation. I need to see the original DNA report.' Kabir looked at his watch, which made him conscious that they had spent the entire day discussing the case. And drinking.

'Okay.' D'Cunha got up to leave.

'And keep the return tickets open, like last time.'

'Sure, Kabir. Good night.' D'Cunha walked out of Kabir's apartment into the waiting car. Kabir, the gentleman, had asked his driver to drop the DSP home.

34

Malaga Airport, Spain
January 7th, 2002

Serena waited for the baggage while Raaj was at the Hertz counter completing the formalities to hire a large MPV. He had been cautious not to book one from London and leave a trail. As intended, they had left for Athens, from London, spent a few days honeymooning and then flew into Spain. It took them over an hour before they comfortably piled the luggage in the car before driving off to their dream villa.

'I can't wait,' Serena said as they left the airport.

'We'll be there soon, *señora.*'

'*Muchas gracias, señor,*' Serena responded.

They drove up their little private hill and sat in the car for a while admiring the villa and its views. 'Your new home…' Raaj got down from the car to take in the view.

'It's *our* new home.' Serena corrected him.

Raaj lifted Serena in his arms, and carried her up the steps to the main door of the villa. Unlike Alfredo, he took out the right key first time and put it in the lock. It didn't turn. He put Serena down and tried again. And again, but it wouldn't open.

'What the f…!' Raaj was infuriated.

'What happened?'

'The bloody thing won't open.' Raaj said, in disgust, and then pulled out his phone to call Alfredo.

'Hola, soy Alfredo. How can I help?' Alfredo cheerfully asked, in Spanish, picking up his phone.

'Hello Alfredo, this is Nikos – the keys of the villa…' Nikos complained politely.

'I'll be there in ten minutes, Mr Nikos. I'll explain when I get there.' Alfredo rushed out immediately.

Raaj and Serena walked around the villa enjoying the views of the sea, despite their puzzlement at being locked-out. They felt amazingly successful and were in the mood for celebration. They embraced and kissed with the sound of sea in the background, which was shattered by the sound of a motor as Alfredo turned into their drive.

'I am very sorry you had to wait,' Alfredo apologised before saying anything else, and handed over a bunch of keys to Nikos. 'Why didn't you call me from the airport?'

'What happened?' Raaj was noticeably irritated.

'Three days ago, someone broke into your villa and got away with some kitchen appliances, like the microwave and toaster. One of your neighbours saw the front door ajar during his morning walk and gave me a call, thinking I was still responsible for it, so I turned up and got all the locks changed,' the chatterbox chirped incessantly.

'Thank you so much but…'

'I tried your number but it was out of reach.' Alfredo interrupted as usual.

'When was this?'

'It was about three days ago.'

Raaj calculated that they had left on the fourth and hadn't used the UK SIM card since then, aware that technology, these days, could locate the co-ordinates through mobile phones if the phone was used. 'Oh I see,' he said.

'I tried many times but then I thought you might be away with your pretty wife.' Alfredo looked at Serena who wore a short red skirt with knee-length leather boots.

'Thanks.'

'No worries. I wanted you to contact me and you did, that is what matters.'

'Do I owe you some money?'

'Don't embarrass me, we are friends now…' Alfredo smiled.

Could you ask him to shut up and leave now please? Serena wanted to say.

Alfredo waited till Raaj tried the new key and got into the villa. The couple were not interested in the old kitchen appliances hence the small loss did not bother them.

'Does burglary usually happen in this area or was this a one-off incident?' Serena asked once they were inside.

'Not at all, madam, but this villa had been lying vacant for several months now, so it might have been targeted,' Alfredo, the super salesman, replied. Despite being a chatterbox, Alfredo seemed a nice guy. He helped Raaj unload the baggage from the car, stealing opportunities to look at Serena, and moved it into the villa. 'I must leave now,' he finally said.

Better late than never, Serena almost said.

'Muchas gracias, señor,' Serena uttered the few words she knew in Spanish.

'Madam speaks Spanish too.' Alfredo, joyously, stepped forward and kissed Serena on both cheeks. 'I hope you enjoy the villa. If you need anything, please give me a call.'

'Thanks Alfredo.'

'Finally…' Raaj sounded relieved as he closed the door. 'He's a good guy… and he's now my friend, he told me.'

'He's really helpful and extremely annoying at the same time.' Serena came into his arms, and they kissed. 'They say the first thing one should do in a new house is to make love.'

'Who says?'

'I do.' Serena, in one swift motion, pulled both her jumper and T-shirt over her head. 'Come on my love.'

'Here?'

'Do you want to come to the deck and do it in the open?' She dropped her skirt.

Lying on the deck, later in the evening, under the moonlit sky with a bottle of red wine that Raaj had opened a while ago, they excitedly made plans to buy new furniture, furnishings and electronics to set up their new home.

'We'll get some signature art too.' Serena sounded excited.

'Why not… we can afford the originals and you know…' he started.

'You hate fakes.' She completed his sentence.

'You're so damn right sweetheart.'

'To be honest, I was scared all along. There were so many things that could have gone wrong in our plan.'

'It's all in the past, sweetheart.' Raaj urged Serena to stop worrying now.

'I was just wondering…' she carried on.

'I hope you aren't scared now.'

'No. I am with you now, why should I fear anything?' She looked at him like a little girl, tears of joy in her eyes. A dream they had seen together almost eight years ago, on an island in the Indian Ocean, was coming true in their own villa on the coast of the Mediterranean.

35

Mumbai
January 10, 2002

Kabir and D'Cunha had now been in Mumbai for a few days, but Kabir was keen to go through the whole file, and the related investigation, before approaching Kim with any questions. He had spared Mr Gill the details of the homicide case they were investigating to resolve the one at hand. Without divulging many details at this stage, except that the cases were, conclusively, linked like two parts of the same story, he convinced Mr Gill to authorise some files to be taken out of the police station on a promise that they would be used with due diligence and returned as soon as they were not required.

'They are your responsibility.'

'I know what I am doing sir. I wouldn't let you down,' Kabir promised.

Kabir was intrigued – and fittingly so - by the details in the file. The investigation, the postmortem report, the faded DNA analysis report via fax message, which was hardly legible...D'Cunha had covered every area possible, missing no page in the textbook.

I know you are alive, Raaj, and I know you did it. I just don't know how and where to get you, Kabir was convinced.

'We need to speak to Serena,' Kabir said. He had tried hard to avoid meeting her, but it appeared he did not have a choice any longer. If for no other reason, she should at least be informed that her husband wasn't dead.

'I checked her out while you were buried in the files. She moved to London last year,' D'Cunha replied immediately.

'Are you serious?'

'She might have been part of the plan too,' D'Cunha suggested.

Kabir had already worked out that Serena *could* be part of the whole arrangement, but his heart was not prepared to face the harsh truth. Not just yet. 'Could we see Kim?'

'The famous model…?' D'Cunha knew the answer but he still wanted it confirmed.

'Yes, and I would prefer to see her without clothes please.' Kabir hadn't lost all his humour. He had a knack of moving, seamlessly, between seriousness and frivolousness during a conversation.

'I'll arrange that for tomorrow.'

'Arrange her, without clothes, for me?' Kabir smiled.

'I'll arrange the meeting with her tomorrow.'

'Should we go to that place we went to last time – Geoffrey's – and get drunk again tonight?' Kabir suggested.

'That's a brilliant idea.'

D'Cunha asked one of the staff at the Worli police station to call for a cab for the two of them.

'Will it take long to get there?' Kabir asked.

'Half an hour…'

Geoffrey's, Marine Plaza
Mumbai

The duo were barely halfway through their first drink when the crowd started cheering, as if they had sighted a minor celebrity walking into the bar. Kim had walked in, dressed to kill, as always. Her long, bare legs were highlighted by a short black dress that hung on spaghetti straps from her shoulders. The high heels she wore made her long legs look longer. She had recently been married and her husband was holding her arm when they walked in.

'She is mesmerising,' Kabir uttered, involuntarily, raising his glass and finishing his Jack Daniels in one large sip.

'Isn't she?' D'Cunha knew it from the very beginning.

'Who's the guy?'

'She got married only a few days ago, so I'm guessing it must be her husband Ron.'

'Does your wife know that you know about every woman in town?'

Kim and Ron moved to the bar, ordered their drinks and sat down at the table next to Kabir and D'Cunha.

'Hello Ms Kim.' D'Cunha acknowledged her presence as she sat down.

'Hello officer.' Kim had obviously not forgotten him.

'You still recognise me?' D'Cunha asked.

How can I ever forget you, officer? Your baseless accusations meant that I had to do something really disgusting to get out of it, she thought.

'Of course I do. Inspector D'Cunha was the chief investigating officer in Raaj's accident…' she explained to Ron.

'Was it?' Kabir jumped in, before she could finish.

'What do you mean?'

'Was it an accident?' Kabir reiterated.

'It was so long ago and Inspector D'Cunha did all the enquiries.' Kim's face grew pale remembering the rough time she had at the Worli police station and then having to sleep with Adi to get out of the whole mess. The whole episode of Adi carrying her worn bikini in his briefcase and stripping it off her in bed came back to her in a matter of seconds and made her sick.

'You alright honey?' Ron asked seeing her visibly getting uncomfortable.

'Yes. I'm okay Ron.'

'I am sorry, the idea was not to spoil your evening, but we might have to open the enquiry once again.' Kabir never minced words when it came to work.

'Why don't we go to some quieter place for a drink and discuss this at leisure, rather than in this crowd?' Ron offered.

'Wouldn't you like to ask your wife?' Kabir suggested.

'Oh, yes.' Kim realised this sordid problem wasn't going to go away. *It must be serious enough for them to reopen a case after more than five years, she reckoned.*

Ron was classy. His chauffeur-driven black Mercedes arrived at Geoffrey's door the moment they stepped out. He gave some cash to the driver who immediately vacated the driver's seat for Ron. Kim took her seat with her man in front, and the two men sunk into the back seat comfortably.

'By the way, I am Ron.'

'Kabir.'

'What's the story, officers?' Ron asked after a few minutes in the car.

'We've been investigating another case that seems linked with Raaj's death, so we need to solve this mystery first.' Kabir wasn't giving away much.

'May I ask what the other case is?'

'I'd rather you didn't. We are under oath not to divulge it.' Kabir made it clear.

'Are you from the Mumbai police?'

'We are currently working for CBI.'

'My cousin is the head of CBI for the northern region,' Ron stated without changing the pitch of his voice. Kim looked at Ron, for she hadn't known the connection. It came as a relief to her – she realised she wouldn't be humiliated once again.

'Oh I see. Then I sincerely hope you will cooperate with the enquiry,' said Kabir.

'Of course we will. I didn't want the whole bar listening to our conversation considering almost everyone there knew Kim... why don't we go to our house? We can sit comfortably and discuss this…'

'We are fine with that, if you are,' Kabir responded immediately.

It was a long drive from Marine Drive to Versova, where Ron and Kim lived. They owned one of the few remaining bungalows in the area, unlike everyone else who lived in an apartment.

'Here we are.' Ron turned into their drive.

The house was a palace by Mumbai standards, furnished immaculately with artefacts and a few of Kim's photographs. She had shifted some of her belongings from her previous apartment and taken time to make this place as distinguished as her old one that was only a few blocks away. They all made themselves comfortable as Ron asked the men to choose their drinks and went to his bar in the corner to get them. Without detailing the scam that they had originally started investigating, they quickly came to the subject of Raaj's disappearance.

'Why do you even think Raaj's death was not an accident?' Kim asked, referring to their conversation left incomplete at the bar.

'Because he did not die…'

Kim looked stunned. 'What do you mean – *he did not die*?'

'Ms Kim, according to the file, Raaj died in the accidental fire in 1996 and I saw him in Frankfurt in 1998,' Kabir explained.

'What...?' Kim almost spat out the wine she had just sipped.

'I am serious.'

'How did you know Raaj?'

'I went to college with Raaj and Serena.'

'Oh my God... what a small world this is.' She made no attempt to hide her astonishment.

'I believe Serena has moved to London.'

'Yes.'

'Are you in touch with her?'

'Yes. She called me last month – she was getting married to a Greek guy on the same day as me – January 7th.' Kim became silent for a few minutes reflecting on her last conversation where she had told Serena to forget Raaj and get on with her life.

'So, she doesn't know about Raaj then?' Kabir did not know if he should have been excited that Serena was not involved in the crime, or unhappy that he had lost her a second time to another guy, but he did not want to show any emotion.

'Obviously not... Serena couldn't have known Raaj is alive. In fact she even asked me for advice about getting married to this Greek guy – she still missed Raaj, but I told her to move on with her life... officer...'

'Kabir...my name is Kabir.' Kabir displayed his friendly side, especially since Ron and Kim were being such courteous hosts.

'What do we do now?' Kim asked.

'Most importantly, why would Raaj have done something like this? All the insurance money was paid to Serena, so what did he get out of it?' Ron asked, he wasn't privy to the information about the other scam and the money involved in it.

'Let's just say there was another, much bigger scam that has been unearthed that could make the insurance payouts look puny. I am really sorry but, as I said before, I cannot let that cat out of the bag, not as yet,' Kabir explained again.

'That adds up. He forged his own death, escaped to another part of the world, and let Serena have the insurance money to be content with while he may have started a new life,' Ron surmised.

'That is likely, if Serena were not involved.' Kabir made it clear that he wasn't giving up on Serena yet.

'But, she's got married to some other guy,' Kim protested.

'We'll see. Could you give me Serena's number and contact address please? It will save me the bother of collecting it from her local office here.'

'Wait a minute.' Kim got up to go into the other room to get the details. Neither of the men missed the chance to see her walk the length of the room in her short dress and heels, while Ron picked up the glasses for a refill and went to the bar.

'She is agonisingly gorgeous,' Kabir murmured.

'You bet.'

The couple was back. Ron refilled the men's drinks, and Kim handed over a piece of paper with Serena's telephone number and email address scribbled on it.

'Do you want to call her now?' Kim asked.

As an instinctive reaction, both Kabir and Ron looked at their watches. It was getting to half past ten in the evening.

'How about dropping her a line?' Ron asked.

'Could I ask you for a favour please?' Kabir requested.

'Sure,' Ron answered for Kim.

'Could you, as a friend, send her an email asking how the wedding was, to confirm if she is in town before we make any plans to travel overseas, please?'

'Now?' Kim asked.

Kabir nodded.

'Let's go into my study, we can frame the words together.'

Kabir had trusted Ron and Kim more than usual for a first meeting. Part of it came from the fact that Ron was connected to the CBI, through a blood relation, and in any case he hadn't given out anything on the scam. But he knew from experience that his instincts for trusting people had become a science over a period of time and had rarely let him down. He got up to go to the study followed by the faithful D'Cunha. Kim typed the email as agreed, with all the pleasantries, asking Serena about her wedding. She asked if they had firmed up the plan for a joint honeymoon as discussed. 'Let's see when she responds.' Kim clicked *Send*.

They got up without Kim logging off and had barely moved a step when a pinging sound announced a new email in Kim's inbox. Kim glanced back at the screen to see an *Out of Office* response.

'She might be away for her wedding. Everyone's not like Ron who has work right after marriage and has to postpone the honeymoon,' she affectionately complained, looking at Ron and sitting down to open the response.

'Please note that as of 21st December 2001, I have left the company and will no longer have access to my emails. You are requested to resend this email to Andrew Harrison for any matters relating to retail banking.

Sorry for any inconvenience that this may cause.

Best regards,

Serena Kumar.'

The silence that followed shattered all four of them.

'She might have moved to Greece with her husband.' Kim was protective about her friend.

'Who knows?' Kabir was disillusioned.

'What are you thinking?'

'I cannot think.'

'Serena cannot do this…' Kim broke down.

'Calm down darling.' Ron put his hand on Kim's shoulder. She was still sitting in front of the computer.

'I am not saying she is involved in the crime, but something's not right here. When did she speak to you last?'

Kim pulled out her mobile phone and scrolled through the incoming calls, but unfortunately it had been a while ago and her phone could only store the last twenty calls. 'I am sorry. But... it was the last week before her Christmas break she told me… it was the Monday Ron was travelling for the Kodak shoot to Bangalore,' she recollected.

Ron looked at the calendar on his mobile. '17th December.'

'So your friend spoke to you on the 17th, gave you her number and forgot to tell you that she was quitting her job the same week?' Kabir did not want to make it sound like a question.

'Maybe she wanted to surprise me.'

The three men looked at her. She was either being naïve, or was being unthinkingly loyal to her friend.

'It could well be a coincidence, Ms Kim. But I would have imagined that this case had run out of its fair share of coincidences by now. That is not to say that I am accusing your friend of anything, but the fact remains that someone died in your friend's apartment on the night of August 18th 1996, and we need to go on with the investigation till we expose the truth. The only request I have for you both is...please don't talk to anyone about this case,' Kabir requested and got ready to leave.

'You have our word.' Ron promised for both of them and shook hands with the officers. 'My chauffeur is here, he'll drop you at the hotel.'

'That's so nice of you.'

'Thanks,' D'Cunha said.

'Good night.'

'What do you think of her?' D'Cunha asked softly in the car.

'She was used as a distraction, a consuming distraction,' Kabir responded without any ado. 'Do they have a flight to Jaipur?'

'I am sure there is. Why?'

'To reach the end, we might need to start from the beginning. Sometimes just the one thing you miss can haunt you forever… I do not want to leave anything to chance… coincidence, if you will,' Kabir said mockingly.

'I will check the flights when we reach the hotel.'

'You can leave all the documents, in the file, back at the Worli police station but carry Raaj's passport.'

'Do you suspect anything?'

'Yes. Let's check it out.'

'Okay boss.' D'Cunha understood that Kabir had something in mind, but would only share when he was sure about it.

St. Xavier's School
Jaipur, Rajasthan
The elderly principal of St. Xavier's School at Jaipur warmly welcomed his guests. He had received a call from Kabir earlier, requesting a meeting to find out about an old friend. 'I was a very close friend of Raaj. Any help will be greatly appreciated Father,' Kabir, respectfully addressed the principal by his title in the Catholic school.

'It must have been in the eighties,' he responded in his old gruff voice after listening to Kabir's request.

'It should be the class of 1982.' Kabir had calculated back from FMS years.

Black and white pictures, of most of the student batches in their finishing year, hung along the hallway; they came across the 1982 class, merely a few metres down the aisle.

'There it is, now I remember.' Despite his fading memory, the principal, vividly, recollected Raaj Kumar from the photograph as one of the good all-round students and the head boy in his batch.

'Has he been here of late?' Kabir asked.

'I cannot remember that. But I recall he was an exceptional student and very good at tennis, debates and drama.'

He could have given a serious lesson or two to the bard in playwriting if you ask me, Kabir wanted to say.

Surprisingly, the name of Raaj's father was blank in the school records, but they got the address of the place where Raaj stayed during his school days, which was their second port of call. It wasn't a slum, but it wasn't far from it, explaining the hardships Raaj had mentioned to Kabir in the first term at FMS, when they were close friends. Only a few old neighbours remembered him and his mother as a nice incomplete, family. There was one old man who had met Raaj when the latter's mother passed away, but he hadn't seen Raaj since. He dimly remembered that Raaj had got married in the city some years later, but he was not invited to the occasion. No one had ever met, or seen, Raaj's father, which was in line with what Raaj had told Kabir, years ago, at college.

'There is only one more thing to do,' Kabir told D'Cunha.

'What is that?'

'You've got Raaj's details on the passport, let's go and check out the municipal office, first thing tomorrow morning, to confirm the name of his father. We might be able to reach the son through his affluent - departed - father.'

'But his father's name is on the passport?' D'Cunha asked innocently.

'You really want me to believe that?'

The municipal office that held birth records was the dirtiest place either of the two officers had ever seen in their lives. 'You will have to come tomorrow.' The only peon present was immersed in the local newspaper, sitting at the front desk, and was certainly not used to helping without getting any monetary incentive from his visitors.

'Will this help?' Kabir put his hand in his pocket. For a moment the peon thought that he was getting some cash in lieu of the favour, but when Kabir pulled out his identity card he sprang up from his chair as if an electric current had passed through him.

'Come with me, sir.' He was already moving towards the room where the files were stored. Kabir and D'Cunha followed him to another misty and exceptionally filthy room where the files were kept in a disorganised manner. 'What year did you say sir?' the peon asked, wishing to exhibit his efficiency.

'June 1964.'

'Here they are.' He pulled out a bundle of files for the year in less than five minutes, even in this dimly lit pigeonhole.

So there is a method even in this chaos. It would have taken the same amount of time to search out the damn thing on a computer, Kabir thought and smiled.

June 1964 had two files and Kabir and D'Cunha took one each. Kabir quickly turned the pages and there it was… their manna from heaven. D'Cunha took the file from Kabir, read and gazed into his supervisor's eyes and almost bowed in reverence. It only took him a second to comprehend the whole story. The conundrum was finally over.

'Did you know this?' D'Cunha asked.

'I had a doubt. Remember Agatha Christie?'

D'Cunha had heard about the queen of crime, but he hadn't read her books, and clearly didn't grasp what Kabir was referring to.

'The impossible cannot have happened, therefore the impossible must be possible in spite of appearances,' Kabir, eloquently, quoted Monsieur Poirot. 'I had an inkling of this after I saw the original DNA report in Delhi, the other day. I only wanted to see Kim to check if she was involved. In fact, there was another reason…'

'What?' D'Cunha wanted to know if he had missed something again.

'I wanted to see her.' Kabir smiled. 'She's gorgeous.'

'Should we see Mr Gill?' D'Cunha asked, after the initial euphoria was over.

'No. We are not reporting to him on this case, and the scam we're investigating isn't resolved till we find Raaj to substantiate it.' Kabir made it very clear. 'For now, only you and I know about this. I will talk to Mr Gill without troubling him with the intricacies of this investigation.'

'But how will you arrest them?'

'We need to get diplomatic papers processed for one of us to travel to London… or Greece to find him… or… them.' Kabir corrected himself twice in the sentence.

'I don't even have a passport.'

'That means only I will have a vacation.'

'London… then somewhere exotic in Greece…?' D'Cunha regretted having missed the opportunity.

'The guy is too smart to be in Greece.'

'Where will you find him?'

'I will only know after I reach London.' Kabir walked out of the dirty municipal office in Jaipur, followed by D'Cunha.

36

London
January 31st, 2002

It was a long and agonising flight for Kabir. Thirty thousand feet above the ground, his mind went back more than fifteen years in the ten-hour journey – the college years, their first few months of togetherness in the first term at FMS, Raaj proposing to Serena, him moving away from the couple to give them space, the painful parting... it had taken him an extraordinarily long time to let go of the past, only to be obsessed by it all once more. Some memories are never pleasant. He had never even once imagined - or desired - to meet Raaj and Serena again, much less as adversaries or in the circumstances in which they might meet now, after all these years. His prophecy of meeting them again, which he had discredited long ago, seemed to have had a reversal of fortune, albeit almost fifteen years late. He drank till midnight on the flight, and tried convincing himself he wasn't going after his friends; he had a job to do and his duty demanded that he did justice to it. But, it wasn't a simple switch that he could turn off.

It was only natural that his mind drifted from the crime, to Serena. He lamented having rushed into his first relationship. That had turned sour and led him to miss the second one because he delayed it, just that little bit longer, to make up his mind on Serena. He hadn't lied when he told her to consider him if she declined Raaj's proposal, almost seventeen years ago. Against all the evidence, he still wanted to believe that Serena's marriage to the Greek guy, and her sudden move, was purely coincidental, that Nikos was a genuine Greek guy and Raaj was at large, somewhere else.

London was cold and wet, but the real gloom was in Kabir's mind. He kept trying to push the disquieting conclusion away. His heart compelled him to believe that Serena's marriage to the Greek guy could well mean that she was out of this felony, however he did not really believe that. Out of the airport with little baggage and a suitcase full of bittersweet memories, he got into a cab to go to the New Scotland Yard office of the Metropolitan Police at Broadway and report his arrival. The officer in charge, Julie Bird, had been through the case, in brief, before Kabir's arrival and was extremely courteous. She explained to Kabir that he could carry on the investigation, and all help required would be extended, but he couldn't use firearms in the country or make any arrests. And if extraditions were required in the end, it would be a matter of diplomatic debate, not a police function. He had been booked in a transitory studio accommodation in Docklands where he had to meet a few people.

Andrew Harrison was waiting for Kabir when he arrived at the bank. 'Hello officer… I am Andy,' he said, getting up and shaking hands.

'Kabir Singh.'

'How may I help you?' Andy asked politely.

'I am sure you are aware that I am a police officer investigating an old case, but I would request you to introduce me to others as Serena's friend, please.' Kabir wasn't insincere.

If Serena met me without knowing that I was in the police, she might meet me as an old friend.

'I can understand. We shouldn't malign anyone before the case is resolved.'

'You're right.' Kabir was happy that Andy shared his view. Both the men sat down. 'Tell me all you know about Serena please.' There was no time to waste.

'She joined us early last year and I would have to say that we were extremely impressed with her work, the way she managed people, until she started dating this Greek guy, and as with all love-struck people, she got preoccupied with her emotions. That's not to say that she wasn't good at the work any longer, but her commitment had certainly lessened. She announced her wedding before the Christmas break last year and we all thought she would be back to work after that, but she decided to quit and move to Greece.' Andy summed up her appraisal, love life and relocation in a few brief sentences.

'Where was the wedding?'

'It was somewhere in Greece.'

'Did anyone from the office attend her wedding?'

'No. Paul was the one closest to her, but even he couldn't make it because it was immediately after the holiday,' Andy explained.

'Did she say where in Greece?'

'I am not sure, but from her conversations in the last week I gathered that it was on the coast, as she mentioned the beach a few times.' Andy was quick to demonstrate his sharpness.

'Did you meet her Greek boyfriend?'

'No.'

'Did anyone you know?'

'Paul has surely met him. In fact, he was the one who introduced Serena to this Greek guy. He lived below Nikos' penthouse in the same building.'

'Could I see Paul, please?'

'He's out of town and will only be back after the weekend.'

'Okay. Could I have Serena's UK address please?'

'Yes.'

Andy called up Human Resources who were very pleased to oblige. 'Thanks for all the help. I shall see you again on Monday, then.'

'Bye, Kabir. If you need any help, give me a call please.'

'Sure. But please don't tell Paul about me. I will drop in on Monday to see him as Serena's friend.'

'Don't worry about that.'

Kabir got little sleep on the flight and was exhausted by the time he left Canary Wharf at four. He walked back to his studio, picking up a sandwich on the way as he had no intention to venture out in the wet and cold again. Sleep eluded him for a long time. He was happy, for some strange, unknown reason that Paul was away. Serena would remain presumed innocent for another four days, at least, in his mind.

He woke up, feeling fresh, at nine in the morning. The jet lag and the alcohol had gone from his system. He looked out at the cold February morning from his window and a chill ran down his spine. He had an hour before his first - and only - appointment of the day with Nick, the estate agent, who had arranged the rented apartment for Serena. He had a shower, got into his faded blue jeans with the white button-down shirt that had become his attire since he had stopped wearing the uniform for this assignment. Given the weather in London, a navy blazer and a coat were added. Since the estate agent was also in the same area Kabir decided to walk, picking up a coffee on the way.

'The apartment has been rented to another family only three days ago,' Nick told Kabir.

'I can understand that. Did she leave any forwarding address for her mail? Or any bank details in Greece?'

'No. She had planned to move in advance, so we refunded the deposit to her UK account.'

Kabir had checked the bank account through Andy already. Almost all the money had been withdrawn from the account except a few hundred pounds, and she had not bothered to close it. It would have been juvenile to expect people as razor-sharp as the ones he was dealing with to withdraw cash or use UK debit or credit cards anywhere near their new home. 'Was there any post for her after she left the apartment?'

'There were her monthly bank and credit card statements and some utility bills which were passed on to the owner of the property,' Nick said. 'Let me speak to the current residents to check if it's okay for us visit the apartment.'

'No harm in trying.' Kabir wasn't prepared to give up even a disappointing opportunity like this.

What if there was some post that came in after the agent had collected the bills?

'Good news,' Nick said, putting the receiver down on the cradle. 'The new tenants haven't moved into the apartment, and they are happy for us to visit the place in the afternoon.'

'That's a good start. Thank you for arranging this, Nick.'

'It's always a pleasure to help the law.'

Serena's erstwhile apartment was a furnished one and she had left it in good order. She had hardly stayed in it after May last year, except infrequently visiting to collect her post and bills, or sometimes with Nikos for a nightcap. Nikos's penthouse was a better place to party and spend time in. There was nothing in the apartment that provided Kabir with any clues. As confirmed by Nick the post had already been at the estate agent's office, and nothing had been delivered after that.

She wouldn't have painted her forwarding address on the walls, I suppose. Kabir laughed at himself.

Kabir spent the weekend in his guest apartment eating microwavable packed food he had picked up from the nearby ASDA. There was little he could do until Paul returned from his vacation since, according to Andy, Paul was the only guy who knew Nikos.

Kabir was mindful of the time constraint he was working under. He was only a little distance from the bank, but didn't want be the first thing Paul had to attend to after his holiday. He was in Canary Wharf at four and met with Andy again.

'Hello Kabir. How was your weekend?' Andy asked.

'Fine, thank you. How about you? Did you do anything exciting?'

'With two growing kids, there's hardly any time for something exciting.' Andy laughed it off.

'Is Paul in today?' Kabir came to the point directly.

'Oh, yes. Let me take you to his office.' Andy got up and the two of them walked down the corridor to Paul's office.

'Paul… this is Mr Kabir Singh – he's the old friend of Serena I told you about,' Andy made the introduction.

'Hello Paul.' Kabir walked in behind Andy.

'Hello,' Paul said, gesturing for both of them to sit.

'I've got a meeting in ten minutes, so I'll leave both of you. Kabir, if you need anything else, please drop by my office.' Andy apologised and left.

'Thanks, Andy.'

'How may I help you?' Paul asked Kabir.

'I was looking for Serena.'

'How do you know Serena?'

'We went to business school together, but lost touch after that.'

'Oh… you know she got married last month?'

'I know… to a Greek guy…'

'A Greek millionaire.' Paul couldn't resist adding the qualifier. 'Would you care for a coffee?'

'That would be lovely.'

'I don't have any meetings now, so let's go to the café.' Paul pulled out his wallet from the top drawer on his desk.

They picked their drinks and sat in the café. Given the time of day, there weren't many people around.

'Thanks for the coffee. I want to be honest with you. Although I did attend business school with Serena that is not the reason I am looking for her. I work for the Indian Police and am currently investigating an old case that has been reopened due to an even older one. I am hoping Serena could fill in some gaps,' Kabir explained.

Paul's casual demeanour suddenly changed, and he inadvertently became more attentive. He obviously gauged this wasn't a friendly search, and for someone to come looking for facts from another part of the world spelt something significant. 'I'll do anything I can to help you.' He recomposed himself.

'How well did you know Serena and Nikos?' Kabir pulled out the name of the Greek millionaire who Kim and, then, Andy had mentioned a few times.

'Serena and I started as co-workers. She came to me because someone told her that I lived in the area where she was looking for an apartment when she moved here from India. She found one, and she was nice enough to take me out for a drink to thank me, hence we became friends. We occasionally had coffee together in this very café during office hours, and even met outside the office for a drink or a film. I invited her to a party at my place where she met Nikos for the first time,' Paul narrated.

'Do you know where she is now?'

'She moved to Greece before the wedding. As a friend, I expected she would leave her contact details, but she didn't. Maybe, she'll drop me a line or a card after she's finished honeymooning on the yacht,' Paul said with a smirk, but he was visibly disappointed that Serena hadn't bothered to keep in touch.

'And how did you meet Nikos?'

'He lived in the penthouse above my apartment. In fact he moved in February last year. He used to play loud music at odd hours, so I had to knock on his door once, to tell him to stop. He was very apologetic, and when he met me the next time invited me over to his place for a drink. That's how we got to know each other.'

'Anything more you can tell me about this Nikos guy?'

'The guy was extremely suave and sophisticated. He had an unrivalled selection of antiques, artefacts and a classic sports car. He came from a Greek shipping family, but he had branched out to become an antique dealer.'

Nothing was ever unassuming about you Raaj, Kabir cerebrated.

'So why did you invite them, together, for a party?' Kabir was without uniform, but his policing instincts made him question everything.

'When Serena came to know that there was a bachelor staying above my apartment who was, also, a millionaire, she wanted to be introduced to him, so I planned a party with her, Nikos and a few of my other friends.'

'Do you have any pictures of Nikos?'

'No.' Paul shook his head.

Kabir pulled out Raaj's passport, turned the pages and put his picture in front of Paul.

'That's Nikos.' Paul still, did not cry *Eureka.* 'Where did you get that from?'

The eventuality Kabir had dreaded to discover was, foreseeably, inevitable now. Serena had been as much a part of the scam as Raaj and would, therefore, have to face the consequences.

Raaj being the force that he was, would have convinced Serena to be part of the dreadful crime, he finally admitted to himself.

'I'll explain. What time do you get off work?'

'I normally leave after six.' Paul looked at his watch; it was already half past five.

'Is the penthouse above you vacant now?'

'Oh yes. It is so horrendously expensive, only millionaires can afford the rent,' Paul said.

'Who has the keys?'

'Most likely they'd be with the estate agent. I saw the "Penthouse for Rent" sign when I left the building in the morning, so we can call them. But I'm sure there's nothing in there. He would have definitely taken all the beautiful antiques and…' Paul trailed off.

'Do you have the estate agent's number?' Kabir was on a different track and displayed no interest in Nikos's antiques.

'I can give them a call, but they would have closed for the day. You can most probably see the place tomorrow morning. But how do you have Nikos's passport?' Paul asked again.

'Let me have the honour of taking you out for a drink after work today,' Kabir said.

'That would be great. Let's go down, I need to shut off my computer and then we can go somewhere.'

'I should say thanks to Andy in the meanwhile and then wait for you in the main reception area,' Kabir said.

'Okay.'

Paul took Kabir to Slug and Lettuce. 'This is where Serena and I had a drink a few times after work,' he told Kabir, as they entered the pub.

'Nice place.'

Fortunately it being a Monday, the place wasn't crammed with people as it normally was towards the end of the week. It was full, but not crowded. They could walk to the bar and pick up drinks without losing thirty minutes.

'Tell me now. What's the whole case about? How do you have Nikos's passport?' Paul was - hardly surprisingly - getting curious now.

What if Paul was still in touch with Serena and Nikos and forewarned them about the whole thing? But with Nikos actually being Raaj, it was highly unlikely, Kabir reflected.

'I know it will hurt you, but there isn't an easy way of putting it. They made judicious use of your acquaintance, my friend. Everything had been planned, and was not a coincidence, though it was designed to appear as one to you.' Kabir took a sip of his beer.

'How?' Paul was stunned.

'They had nothing personal against you. They needed a Samaritan to help them carry out their plan.'

'Could you explain that in plain English, please?' Paul was polite but assertive. He was an honest banker and had never made any claims to being a detective. Kabir's cryptic language was beyond him.

'Serena came to you looking for advice on the area around January last year?'

'Yes.'

'Nikos moved into the penthouse above you soon afterwards?'

'Yes.'

Kabir realised that he should stop phrasing every sentence as a question, or Paul would cut him off after every sentence with a *yes*. 'Serena befriended you by taking you out for a drink, and Nikos caught your attention by playing loud music so you got to know him. Then, he invited you over to his house to impress you with his antiques, sports car and grandeur and you fell into the trap. You thought they were two separate individuals who, coincidently, became friends with you around the same time?' Kabir made the mistake of asking again.

'Yes.'

'By your own admission, the penthouse above you is too expensive for most people to rent, therefore you were the best bet. Serena zeroed in on you for help because the penthouse above you was vacant, hence it was only a matter of time before they ensured that you - Paul - introduced them to each other in the company of others, so that they could, apparently, fall in love and get married.' Kabir thought he had explained enough for Paul to tie up the loose ends.

'But why would they need me if they knew each other already, and why would they plan such...'

'I am sorry, I forgot to tell you. Nikos is actually Raaj - Serena's ex-husband who, supposedly, died in a fire accident in Mumbai. In 1996.'

Someone needed to pinch Paul to bring him back to reality, as this was, indeed, more than he could grasp. 'You mean…?'

'And it was all done to cover up another crime that I cannot disclose.'

'Both of them looked respectable people to me. I never even once doubted that they could be impersonating…'

'It was all a pretence.'

'How will you find them in Greece?'

'The challenge is much bigger here. They are more intelligent than that – they wouldn't announce it to the whole world if they were going to Greece. Don't you think?'

'But Nikos was Greek…' As Kabir waived the blue passport in front of him, Paul realised, mid-sentence, that Nikos was not actually Greek.

'Why don't we go to the estate agent first thing in the morning?' Paul asked.

We? Kabir wondered for a moment.

'I have no issues with you coming along, but what about your office?'

'I'll call up and say I'd be coming in late.' Paul was keen to know if anything could be found in Nikos's apartment that could lead them somewhere.

'Okay.'

'What are you doing for dinner?'

'I have no plans,' Kabir confessed.

'Where are you staying?'

'On Manchester Road...'

'That's very close to where I live. Why don't we go to this brilliant Thai restaurant near my apartment?' Paul suggested.

'Only on one condition - I will buy dinner for you.'

'Be my guest.' Paul did not want to get into an argument on this one.

'No. You be my guest.' Kabir smiled.

Paul and Kabir met outside the estate agent's office, as decided, shortly after nine the next morning. Kabir had already called up his contact in Scotland Yard that morning, to leave a message for the agent to attend to Kabir's request into the enquiry. A bouncy Catherine was waiting for them. After the usual introductions, Kabir asked about the penthouse. 'I understand no one's currently living in it, so I was hoping you still have the keys.'

'You're right,' Catherine said.

'Have you picked up any post from there?'

'No. Mr Nikos had got the apartment professionally cleaned before vacating it, so one of my colleagues tallied the inventory and collected the keys. I haven't been there lately. Do you want to see it?' she asked, without being prompted.

'That's really nice of you. When could we see it please?'

'We could go now, if you guys want.' She looked, questioningly, at Paul.

'I live in the apartment below,' Paul told her as both the men got into her car for the short drive.

'Do you do a reference check on the tenants?' Kabir enquired.

'Of course we do. Mr Nikos caused no suspicion. He had been living in London for years and had a good credit history, so he passed our credit check,' she explained.

'Do you have details of his bank account?'

'I am sure we have it on the file. I'll look into it when we get back to office.'

'Thanks.'

They drove into Paul's apartment block. The penthouse was gorgeous. To Paul and Catherine's surprise, Nikos had left behind all the antiques and artefacts. 'These fake antiques, to a random amateur eye, are quite indistinguishable from originals Paul.' Kabir saw Paul aghast at seeing all the counterfeits in the penthouse.

You are the best counterfeiter Raaj…you faked share certificates, displayed fake antiques, faked your origin, you even faked your own death. Kabir was disgusted.

Some post was lying on the floor, which Catherine collected and handed over to Kabir. There were various bills, a *Newsweek* and some local take-away flyers. Glancing through it, his eyes noticed an envelope with a Spanish postmark on it. He tore it open to reach for the letter from Alfredo:

'Dear Mr Nikos,

I tried calling you many times, but there is something wrong with your mobile phone, it is not even going to your voicemail.

Someone broke into your villa yesterday and I have got the locks changed. Nothing to worry about, just give me a call when you get this letter or when you arrive at the airport and I will be at your villa to deliver the keys to you.

Give my regards to madam.

I look forward to hearing from you soon.

Yours faithfully,

Alfredo'

It was dated January 5th 2002 and carried Alfredo's office details.

'Spain is the new Greece.' Kabir passed on the letter to Paul and Catherine.

'Goodness gracious!' Paul was open-mouthed.

'They might have to correct some literature for the new students.'

'What?'

'It should be called Alfredo's heel,' Kabir gagged, pointing towards the letter in Paul's hand.

37

Almost noon, Marbella
February 14th, 2002

It took a while before Kabir could get the diplomatic papers processed to visit Spain for the investigation.

'Kabir, are you sure this is the same investigation that I put you on and the state is not funding your exotic vacation?' Mr Gill had laughed.

'Mr Gill, Spain should be the Armageddon.'

'I'll get things moving but why haven't you given me any details? Who is this man?'

'It's only a matter of days now Mr Gill. I wanted to get the evidence before bothering you with the trivia,' Kabir promised again.

'Okay.'

The instructions to Kabir from the Spanish police were no different from those of the British. No firearms, no uniform and no arrests. They couldn't take part in the investigation, but would be happy to extend any help if required.

Alfredo had a small, yet, posh office. He was sitting in front of his computer with a cigarette in his hand when Kabir walked in.

'Mr Alfredo?' Kabir asked.

'I am Alfredo. What can I do for you?'

'I am looking for my friend Nikos…'

'You mean Mr Nikos… the Greek gentleman with a pretty Indian wife? I got them the best villa in the region. I have another one similar, but it is a little distance from the village, though it is equally scenic…' Alfredo started. The chatterbox certainly did not discriminate between his audiences.

'I am not here to buy property, I am looking for my friends.'

'How did you find me?' Alfredo was curious.

'You recognise this letter?' Kabir showed him the envelope.

'Oh, yes. Where did you find it?'

'In Mr Nikos's old apartment. Thankfully, he had left the place before this arrived, so I got it.'

'That's surprising. I thought he had received the letter and that's why he called me, though I wondered why he did not call me from the airport to save time.' Alfredo thought aloud.

'You are the only person he knew in this region...you sold him the villa, so it was only natural that he called you when he couldn't get in. But I am grateful that you wrote this, or how else would I have found him?'

'It is so nice to get in touch with old friends.' Alfredo was excited. 'Let me call and give him the good news.'

'I think I should give him a surprise in person.'

'That's a brilliant idea. Let me just go to the washroom before I take you there.'

'Could you give me their address, please? I need to tell another friend to join us there.'

'Of course Mr…'

'Singh.' Kabir intentionally did not give his first name.

'There you are, Mr Singh.' Alfredo scribbled it on a piece of paper.

'Could I use your phone for a moment?' Kabir extended his hand for Alfredo's mobile to make sure he did not spoil the 'friendly' surprise.

'Yes of course Mr Singh.'

Kabir used the desk phone to call the local police and gave them the address. 'How long do you think it would take you to get there to make arrests?'

'Armed or unarmed?' asked the voice.

'You'd better be armed, but no alarms or sirens please.' Kabir did not see the likelihood of firearms being used but, given the circumstances, he did not want to take any more chances. He was dealing with a very smart - and maybe dangerous - couple.

'It should take anything between thirty and forty-five minutes.'

'Thanks.' Kabir put the phone down and dialled a random number as he saw Alfredo walking towards him. He didn't want anyone to redial the police.

'You did not use my mobile?'

I did not want you to know the last number dialled out.

'I couldn't handle such a sophisticated instrument.' Kabir smiled and returned it to Alfredo.

'Let's go Mr Singh.' Alfredo's assistant wasn't in the office, so he put a note on his door saying he would be back in fifteen minutes.

'Could you take a detour to show me the other villa you mentioned with similar views please?' Kabir had calculated the time, and knew he wanted to spend the minimum time with his old friends before the police arrived.

'That will be my pleasure.' Alfredo checked to see if he had carried the keys of the property.

'You can just show me the location from outside for now.'

'Okay,' Alfredo said and sat in the car.

Although Kabir was completely engrossed in what lay ahead, he couldn't help but notice that the location of the villa was incredibly picturesque. Nothing the blabbermouth described about the property, its accessibility, its views, its reasonable price, registered. The azure Mediterranean was calm, but his mind was weathering the storm inside. He looked at his watch again, calculating that he had managed to spend twenty minutes since he had called the local police, and reckoned it was time to see Raaj… and Serena.

'It's beautiful. But I need time to think before I can decide on an expensive place like this,' he told Alfredo.

'Good. I knew you would like the property – the views are amazing, as you can see for yourself, and if you can manage to do a part-cash deal like your friend, I could get you a generous discount on the price…'

'Should we…?' Kabir opened the car door indicating it was time to leave.

'Oh yes.'

'The weather is great today, why don't we go for a swim in the sea?' Serena asked, looking out of the bedroom window that provided bewitching views of the Mediterranean.

'Not a bad idea, sweetheart. Let's have a dip and then go to the golf course,' Nikos agreed. 'What do you think?'

'I am wondering what I should wear.'

'A bikini will be nice.'

'I know but which one?'

'Anything that does not weigh more than a gram, please. You fascinate me…' Nikos was halfway through his sentence when the doorbell interrupted him.

'Who can it be?' Serena asked. Surely they were not expecting anyone.

'I wasn't expecting any visitors… we hardly know people around here.' Nikos was equally surprised. 'Why don't you go down and see while I choose a bikini for you from your collection?'

'Okay.' Serena came down wearing short cut-off denim hot pants and a snug white knitted top with slippers. She could see Alfredo's car on their drive from the window and thought for a second of returning to change into something more respectable considering she had seen Alfredo ogling at her.

Let me tease this man a bit more, she thought and opened the front door.

'Hello Mr Alfredo. What brings you here?'

'I've got a surprise guest for you.'

Kabir had purposely stood to the side before the door opened to avoid being seen, lest someone peeping through the eyehole might spoil the surprise and prompt unnecessary action. 'Hello Serena.' He was now in front of the open door.

Serena was taken aback for a moment. She recognised Kabir instantly, but she couldn't comprehend the motivation for the surprise visit after years. Kabir had never stayed in touch and was long gone from her memory. 'Kabir…! What a nice surprise,' she exclaimed, throwing her arms open to hug her old friend.

She's still so attractive and even more so in this tiny outfit, he thought.

'You still look gorgeous.' Kabir hugged her.

'Thanks. Come in.' She opened the door wider.

Seeing Serena in tight little shorts, Alfredo wanted to stay a bit longer, but he was aware his assistant wasn't in the office and knew he should return quickly.

'I'll leave you friends together as I need to rush.' He turned to go.

'Thanks Alfredo.' Serena closed the door and walked into the living area. 'How did you find us?' she asked, though she would rather have replaced *how* with *why* in her question.

'It's a long story. Where's Raaj?' Kabir deflected her question with his.

'He'll be down in a minute.' She knew there wasn't much sense in telling Kabir to call her husband Nikos, as he would recognise Raaj the moment they met. She was totally ignorant of the fact that Kabir had joined the police after his MBA, thus she didn't perceive the danger. Her mind was trying to work out how Kabir came to know about their existence in this remote part of Spain.

Maybe it came out in conversation with big-mouth Alfredo who mentioned about them being here. But Alfredo did not know that Nikos was Raaj... she was baffled.

'Could I get you something to drink?' she asked, wanting to get away until Raaj came down, as there was a discomforting silence in the room.

'Don't bother.' Kabir looked at his watch. It was getting close to thirty five minutes since his call. 'I won't be long.'

'I'll call Raaj.' She got up seeing Kabir look at his watch, but they heard footsteps coming down the stairs.

'Who is it, sweetheart?' Nikos asked.

'It's an old friend,' Serena said, as he came into the living room from behind Kabir.

'Hello Raaj.' Kabir got up and turned.

'K a b i r...!' Raaj hollered loudly without thinking whether he should be excited or sensing trouble seeing Kabir after all these years. His mind went into overdrive as he hugged his old friend. 'How are you my friend?' He asked after a long hug, gesturing Kabir to sit on the sofa.

'I am fine, and by the looks of this place, you guys seem to be doing extremely well.' Kabir commented looking at both of them.

'We've kind of retired early and thought this was a good place – brilliant weather, great food, excellent lifestyle. It's been ages since I saw you last...' Raaj showed excitement.

'Four years is not, exactly, ages Raaj,' Kabir said with a smile.

Raaj looked up to think.

'Remember we crossed each other at Frankfurt in 1998?' Kabir reminded.

'Oh, yes.' Raaj recalled his flight back from Dubai via Frankfurt where he had waved to Kabir.

'When I passed out of FMS, I did not go into the corporate world like you two and I am glad I didn't. I joined the Indian Police Service,' Kabir said with pride. Raaj and Serena looked at each other. They could sense that Kabir wasn't on a friendly visit, but kept quiet and maintained their composure.

'What brings you here?' Raaj wanted to know.

'There was a counterfeit share certificate scam that got exposed in the late nineties, which I am sure you will have heard of. The first enquiry sadly failed, but it got opened again and the investigation was passed on to my colleague, Michael D'Cunha, and me.' Kabir glanced at Serena and her expression convinced him that she was familiar with the name he had just mentioned. 'I confess that the perpetrators had excellent knowledge of the market to have devised a fraud of this sort and get away with the money, but you have to commend our outstanding job - we traced the path to find that almost all the counterfeits emanated from a single firm. Savvy Consultants.' Kabir paused to look at the faces of the couple as he mentioned the name of Raaj's company. Despite Serena looking as sexy as hell, there was no doubt left in his mind that she was an active accomplice, a co-conspirator in the whole crime.

'What has that got to do with us... or you being here?' Raaj had the nerve to ask. Serena was scared. She realised that the past had, finally, caught up with them.

'Let me refresh your memory again, my friend. Savvy Consultants belonged to you… although you died in, an inexplicable, fire accident in 1996 – two years before we saw each other at Frankfurt. I have been on this case for quite some time now and request you to stop the pretence,' Kabir said, with a penetrating gaze.

'There is no pretence. I don't know anything about Savvy Consultants.' Raaj raised his voice.

'You counterfeited share certificates and sold them in the market, keeping the originals. When you realised that the SEBI ruling would expose your scam, you staged your own death and escaped, leaving everyone to believe that you had died in an unfortunate fire accident. To give her credit, Serena acted her part of a mourning wife with finesse too. She stayed on in India until the smoke had cleared, and then asked for a posting abroad to meet you. You guys got together again, using Paul, and moved to Greece… sorry, Spain. Correct?' Kabir outlined the whole story back to the scriptwriters.

Before Raaj and Serena could react, or deny the reality any longer, there was a noise in front of the villa; through the windows they could see armed Spanish police quickly crouching down and coming towards the front door.

'Sorry for having to write the last page of your brilliant script but…the case is closed now - Serena and Raaj… or Nikos, whatever you prefer. I arrest you for fraud, murder and impersonation. I request you to stop playing games.' Kabir got up and opened the door for the police to come in.

PART FOUR

'Pleased to meet you, hope you guess my name
But what's puzzling you is the nature of my game'
— Sympathy for the Devil [The Rolling Stones]

38

Worli, Mumbai
August 10, 1996

The tension in Raaj and Serena's household had been mounting with every passing week since the SEBI had decreed the dematerialisation of shares that had sealed their fate. The mood, in general, remained grim and the second-stage devious plan of role-playing Raaj's death was approaching faster than they had anticipated. 'It's time now. When are you off to Singapore for your trip?' Raaj asked Serena on Saturday afternoon.

'I am off next Monday.'

'19th?' Raaj confirmed.

'Yes.' Serena looked at the calendar to confirm.

'Is it flexible?'

'I am going for a conference that starts Tuesday, in the early morning, so...'

'Perfect,' Raaj said.

'What is it?'

'I'm sure you can go a day earlier.'

'You mean on Sunday?'

'Yes. What time's your flight?'

'At noon, I think. Why?'

'Remember Rana - the guy we met in Zurich? He said he was packing up from London to move to Sydney on a new assignment. This means no one will be looking for him in the UK, and nobody in Australia should miss him anyway. His flight comes in around one on Sunday afternoon and he's decided to do us a favour by breaking his journey and spending a day here, before he takes the flight to Sydney on Monday morning. It's only courteous that I return the favour by allowing him to help us out of our mess.' Raaj had a crooked smile on his face.

'Next week?' Serena had known about the plan for a few months now, but the timing hadn't been set. With her Singapore trip coinciding with the guest's travel plan, Raaj was quick to grab the heaven-sent opportunity.

'We don't know if we will ever get such a great chance again,' Raaj explained, seeing Serena in tears.

'Can't we postpone it by a month or so? He would, I am sure, travel again in September, as he said, and I can always make another trip…it would give me some more time to prepare for it mentally,' Serena pleaded.

'What if he changes his plan next time around? Or the flights don't coincide? Or your trip gets cancelled? Or he decides to travel with a companion? We can't afford to take the risk. Let's do it and get it over with. Why are you crying, sweetheart?' Raaj took her in his arms.

'I don't know if we will ever succeed in this plan, and even if we did - when, where and how will we meet again?'

'We will certainly succeed, though it may take time. But it's good that you feel so strongly about our separation, it will convince others that you are actually mourning.' Raaj found something positive in her despair. He knew Serena wasn't acting, she was genuinely concerned.

'How will I live without you?'

'Would you rather prefer that our counterfeiting operation is uncovered?'

'No…' she sobbed, and hugged him tightly. There was a tinge of sadness in the house. They had, finally, found the solution to their problems, but the risk involved could cost them, perhaps, everything they had, including their liberty. Even if they succeeded, it would be preceded by a very long goodbye. 'We shouldn't have got into the counterfeiting in the first place.'

'The milk is already spilt, baby.'

'Is there no other way?'

'No. Let's go out for dinner tonight?' Raaj wanted take the gloom away. Or, maybe, run away from it.

'Okay.'

August 11, 1996

'How will I know if you've succeeded in this plan?' Serena asked after she had slept on the previous day's conversation, which had, now, convinced her that this was the only way out.

'I've thought about that. I'll post a blank letter to you at your office address. I imagine that you will take some time off for mourning, so don't be in any kind of haste to get it. Give it a few weeks for things to resolve a bit before you call up your office to ask for something and also check for any mail. In case anyone intercepts it, an empty sheet of paper with a typed envelope will be seen as some kind of a mistake.' It was evident Raaj had worked on this plan for months now.

'How will we stay in touch? I am sure you've thought about that too.' She came close to him, still in her little nightdress she had worn the night before.

'Oh yes.' He took her in his arms and kissed her, his hands moving all over her body.

'We've got just one week left… let's make the most of it.'

'If you insist...' He pulled the slip-nightie over her head, picked her up in his arms and turned towards the bedroom.

'Let's do it here, in your office.'

'As you say, my lord…'

'Lady,' she corrected.

August 12, 1996

'Don't let your mood or expressions change just yet.' Raaj told Serena when she was getting ready for the office the next morning. They had decided to keep their schedules unaltered before the planned event to avoid any needless attention.

'See you in the evening.'

Serena was back in the evening and the couple started crystallising the plan further, rehearsing their parts. This was one performance that would not allow retakes.

'I have your Lotus Notes ID…' Raaj said sitting down for dinner.

'I'm listening...'

'Once you get the blank letter, it will mean that I am safe and that our plan has succeeded. I will not be able to contact you for quite some time after that… say six months… that should allow a reasonable time for any enquiry to finish. I'll send you my contact number after that… on your office email, without any message. I will make a false email ID every time I need to update you on my moves or change my telephone number, so when you receive an email containing only a contact telephone number with the country code, it will be me. Just memorise it and delete the mail – treat it like an ATM PIN.'

'Six months?' Serena sighed.

'One important piece of advice - never, ever, call from your home, office or mobile phone. Always use a public telephone booth,' Raaj warned assertively.

'You think they would trace my calls?'

'They might.'

'Can they?' she asked like a novice.

'Of course they can, which brings me to another point. Between the times I drop you at the airport and pick up Rana, I will make several lecherous calls to Kim…'

'I always knew you wanted to get into her pants, you cheeky bastard,' Serena shouted.

'Hold fire sweetheart… you haven't heard me out. The reason I would make these lewd calls is because I want her to avoid telling you about them, even if you ask.'

'I am not sure I follow your reasoning here.' It wasn't quite clear to Serena.

'If I were to make passes at her in ordinary circumstances, she would come running to confide in you. But when I am gone, she'll only worry about why I did what I did, but she wouldn't tell you about my rude or nasty behaviour when you are mourning my death - would she?' Raaj was looking for assurance.

'I don't think she would. But how does that help us?' Serena asked.

'Simple. If I die in an accident with you being the only beneficiary from my insurance, sthe police will look at you as the prime suspect. To defocus them we have to provide them with another interesting suspect and a plausible storyline.'

Serena nodded, but she still wasn't catching up with Raaj's complete proposal. 'You won't sleep with her for sure?'

'No, sweetheart. Why would I?' Raaj was a bit agitated that his wife was more concerned about the wrong issues.

'Promise me?'

'I promise,' Raaj said and without stopping to give Serena a chance to ask any questions, he carried on, 'during the investigation, whenever you get a chance to be with Kim alone, you should ask her whether she got any calls from me after you were gone…I reckon that she would deny it because of the nature of the conversation. I am equally sure that in an accidental case like this, with huge insurances to pay out, the police would want to confirm everything, and they will pull out the telephone company's records. If they ask you about any relationship between me and Kim, you should initially throw a fit, but later admit that you had asked Kim about any such calls and she had denied them. That should provide them with enough evidence to follow the trail.'

'What else have you thought of?' Serena couldn't help but admire Raaj's anticipation of the events following his disappearance.

'I'll tell you tomorrow, honey. We've got a few more days,' Raaj said, gallantly, bustling with pride.

'…And nights,' Serena was quick to add.

August 13, 1996

'I've borrowed Sonny's Ducati,' Raaj mentioned when they got into bed at night.

'Why?'

'You don't want me to be seen with Rana, do you?'

'So how will you hide on a motorbike?'

'I forgot to tell you, I also borrowed both his helmets. I told him I want to take you for a motorbike ride as it's been a quite some time since the college days.'

This was how Raaj had explained things to Sonny.

'Will you?'

'Of course I will, and we will make sure the security on the gate sees us going out on it.'

'Are you thinking of all this as the days progress, or are you giving all this information to me piecemeal,' Serena asked, snuggling against him.

'It's the latter, sweetheart. I just didn't want to bore you with every little detail till the day.'

She was asleep in a few minutes, though Raaj lay awake going through the plan, a hundredth time, in his mind to ensure that he hadn't missed anything that could give them away.

Is there anything else I could do to mislead the police, he fell asleep thinking.

August 14, 1996

Serena got up feeling low. It had started dawning on her that in a few days time the house and her entire belongings would be gone. And along with that, Raaj and the memories she had of all the good times they had spent together in the house since they moved in a while ago. Her parents had passed away after her wedding, so there would be no support, no one to turn to for love, or a shoulder to cry upon, after Raaj had gone. 'Take me away with you.' She was almost crying in bed as Raaj brought the morning tea in for them.

'Don't do this, sweetheart, this is the only option we have. If you get cold feet now, I'll rot in some prison all my life, anyway, and you would have to live on your own for more than just a few years for certain.' Raaj reminded her of the only other choice.

'No.' Serena burst into tears. 'What can we save from the house...?' she asked after she was a little more controlled and sipping her tea.

'Nothing at all, I am sorry. No one can prepare for an accident. If anything of value goes missing and gets noticed by neighbours or friends, the police would have a suspicion that it was engineered.'

'What about my jewellery?'

'Carry whatever you would normally take on a business trip. Anyway, most of your valuable jewellery is in the bank lockers, so why worry?'

'But... all these paintings... furniture that we bought together... clothes...'

'We can buy all this together again, Serena.' Raaj kept his calm to cheer his wife up.

'But I can always come back and collect what is left.'

'This bedroom is where the fire will start so that it reaches my office next door. This will ensure that my computer is burnt beyond recovery. I am not sure how long it will take for the neighbours to raise the alarm, and the firemen to reach and extinguish the fire. If there's anything left in the living room, or the other bedrooms, you can collect it after the police let you in.' Raaj couldn't imagine much would be worth collecting after the fire.

'And where will I live?'

'With Kim. Or check into a hotel, temporarily. Our Bandra apartment is vacant since the last tenants left, you could move in there.' Serena kept silent for a while. 'I think you need to be quick if you don't want to be late for work.'

August 15, 1996

'What if they get to the truth?' Serena asked. She had got up late to enjoy the bank holiday.

'There is no way. But if they do, disassociate yourself from everything. You should, at all times, maintain that you had no inkling about any such plan. Act cheated on by a deceitful husband.'

'It's not as easy as you say…'

'It's equally hard to carry out what I am about to do, sweetheart,' Raaj said. She didn't contradict him. 'After I drop you at the airport and make the calls to Kim, it would only be logical that I drive to her apartment block and park my car there for a few hours. Her building is right by the sea, it would be easy to park the car, walk through the hallway, take the rear exit...the pedestrian gate that opens on to the beach.' Raaj was adding tasks for the police by supplying another element that would be difficult to isolate from the investigation.

'If you want to have a jolly with Kim, why don't you say so?' Serena smiled, now that she knew the plan better.

'You know that's not the case.'

'What happens if she does not object to your rude passes?'

'You think that's likely?'

'Who knows?'

'Well, in that case, why didn't you tell me till now?' Raaj teased.

'You want her?' she said throwing a pillow at him.

'So,' Raaj carried on, completely ignoring Serena's comment, 'on Saturday we will go out, in the evening, on the motorbike and park it at the airport. After I drop you on Sunday, I will drive straight to Kim's apartment and leave the car in the visitor's parking, then slip out from the rear gate, take a cab, go to the airport and collect the motorbike to pick up Rana. When Rana and I arrive at our apartment, I will give Rana the keys and tell him to go in while I make an excuse to leave, return the motorbike to Sonny, take a cab to Kim's place, slip in through the rear gate and drive back. So if and when the police investigate, they will have a raunchy tale leading them into another dimension – *Raaj made calls to Kim but she denied this to his wife, Raaj's car was parked in Kim's apartment block for a few hours the same day…*'

Raaj's story had no fracture that Serena could detect.

'What if they build a case against Kim and actually arrest her?' Serena came to her friend's defence.

'Even if they believe that there was something going on between Kim and me, they cannot, in any way, establish that my accident had anything to do with it. If they carry on with that line of investigation, the only thing they might be able to suggest is that it could be a suicide. The worst-case scenario would be that the insurance policies would become void. We still escape the counterfeit scam and…' Raaj stopped, not prepared to say the words 'arrest' or 'punishment'.

'But how long would you let Rana be alone in the apartment?'

'He will have to spend an hour in the apartment without me, at least, for which I will apologise profusely,' said Raaj.

'Shouldn't we go riding on the motorbike today, too?' Serena asked like a little kid.

'That's a good idea. Let's take a shower quickly.'

'Why should we take it quickly? Let's get into the shower together,' she said, flirtatiously.

Raaj undressed and got into the shower. Serena followed him.

'You've got very beautiful feet, sweetheart.' He pointed out when she put her feet into the shower.

'Are you saying that's the only beautiful thing about me?' She was unclothed and didn't want to miss his attention on what could be one of the last occasions for a very long time to come.

'You're gorgeous, my precious.' He pulled her into the shower.

August 16, 1996

Serena was early in the office trying her best to put up a natural front. Though she felt weak at the knees, she did not want to reveal it to anyone in the office, and absolutely not to Raaj. She understood well that he was undertaking whatever he could to get them both out of trouble; he would be the one playing the bigger role, taking the larger risk. Any impulsive behaviour on her part could be demoralising for Raaj and could defeat the whole plan. This was one time she knew she had to play the doughty booster. She worked late that evening to complete her presentation for the Singapore conference as she had to send it for review. GK had left for the day, but insisted on seeing the final numbers; Serena was presenting facts and figures on the country's retail banking and he wanted to be absolutely sure about the statistics.

Back home it was a sombre evening. The couple decided not to go out and instead simply enjoy each other's company. 'What are you wearing for the party on Saturday?' Raaj broke the dreadful silence.

'I haven't decided.'

'I want you to dress up for me, please.' Raaj could feel himself choking with emotions.

'Anything you want me to wear or not wear darling…' Serena was quick to turn the mood lighter.

'Not wear? What can I ask you not to wear?'

'You're getting old…' she commented at him having not caught her clue.

'I want you to wear a nice black dress for me.'

'Only?'

'Yes.'

'Nothing… underneath…?'

'Now I see what you've been referring to. Since when have you become an exhibitionist?' He was astonished at his wife's question.

'Who would know except you?'

'Of course, if you wear a dress and nothing underneath it would be pretty obvious, wouldn't it?' He didn't want her to believe that it would go unnoticed.

'Oh, really? When did you last notice someone without brasserie and knickers?' she asked, playfully.

'That's an awkward question. I don't think I have seen anyone at our parties like that.'

'What if I tell you that Kim regularly comes to parties without them?'

'Are you serious?' He jumped.

'Caught you… that really got you excited, didn't it?

'I don't care, but I don't want you to excite anyone so you would not do any such thing, please.'

'Do I excite you?' Serena never gave up once her mind was set on something.

'Of course you do.'

'Then why don't you finish eating and come to bed with me honey.'

'We haven't tried the dining table as yet, have we?'

August 17, 1996

'Barely one more day left to wake up with you...' Serena stretched on the bed.

'Hopefully we will escape from the mess.'

'I pray to God.' Serena closed her eyes even though she couldn't envisage God being on their side in this venture.

'Let's go through the whole plan all over again. What time do we have to leave for the party?'

'Around nine, I think.'

'We've got a lot to do today. We will leave on the motorbike for the airport at six and be home by seven to get dressed and go to Kim's party.' Raaj timetabled everything.

'What am I permitted to wear to the party?'

'Everything you *should* wear.'

The rest of the day passed quickly. They went over the plan in detail for the last time and Serena packed her bags for the Singapore trip. As decided, they took the motorbike out around six, went straight to the airport parking area and took a cab on their return that dropped them a little away from their apartment. In case someone saw them, they would appear to be returning from a leisurely walk on the sea front, rather than coming from a distance.

'Let's get dressed for the party, or we will be late,' said Serena, entering the apartment.

'One more thing... tonight I will pay special attention to Kim.'

'Why is that?'

'So if the police question a few of our friends, the recollections of my closeness with Kim should be fresh in their minds to mislead...' Raaj elucidated.

Raaj changed in ten minutes into faded denims and a navy long-sleeved shirt, but had to wait for better part of an hour for Serena to dress up, though when she came out every minute spent was justified. The wrap-around black dress she wore curved into her valuable assets, thanks to its flattering snug styling which shaped her petite waist. The attractive A-line flare had a long slit on the left leg that went all the way up the middle of her thigh.

'How do I look?' She posed for him flashing her leg like a catwalk model.

'Let's forget the party and get into bed sweetheart.'

'I am ready.'

'To go to bed or for the party…?'

'Both, but the party first.'

If Serena was dressed to kill, Kim was clad for mass murder in a chic and sexy crushed pale yellow chiffon dress, deeply cut with dainty lace borders that ended well above her knees. Actually, most of women wore party dresses, while their men, it seemed, had decided on jeans.

Serena made it a point to visit the ladies a few times, or disappear to the balcony for a smoke to allow Raaj a close dance, or tête-à-tête with Kim in full view of the others. As predetermined, he moved closer to Kim as soon as Serena left the room and was back with his wife quickly when she returned. It, did, raise some eyebrows. If some sucker was focusing on him, it would indeed look like the man was trying to manage his wife and mistress, which was the plan.

Kim left early. She had a shoot the next day. Raaj and Serena mingled with the others for some time revealing nothing that would give anyone in the crowd a clue that there was anything different about the day ahead. They finally left the party at midnight.

Do not even mention that we are having a guest over from abroad tomorrow Raaj had warned Serena before the party.

Serena was cross. Nervousness, fright and panic had started setting in, and all that combined with Raaj's flamboyant flirting with Kim had got to her. 'You had no reason to get so close to her,' she said loudly when they walked into their apartment.

'I was making sure that people get the wrong idea,' Raaj shouted back in a higher pitch than her.

The shouting and screaming did not continue for more than five minutes, as Serena started weeping. Raaj calmed down immediately, realising that she wasn't upset about the party incident, but was distressed over the day ahead.

'I love you,' he said as if it was an antidote to everything.

'I love you too… I am going to miss you very much. I hope everything goes as we have planned and we get back together soon.'

'It will sweetheart. It will.' Raaj kissed Serena and both stood in an embrace for a long time.

'What about the second place you wanted to take me after the party?' she asked.

Raaj didn't need to be reminded.

39

August 18, 1996

The day of reckoning had finally arrived. Serena woke up to find Raaj missing from the bedside, searching for something around the house.

'What are you looking for?' she asked loudly.

'I can't find my passport.' Raaj looked worried when he returned to the room.

'It's in the top drawer of your office table.'

It was there.

'How would I find anything without you?' Raaj came into the bedroom with the passport in his hand.

'What would *I* do without you?'

'It's only a brief parting sweetheart,' Raaj said to avoid going into the upsetting discussion again.

'Promise me you won't fall in love with someone else?'

'Don't even think about it. I love you...' Raaj stooped to kiss her.

They were ready by nine, ate little breakfast, but kept sitting at the dining table in silence looking into each other's sad eyes. It would be a long time before they could repeat even a simple ritual like this. 'It's time to leave,' Raaj said, as he looked at the time on the wall clock.

'I guess so.'

They locked the house around ten and carried Serena's baggage, in the lift, into the basement parking area and put it in the car. Raaj drove up the ramp and out of the gate waving at the security guard. They hardly spoke in the car. Both of them were gravely engrossed in fighting strange fears, but exhibiting normalcy for the sake of each other.

'Take care of yourself sweetheart and remember I'll send cryptic messages on your office email after six months, not before.' Raaj stopped the car as they approached the drop-off point at the airport.

'I wish you all the best. Please be careful.'

'Be brave, sweetheart.' Raaj took her baggage out of the boot, kissed her, got back into the car and quickly drove off. He didn't want to hang around to make the parting any more difficult for either of them.

It was nearly eleven. He drove a few yards and made his first call to Kim. 'How are you doing gorgeous?'

'Hello, Raaj. Has Serena left?' she asked.

'She has, but you are here.'

'I know. I wish I could travel to Singapore with her…'

'Why with her? I am your friend too.'

'Of course you are.'

'Is that it?' Raaj was arduously trying to turn the conversation lewd but, so far, was failing miserably.

'What kind of a question is that?' Kim hadn't understood his intentions but still found it a bit vague.

'How about having some fun together?'

'What kind of fun?'

'Like some man-woman fun?' Raaj found a way to steer the discussion into the pre-determined lane.

'What's wrong with you this morning? Are you drunk already?' Kim still thought he was playing some kind of a joke, which was his usual habit.

'I'm not drunk. I just dropped Serena at the airport and thought if I could come down to your place for some steamy time in bed with you…'

'How dare you think I would sleep with you? Serena is my best friend...' She cut him off.

'But she's not in town.'

'Raaj, stop misbehaving, or I'll have to tell Serena.'

'And I'll let a few women know about you getting into the sack with their husbands,' he warned her.

'Are you blackmailing me?'

'No, I am only making an offer. I promise I won't let tell anyone.'

'Stop it, Raaj.'

'I have been thinking about you since last night when I held your body close to mine, I know you weren't wearing anything underneath your little dress...'

She banged the phone down on him.

He made a few more calls as he drove to her apartment block, but she disconnected after only a few sentences each time. He parked the car, checking for some onlookers around to see him. There wasn't anyone around and he was mindful that the car could well be missed being parked there if no one observed him. He kept sitting in the car until he saw a guy from the building's security. He got down from the car with the packet of cigarettes, looking for a light.

'Would you have a match, please?' Raaj intentionally walked closer to the guy as he asked.

'No sir. I don't smoke but there is a little shop in the vicinity... I can run and get a matchbox for you,' offered the polite building guard.

'Please...' Raaj gave him a few coins and he went off, making Raaj's disappearance from the scene simpler, knowing well that no one would observe him taking the rear gate. He promptly took out the two helmets from the boot and without waiting for the guard to come back with the matches or the change, slipped out of the gate, walked on the beach for a few yards to join the road he knew well, and then stopped a cab.

'Sahar Airport please,' he told the cabbie as he sat down, lit a cigarette and looked at his watch. It was a quarter past eleven now. He had enough time to reach the airport to pick up Rana.

'Arrivals or departures?' the cabbie asked putting his meter on.

'Departures...' Raaj said.

If anyone should see me, it should be at departures where I dropped my wife, he was sufficiently careful to have thought about it already.

Raaj arrived at the airport, paid the cabbie and keeping his head down all the time, dashed to the parking area with the two helmets in his hands to pick up Sonny's Ducati, which had been parked since the evening before. He wore one of the helmets and balancing the other one, carefully, between his thighs over the petrol tank, he slowly travelled towards the arrivals pick-up area.

It was exactly noon by his watch.

Serena's flight should be on the runway now and Rana's should have landed sometime ago. If Rana had kept to his plan of travelling light, he should be out within the next fifteen minutes or so, he estimated.

There was a plentiful crowd at the airport but thankfully he knew no one, which was precisely what he needed at this hour.

No acquaintances, also, meant no witnesses.

12:10

Raaj parked himself on the motorbike at a reasonable distance to avoid causing a needless traffic jam, but close enough to see people coming out of the airport terminal. He was quite certain that he would easily recognise Rana.

And he wasn't off the mark. At all.

Dressed in a natural linen suit for the hot and humid Mumbai August afternoon, Rana walked out of the arrival gate just a few minutes later, looking for Raaj. Anyone who knew Raaj, or had even seen him once, would have recognised Rana. In fact most people would have had difficulty in distinguishing between the two. Rana was Raaj's identical twin who was taken away by his father when the parents separated. No one knew this fact except his parents and the local government officials who had put it on their records when the twins were registered at birth. Even Raaj came to know about it much later when his mother told him just before her death. When he had called up for his father after she passed away, he got in touch with Rana who was working in London. They had agreed to keep in touch and meet later. Raaj hated Rana even before they met – he had seen his mother toil hard for every penny to bring him up, while Rana had had a privileged life, inheriting all the wealth of their father. Raaj got reminded of Rana again when his counterfeiting operation went berserk and it looked like that his con would get exposed. He knew that having an identical twin meant that he had a double that could die for him. He studied enough to discover that although identical twins had different fingerprints, they had identical DNA unless one of the eggs mutated at fertilisation or there was an error in their splitting. This was not easily detectable, but he did not want to leave anything to chance, particularly with his insurance in place and the unexplainable circumstances of the irresponsible accident that would unquestionably be methodically investigated. It would be exceedingly stupid to assume that the police would not send samples for DNA matching. The Switzerland trip was timed to perfection with two agendas: Rana was visiting on work, and Raaj planned another honeymoon that was made to look as if it coincidently overlapped. They had planned to meet briefly for dinner after Raaj and Serena had carefully deposited the cash in the bank.

Raaj kept his identical twin as a surprise for Serena when they went out for dinner. He had to actually elbow her couple of times when she stopped breathing seeing Raaj and Rana together. The men had known about each other's existence for a few years by then, but to see a mirror image of oneself in another person was an altogether different experience. It was a wonderful evening, and the scheduled, brief, dinner date had extended well into midnight. Rana told them about his plans of quitting his current job and moving to Australia in the near future. During the parting hugs, Raaj had complimented Rana on his mane of hair, put his hands through his two-minute younger twin's hair and taken a few strands to put in his pocket. Back at the hotel, he fell down in the lobby and hurt his leg simply in order to be carried to the private hospital the next day. There Serena had asked Dr Bernhard to test Raaj's DNA to know his origins…

'We now know where you come from,' Serena told Raaj that she had got his DNA test done while he was unconscious.

'I don't believe this.'

'It's true. We used your blood sample to determine the same,' D. Bernhard explained.

'What if my hairs do not agree with my blood?'

'What do you mean?'

'Could you do DNA analysis from my hair and prove it has the same origin as my blood?' Raaj innocently asked to check if Rana's hair had the same DNA.

'I can. But there's no point as I already know the result. It's only going to cost you an additional test.'

'Let's see.'

Raaj gave Rana's hairs to the nurse when she came to collect the sample. As Dr Bernhard had foretold, the test results were identical.

With identical faces and DNA, the only thing remaining was the occasion.

When Rana told Raaj about moving to Sydney, the precise moment had arrived. It was a boon that Serena had some flexibility in her travel plan. With her around, a theatrical accident would have been a bit difficult to achieve.

'Hello brother.' Raaj pulled up close to Rana to greet him.

'Oh, hi. I wasn't expecting you on a motorbike.'

'A close friend borrowed my car at the last minute so I thought I would pick you up on this rather than go home to get the other car. Hope this is okay…' Raaj handed the second helmet to Rana.

'Of course, it's fine.'

'How was the flight?'

'Boring as it always is. I'm glad I'm not flying direct.'

Raaj was comfortable that no one he knew had seen or met either of them individually or together, and now that the helmets covered both their faces, it would almost certainly a trouble-free ride back. Talking wasn't an option with the helmets on, so both carried on quickly to the basement parking in Raaj's building.

Raaj was careful that both of them should not be seen together by neighbours who might be getting in or out of the apartment or lift. If they saw Rana and Raaj independently no one would ever imagine they were two different men. Moreover, he had some unfinished business to attend to before the event. He took the helmet back from Rana. 'Why don't you go into the apartment and make yourself comfortable while I return the motorbike and bring the car home?'

'That's fine. What is your apartment number?'

'401… take the lift to the fourth floor and when you come out, it's on the left. I'll see you in an hour.' Raaj slipped away from the parking.

He went straight to Sonny's apartment nearby, knowing well that Sonny would not be around. He parked the motorbike, locked both the helmets to it, dropped the keys and a pre-written thank-you note through the letterbox and came out of the building. No one was there to see him, though being seen here could hardly hurt the plan.

So far, so good, he thought.

He called a cab. 'Versova,' he told the cabbie as he opened the door and sat down. He knew it would take him a while to reach Kim's place so he lit up. He calculated that by the time he reached her apartment she would have left for the shoot that she had told him about the evening before. He got off on the little link road before the apartment block and using the same rear gate entered the building and walked straight out of the entrance lobby through the front, only to find the security guard sitting there.

'Sir, I got the matches for you.' said the guard pulling out the packet from his pockets with some change.

'Thanks. Keep the change.' Raaj lit up and looked at his watch. It was past one now. He was glad that the security guard had interacted with him on both occasions.

This should give the police some ammunition for the enquiry, he thought.

He finished his cigarette, started the car and left for Worli. It was almost two o'clock when he entered his apartment and there were no signs of the security guard. He kept the car in the basement, took the elevator and using the duplicate keys entered the apartment to find Rana reclining on the sofa with his eyes closed.

'Sorry. It took me more time than I anticipated; the traffic was horrendous even for a Sunday...' Raaj apologised.

'It's okay Raaj, I can understand. London traffic is no better.'

'Why didn't you change into something comfortable?'

'I was being lazy.' Rana got up to open his bag.

'Forget it, borrow my clothes. They should fit you.' Raaj punned.

'They should. What time is it?' Rana looked at his beautiful watch.

'It's two now... wow... you've got a Patek Philippe.' Raaj couldn't help noticing the watch.

'It's Dad's watch. He passed it on to me as an heirloom, just as a Patek should be,' Rana said it with pride.

You're right. Just like it will pass on to your kin soon, Raaj almost said it aloud.

'Have you had anything to eat?'

'Yes. I raided your refrigerator in your absence. Sorry.'

'You don't have to apologise for that, Rana.'

'It's funny, only you call me Rana after Dad passed away.'

'So what does the rest of the world call you?'

'Nikos. After his separation from your mum, Dad remarried a Greek lady who never had any children of her own, so she brought me up as her own child. She rechristened me Nikos. I never met our real mother, so she was the closest I got to having a mum who, despite being a stepmother, showered all her love onto me and never let me miss the real one, even once. In fact I was quite inconsolable when she passed away in 1989. Dad almost became a recluse after her death and even stopped working or meeting anyone, closeting himself away. Because of it, he passed away a year later,' Rana explained the whole story in brief.

'Oh I see. I didn't know that. So, what is your name on the passport?'

'Nikos Kumar. It's funny, isn't it?'

'What would you like me to call you then?'

'Nikos is better, as Rana makes me feel you are talking to someone else.'

'OK, Nikos.'

'Thanks for understanding.'

'You're too formal. Let's get some drinks…'

'Now?' Rana looked at his beautiful Patek again.

'Why not? You go and change into something comfortable while I'll fix the drinks. What would you like to have?'

'Do you have any red wine?' Rana asked politely.

'Wines are still difficult to get here, sorry. Could I get you something else?'

'Some good Indian rum for me, please, if you have it. I haven't tasted any, but I've heard a lot about it,' Rana requested and went into Raaj's bedroom.

If you haven't tasted any before, it's even better, Raaj thought.

He rushed into the kitchen with the bottle of Old Monk, emptied half the contents down the sink and poured in the anti-freeze he had bought in Zurich to top up the bottle. Nikos was out in ten minutes wearing Raaj's jeans and T-shirt. 'It's the exact size.' He smiled.

'I told you.' Raaj poured the rum into the tumbler in Rana's view to avoid any suspicion and mixed it with cola.

'What are you having?'

'I've had enough of this all my life, so I will have vodka,' Raaj said.

'Cheers' Rana took a large sip and closed his eyes, as he found it more potent than he had expected.

'Too strong for you?'

'It is, but great stuff.' Rana complimented him looking at the half empty glass.

'So, why are you moving to Sydney?'

'I got bored of living in London. It was okay when Dad was around, but now that I have no family there I thought I should give myself an opportunity to see the world and work there. I received a brilliant job offer last month and decided to take it up, so I resigned. This is a small trip to complete the formalities for the new job and have a look at the country before I move, lock stock and barrel.'

'So no one is waiting for you to join them immediately?' Raaj got curious. This was turning out to be exactly as expected.

'Nope.' Rana finished his drink. He could feel his head swirling but reasoned it to be the effect of tiredness and travel.

'Can I make you another drink?'

'Yes please.'

Raaj made another large drink for the two of them, as he looked at the time. It would be five in a few minutes.

'Thanks.' Rana took the glass.

'We'll be drunk by the end of the night.'

'Who cares? We've met after ages. I am sorry I couldn't meet Serena, but I'll stop over next time.'

If there is a next time for you…

'What time is your flight to Sydney?'

'It's early in the morning.'

The brothers chatted about everything. Raaj kept manoeuvring the conversation to complete the items on his agenda. He found out everything about Rana that he possibly could in one meeting, pouring drinks for him faster than Rana could handle. He figured out the company Rana had resigned from, the company he was supposed to check out in Sydney, his address in London, his bank accounts, his immediate friends… though he knew well that he would have to move out immediately from the place Rana lived to keep away from any suspicion that could arise from interaction with people.

Rana passed out by eight. He had finished the whole bottle of Old Monk and hence, also, half the bottle of anti-freeze. Raaj checked that he was still breathing. Not giving up just yet, Raaj poured more anti-freeze into Rana's mouth from time to time as he sipped vodka sitting next to his sleeping double and browsed through the little bag and the wallet for the passport, driving license and any other form of identity besides the credit and debit cards. He intermittently looked at Rana, but was sure by now that there was hardly a chance that he would come to his senses before dawn. This would be helpful as it would be a lot easier if Rana slept and let him go around doing what he had planned for months.

Raaj looked at the ticket to Sydney. The flight left a little after 2:30 in the morning, which meant he had to be out of the house by midnight at the latest. It was ten already. He poured some more drink into Rana and carried him to the bed. Out of the bedroom, he cleared his guest's drink tumbler of all fingerprints and kept it washed and cleaned, back in the bar.

The police should never suspect there was another person in the apartment - Raaj knew that well.

He gave a good scrub to the refrigerator, wherever Rana could have possibly touched it, washed the plates Rana had eaten from and put them back where they belonged. He carried the empty Old Monk bottle out of the apartment and threw it down the garbage chute. It was quiet outside. There was only one other apartment on the floor and he tiptoed to the door to check on the neighbours – they had probably retired to bed, or must have been quietly watching late-night television. Either way they were out of his path.

He went over to see Rana one last time at half-past eleven and poured a bit of vodka on the bed to finish his drink. He smashed the tumbler on the marble floor, but even the noise did not wake Rana up. Raaj checked Rana's pulse, stripped off the Patek to replace it with his Tissot and took off his wedding ring and slipped it on Rana's finger.

Still breathing.

Raaj changed into the linen suit that Rana had worn, on his arrival at Mumbai, and dumped his own worn clothes back into the wardrobe. He took out the matchbox that he had got from Kim's security guard, lit up his final cigarette and threw the burning light on the bed. It flamed up the moment it hit the vodka-laced, cotton bed sheets. He sprinted to his little office and set the files under the computer on fire and opened the top drawer just enough for the flames to reach the passport, but not burn it.

Did he care if it burnt totally? It would be good if it survived though.

He waited for five minutes until he was sure that the fire would do its work before he picked up Rana's bag, wallet, passport, tickets and the anti-freeze bottle and walked towards the main door. He waited just a minute to check if he had taken everything before he got out of the apartment, took the elevator to the ground floor and escaped from the building gate into the night.

He had filled up the anti-freeze bottle with water and closed it tight shut before leaving. He flung it into the sea with the duplicate set of keys, to the apartment, and walked to a parked cab with the cabbie sleeping in it.

'Sahar Airport departures, please.'

'Okay, sir.'

'Could you stop near a letterbox, please? I need to post a letter.' Raaj requested as the car got in motion.

'There are letterboxes at the airport, sir.' The cabbie passed on his awareness.

I know that, you idiot, but I don't want to post a blank letter to Serena from the airport he wanted to tell the cabbie.

'I am afraid that I might forget later.'

'Okay.' The cabbie stopped at the next letterbox he saw.

The flight was on time and the boarding was complete by fifteen minutes past two. Raaj was flying business class, courtesy of the Australian company. He had decided that he would call up the company from the Sydney airport itself and decline their offer.

'Would you like to have something to drink, sir?' As the plane reached the skies the airhostess came around.

'A glass of Pinot Noir, please.' Raaj reclined his seat and looked at the time.

Someone must have called Singapore by now, he thought